THE ROMANOV ORACLE

MOLLY TULLIS

PROLOGUE

"I hate purity, I hate goodness! I don't want virtue to exist anywhere. I want everyone to be corrupt to the bones." - George Orwell

While memories of revolutions heavily focus on the fire and ash, let us not forget the humble spark. It's the incendiary device that rips fabric from the seams, pulls hearts from their chests, and babes prematurely from their mothers.

Before the fires and the firing squads, before the wretched rumors and the gossip that tore a dynasty apart — the smallest of sparks, the brightest of flames, brought 300 years of history and divine rule to its knees. Yet, it was not bombs or bullets that provoked a revolution and toppled the gold-drenched domes of Russia.

It was but two people who fanned a spark that became a flame; one that lit the match that burned down life as they knew it; all while the couple danced in the center of the fire's afterglow and kissed the ash from one another's cheeks.

✦✦✦

St. Petersburg was a haven for the rich, the mighty, and the occult. In 1901, she was a glistening whirl of parties, balls, masques, rituals, sacrifices, and holy baptisms — all baking together under fur trappings and operatic arias.

The Romanov dynasty had been in effect for over 300 years, bringing about the belief of a god-divined right to rule Russia. Which, in turn, created a passive view towards their positions as totalitarian rulers. It bred the rationalization that God found them worthy to rule over the country, which meant, whatever happened to Mother Russia had to be His will. Why else would their lineage have stayed in power through the decades?

Tsar Nicholas II believed their only responsibility was to keep up the iron fist under which eighty percent of the country suffered; the Romanovs had increased in power and decreased in commitment. Famine stretched as far as it did wide, and a shortage of firewood plagued the poor — while the wealthy hosted dinners that displayed caviar purely for the aesthetic and held celebrations where half the food prepared was wasted.

But all that glitters is not gold.

In reality, something far more sinister lurked underneath the silver plating and rough-cut gemstones. It was a front that disguised old-world rituals that had been in effect for centuries.

There was an innumerable amount of secret cabinets, courts, and committees — all with one tie to some religion or another or some secret lord of the state — turning the political subterfuge in the Winter Palace into a melting pot of black magic and Latin recitations of the Lord's Prayer.

Every dance held midnight incantations where saints walked the halls of the Winter Palace like shadows, every song was a prayer played backward, and every jewel was cursed; when there was a masque, there was hardly ever not a hidden priest or khlyst devotee behind it.

The Romanovs' increasing paranoia and grip on the edge of their dynasty's gilded seat caused them to seek counsel in the arms of the *dvoryanstvo*, the nobility, and, more secretly, their priests. A delicate balance between money and religion rocked the family into two separate directions, the Tsarina clinging to her priests as the Tsar did to his nobles.

It was this whirling family portrait of fanaticism and opulence that Anastasia Romanova was dropped into, carrying the last of her father's family magic, which her mother had prayed against, and her father had exorcised.

At her fingertips, she held the beginnings of a spark that would incinerate everything around her, leaving behind nothing but ashes that would give way to only two names that rang through history itself: Rasputin and Anastasia.

❦ I ❦

Anastasia hated her prayers.

As she pushed a blonde curl back behind her ear and mouthed the words that she was forced to memorize ten times over, she couldn't help the look of exasperation that worked its way into her features. Even if the only person who saw it was the gleaming marble statue of the Virgin Mother.

"*Anastasia*," her mother, Alexandra Feodorovna, hissed, kneeling at the bench beside her, "Do it again." Her mother's delicate hand reached over and pinched Anastasia's arm so hard she almost yelped, which was impressive in its own right, considering the layers of Anastasia's dress. Apparently, it wasn't just the Virgin Mother that saw her grimace.

The church in the Winter Palace looked more like an opulent dressing room than a sacred space. While it was littered with relics and mystical objects alike, there was an energy about it that kept people on edge. It was far from the kind of consecrated ground that would make one feel at peace or closer to a higher power.

Instead, it felt like something dark and sinister. The

cruelest irony of all was that due to its location inside the Winter Palace, the church only served those who viewed themselves as the mouthpieces of God himself, which didn't include clergy.

With its arched ceilings and gold filigree, the domed ceilings created a permanent echo that made the space feel cold and empty. Thick incense smoke mingled with that of a hundred candles hung in the air and stuck to the plush tapestries on the wall.

Anastasia knew how often her mother traded acolytes like dinner plates, always fawning after some new cleric. Each one allegedly held all the answers to their woes, which always made Anastasia's stomach turn uncomfortably. What woes? They were praying in a golden silo.

"Anastasia Nikolaevna," her mother hissed, "*Do it again.*"

This time, the priest had overheard them, turning towards the duo in prayer with a mocking expression of contriteness. Anastasia didn't know which priest this was, only that he was a new possession in her mother's occultist pockets that she'd spent little time with. Alexandra's face was one of genuine disbelief and horror as she stared at the priest with dismay.

"Father, she won't say her prayers. I told you," the Tsarina's expression shifted from dismay to frustration. "You said that this would work."

Anastasia stopped, sitting up on her knees as she leaned away from the prayer bench.

"What would work?" Her stomach dropped as she saw the look passing between her mother and the priest. At only thirteen, Anastasia had seen enough political and religious conflict to know when she was being used as a pawn.

"It's for your own good," Alexandra turned and grasped her daughter's hands as her face turned white, an expression Anastasia believed her mother could summon on command due to her tendency to fall into a religious fervor. "You must say your prayers, perfectly, one hundred times tonight, so that your child will save our family!"

There were tears in the Tsarina's eyes as Anastasia rolled hers once more. She was used to her mother's fits of religious fancy.

The Tsarina gripped Anastasia's arms tighter, forcing her to face the brewing storm of panic in her mother's eyes. Anastasia was sure that Alexandra had been swindled once more by the priest in front of them. He had shown up during her salon hours, undoubtedly, to relay a terrible premonition.

Anastasia stood up and pulled her hands from her mother's grasp, promptly adjusting her dress, spinning on her heel, and walking out in a bustle of fabrics that echoed off the ivory walls.

She ignored the sounds of desperate pleas from her mother and the protests from the priest that followed her into the hallway, setting off to find her lady-in-waiting.

What Anastasia didn't know was that the Tsarina had good reason to be obsessed over prophecies of all kinds. In the Tsar's blood stirred magic — real magic, true magic — the genuine thing. The trouble was that magic was fickle when presenting itself; how the craft appeared was as unpredictable as the practice itself.

Nicholas's family had fought for centuries to dampen it, tamper it, and tame it, believing the women in his lineage who possessed the gift were cursed, as the Orthodox Church began to rise to more significant and untamable political power.

When Alexandra made it to womanhood without ever expressing any ability, the bloodline was deemed pure, and she was free to have her marriage secured. Nicholas's family jumped at the opportunity to secure a bride who had no ties to the dark practices. She had won the future Tsar for her betrothed.

The Tsarina was obsessed with the burden of being the family's savior and was constantly worried that magic would emerge in her or her children. She spoke to every priest, did every ritual, and went as far as drinking a goblet of goat's blood at a full moon before consummating her wedding to the Tsar.

As she watched Anastasia exit the chapel without a moment's hesitation, she felt a deep dissatisfaction in her bones that no ritual would bind whatever was brewing in her daughter.

"You're fired," she stood up and stared at the newest priest. Alexandra adjusted her skirts, fidgeted with a particularly heavy gemstone on her wrist, and snapped at the guards who jumped into action, dragging the priest through a side door exit, presumably to the dungeons. He would await his judgment day with the other failed occultists of the Tsarina.

♛ ♛ ♛

Anastasia had left the chapel without a moment's concern for the priest's wellbeing. She assumed most of the men were charlatans, and anything that befell them during their con was just.

As she walked down the long corridors to her chambers, she couldn't help but stop and stare — as she often did — at all of the fineries on the walls. Despite having been born and raised amongst it, she knew that it wasn't normal. The ever-increasing wings added to the palace were not necessary but a tool to soothe her father's never-ending desire for conquest.

She had never felt at home in the palace — she had never felt at home anywhere. She despised how stale and archaic the chapel felt, despite how her sisters seemed to find refuge when they knelt in the pews to say their prayers.

Without thinking, Anastasia began fiddling her fingers at her side, something she always did when she felt out of place — which was often.

Tiny light fragments danced between her fingertips like

sparkling pieces of dust. You could hardly see them in broad daylight, especially when each room of the palace had jewels inlaid in the walls themselves.

It was the opulence of the halls themselves that had hidden Anastasia's secret for so long. It had hidden them so well, in fact, that Anastasia didn't even know about the fire sparking beneath her skin. With a twitch of her pointer finger or the tap of her nail, the sparks would kick up and expel some of her nervous energy.

The rooms were so often full of the nobility, overflowing with hundreds of court members who never seemed to leave the palace, stuffed to the sides with servants and housekeepers and butlers, that no one noticed that whenever her fingers danced, so did the lights.

It wasn't just the lights that spoke to her magic. Gas lamps would flicker, candles would shoot up higher, or people would find themselves gasping momentarily for air and blaming it on the wine.

The curse they had attempted to breed out the Romanov bloodline had returned. It was lying among them, hidden in their ostentatious wardrobes, ducking behind the light that flickered off the plated gold walls, tucked behind the ermine robes in portraits of rulers long dead.

The Romanov magic was back, and it was sleeping amongst them all.

The doors to Anastasia's chambers were guarded by two men, rotated so frequently that she never bothered to learn their names. She went to open her doors, only to have them opened for her, Anastasia's presence being announced to her own chambers as though she was the Tsar herself returning to the throne room.

She rolled her eyes and skipped past them, the candles on the wall going out behind her as she snapped her fingers to an imaginary tune.

"Asya!" Anastasia's voice rang out as she began peeking through her drawing-room, "Are you in here?"

A middle-aged woman poked her head out from the bedroom, wiping her hands on an apron and smiling warmly at the Grand Duchess.

"Your *Highness*," she grinned like the greeting was a little secret between the two of them, and in a way, she supposed it was. She despised when people used her title, but Asya had convinced her that it would be a joke between them and only said it when others were within earshot.

Asya Ivanova had worked in the palace kitchens her entire life. Through a stroke of good fortune, she was the only woman available as a wet nurse when Anastasia was born. That made her nonexpendable, promoted to take care of the new Grand Duchess on the spot.

Asya had lost a child of her own, quickly becoming attached to Anastasia. That meant putting her soul into raising the girl, a soul that held something ancient that Anastasia mirrored... Magic.

She knew that Anastasia's magic was different from hers, something far greater and more powerful than she was used to dealing with but similar in its origins. Asya's family had been kitchen witches and healers for centuries, always lending a helping hand and making themselves indispensable in their villages.

As the Orthodox Church began crying heresy on anything that didn't align with their doctrine, those with power had fled more and more underground, forcing Asya to bind herself to nothing more than potions work subtle enough to give her plausible deniability. The more unpredictable part of her gift was the visions — the oracle talent that popped up as sporadically as spring rain.

In Anastasia, she knew some flames could topple entire regimes, which was no sort of revelation to give a girl who was barely a teenager. So instead, she latched onto Anastasia as if she was her mother, slowly telling her stories of her home, the village, her other children, and the struggles the people faced. How hungry many often went, how their homes looked nothing like the Winter Palace, and how they lacked enough firewood to warm themselves in the winter.

Asya had known for years that she would never see Anastasia's full powers unleashed, so she was content to wait, biding her time and encouraging her in every way she could.

She fed Anastasia with the truth hidden behind the opulent smoke and mirrors of the Romanov dynasty until Anastasia understood that there was no reason for nobility to eat sixteen-course meals while the villagers starved. She knew every time she handed Anastasia a cup of tea — that had been stirred counter-clockwise three times for luck — she'd done all she could.

"Are you listening?" Anastasia's voice pulled Asya out of her thoughts as she watched the candles go out.

"Oh, silly me," she grinned and pointed to the cakes on the table, "Are you hungry? Let's sit. Tell me all about the latest dancing bear your mother put in a priest robe."

2

Asya brushed her hands on her apron, trying desperately to keep the flour off her clothes. She didn't have many garments, and she took care of the ones that she owned. She was not as consumed with her vanity as those around her but instead felt it simply a good practice of self-respect and believed that one's appearance was a point of pride.

She'd spent the last thirteen years raising Anastasia but never forgot how she began her career in the Winter Palace.

Now that the Grand Duchess was older and needed less of her constant supervision, she found herself reverting to her kitchen duties when Anastasia was dispensed for lessons or, more frequently, long sessions in the chapel with the Tsarina's zealots. She knew Anastasia hated both and had a sneaking suspicion that the Tsarina wasn't above more aggressive measures, like a switch, to get her latest doctrine across.

Asya cared deeply for the child and felt that protecting Anastasia's magic from getting out or into the court's hands around her was the only goal. As much as she desperately wanted to teach her about the depths of the power that stirred within, she knew that it would likely curse the girl as much as it could bring about her salvation.

While she couldn't focus on the magic she knew resided within Anastasia, Asya did her best to teach her ward about what was happening beyond the palace walls. She thought that the more the girl knew about the unrest growing in the surrounding cities and towns, the more prepared she'd be for the day the gates inevitably fell. If they would fall wasn't the question. The question was *when.*

The kitchens were crowded with the scent of baking loaves of bread and racks of lamb constantly roasting over the fires. There were three main departments of the massive rooms: wine, cooking, and the bakery.

Dinners and fêtes at the palace happened weekly and often saw guests totaling over five hundred — it wasn't uncommon for the kitchen to send out over two-hundred platters of sweets alone. The fires were always stoked hot, and the kitchens were designed to be as extravagant as the rest of the palace. There were gold-painted sconces where there should have been extra vents and paintings that curled at the corners from the humidity of the wineries.

Asya had overheard whispers about the Tsarina having a petty habit of moving portraits of those she felt were prettier than her to the wine cellars.

Asya was lost in her thoughts as she worked her hands tirelessly into the dough in front of her. She kept up her ministrations while taking a quick glance around the room, and upon seeing that every other servant was distracted, quietly slipped pieces of the dough into her apron pocket. The dough was easier to smuggle out of the castle to those in need than baked loaves of bread, which could be easily prepared.

"Mother?"

Asya was startled and turned around, believing that she had been caught. Her shoulders dropped, her face sliding into an easy smile when she saw her son, Mikhail, enter the kitchens.

"*Moy syn*," she grinned, holding her arms out and pulling him into a hug. When he was younger, he would have fought her off with a groan, but now at nineteen — and already having seen so much destruction on the streets — he knew never to turn down affection from his mother.

Asya was able to get a job for her son at the palace as soon as he turned sixteen, which was nothing short of a miracle. She was convinced it had been the tarragon she'd slipped into the head servant's tea during the interview for good luck that had secured Mikhail's position.

"Mother," Mikhail said again, gently removing himself from her grip and holding onto her wrist, "These *people*. They're hardly people. Animals, all of them!" His voice was barely audible, but it was taut with anger. She saw how his eyebrows furrowed at the mention of the palace inhabitants.

"Ssh," she scolded, patting him on the shoulder, "I know, I know. We must..."

"Do you know I just witnessed the master of the horses spit out a bite of food and feed it to a stable boy? For fun? The worst part is, that boy was starving and didn't even hesitate but for a moment..."

Asya sighed deeply and nodded in a passive acceptance. She knew working in the palace would be challenging for Mikhail, who had seen too many of his friends and neighbors die of starvation. Asya had an even greater need to keep him occupied and fed while she kept her sights on Anastasia and her magic.

"I will burn this palace down, brick by *brick*..."

"Mikhail!" Asya's voice turned sharp as she looked at him. "Do not make such idle threats," she paused and dropped her hand when she realized she was shaking a finger at him.

"Nothing about it is idle," his eyes darkened until they were almost black. She could see his arm shaking with the restraint that it had taken him to walk away from what he had witnessed.

"It better be," she snapped. "I don't like this any more than you do, but that's not the point. The time will come for things to burn, my child, and you would be wise not to singe yourself before the firefight."

She turned abruptly and returned to her work on the table as the head of the servants walked by at a brisk pace, undoubtedly to yell at someone for something they did not know they were supposed to do.

It was commonplace for people to request caviar, lobster bisque, or pheasant aspic, only to be forgotten amongst the buffets. On many occasions, the head of servants would come bellowing into the kitchen, and more than one servant girl would leave for home that evening with boxed ears. Asya waited for him to vanish into the depths of the pantries before turning back to her son.

Mikhail loved his mother desperately and, to his credit, bowed his head and nodded an apology. She knew a terrible temper brewed in him with no outlet, and he struggled to watch injustices happen day in and day out, with no reprieve.

Mikhail knew of his mother's abilities and thought her all the more remarkable for them. She imagined he would treat anyone with the same respect, no matter if magic was involved. Still, she had decided not to tell him about Anastasia, and considering he had never even met the Grand Duchess; she'd kept the secret to herself.

After all, Anastasia was in enough danger without a growing crowd of people learning about the magic that slept within her.

Mikhail turned to leave the kitchens and stopped, looking his mother deep in the eyes.

"One day, Mama, I will make sure that they all pay. These priests, those occultists, the pigs. Those who have condemned you for how you *help* people," he scoffed, "I will make them pay.

Each and every one of them who sought to cripple you of your magic and starve our people. They will pay with their blood."

Asya sighed deeply and shook her head, "The destruction of this house will happen by its own mortar, Mikhail," she looked him in the eye, "and I have seen it."

Mikhail's eyes grew wide as he looked over his shoulder and then nodded in the direction of the pantry doors, waiting for Asya to join him behind a row of salted herring in the stores.

"You've seen what?" Mikhail never doubted his mother's magic, as much as she tried to tell him that she was rather pedestrian in her craft. It didn't matter to Mikhail, as much as it didn't matter to those who wished to condemn and ostracize their family for her gifts. Any magic was a threat as the Orthodox Church continued to rise to power.

The Tsarina collected people with gifts like tchotchkes, which was likely the only reason Asya was allowed in the palace. Even though Asya kept her magic benign and under wraps, she wouldn't give it up. It didn't stop anyone from coming and seeking out Asya's help when doctors couldn't be found — or more often when they were too expensive.

However, to keep from becoming outcasts, too, most people avoided them. It was one of the reasons that Mikhail deeply despised the church and vowed retribution on them, as much as the Romanovs.

"I've seen it," Asya said again, shaking her head and holding up her hand to cut off her son from interrupting. "I cannot explain it to you, and now is not the time nor the place for you to know. Beware this, my son... the Romanov magic is sleeping. It is not dead and buried as much as they would like you to believe. When it wakes, you *must* be there to encourage it."

"Encourage it?!" Mikhail was barely able to keep his voice down. Asya had wanted to avoid this conversation at all costs, but it was proving unavoidable. He ran his hand through his dark hair, threatening to pull it out at the end. He dropped his voice to avoid detection, and it came out a rough hiss, "You want *me* to *encourage* the Romanov magic? The very thing that could keep them in power forever?"

Asya cut him off with a quick shake of her head, "It won't. It will ruin them."

"How so?"

"I promise you, son," she looked up at him, "When the Romanov magic returns, it will bring them all to their knees."

♚♚♚

MIKHAIL WAS UNABLE TO FOCUS ON ANYTHING FOR THE REST OF the day. He wandered the halls of the palace, doing what he did best — making himself look busy while never doing a thing. His mother would chide him endlessly for it if she knew that he managed it, but he didn't care. Their principles were different.

He knew that she came from a different time where it was better to wait and be respectful. Where his mother was checks and balances, he was fire and brimstone.

Every time his feet sunk into the deep carpets that lined the floors or he saw his face scowling back at him in polished silver, the overwhelming need to bury the Romanov dynasty made his blood run hot. Mikhail had lost both of his boyhood best friends by the time they were fourteen.

By sixteen, he had been beaten by more than one Orthodox priest before they were kicked out of the church entirely. He waited and watched as the Romanov royalty and the clergy got in and out of bed together, dancing around one another like ballroom partners that couldn't agree on whom to lead.

"Boy," a sharp voice cut through his thoughts and rapidly brought him back to the present.

A priest was standing at the end of the hall, his long robes trailing after him, his *kamilavka* crooked. Mikhail nodded in greeting, having learned long ago never to speak back when addressed.

"Follow me," the man's voice was high-pitched and sounded slurred with liquor. He waved two fingers in a beckoning motion before retreating down the hall.

Mikhail felt heat gathering in his hands as he wished for the opportunity to punch the drunken man in the mouth. Often, the only thing that stopped him was the premise that his mother would likely get fired, too, and he hanged.

Mikhail picked up his steps and followed the man down the hall before the intoxicated steward pushed a tapestry back from a wall and revealed a hidden door.

There were innumerable hidden passageways, doors, and chambers in the Winter Palace. Nearly everyone at court was staging a coup or a religious uprising of some sort, and they needed the space to do it in. Mikhail had never been privy to any of these meetings.

His anger turned to apprehension as the man ducked inside without a second thought and disappeared down a winding set of stairs. There were candelabras on the walls, but only a few of the candles were lit, leaving Mikhail to make his way after the priest in relative darkness.

Soon, he could hear the raucous sounds of others, the last thing that he expected to hear in this nearly inhospitable passage.

A sudden bright light nearly blinded him as the priest opened a door in front of them, revealing a rather unholy tableau.

If the scene in front of Mikhail were found in the Bible, it would be a depiction of Sodom. Five other men were in the room, cramped around a small table where they seemed to be playing baccarat, even though it had been outlawed.

Three of the men were dressed in various orders of religious dress, and two were wearing the trappings of *dvoryansvo.*

The entire room smelled like stale liquor and sweat; it only took Mikhail a few seconds to take stock of the empty vodka bottles that were littering the floor like tiles. It was yet another disgusting example of wealth in the most forlorn of places.

He spied several oil paintings as large as a man stacked up against the walls and a discarded marble bust in one corner as if the Tsarina had decided that one wasn't up to par. Statues were lining the other side of the room, the marble itself valuable enough to feed an entire village.

The men were yelling and laughing at one another at a volume that could only be explained by intoxication, and it took Mikhail a few seconds to realize there were women in the room.

Two servant women, both of whom he knew by sight, were perched on the lap of a priest and another lord. He could see their disgusted expressions every time the men leaned over the baccarat table and inevitably touched them with their sweaty hands.

He was about to intervene and pull the servant women out of the room when the other priest's booming voice cut through his thoughts.

"Who is this now?" He laughed heartily, his reddened cheeks betraying the constitution of a very unhealthy man, who was very, *very* drunk. The priest who had summoned Mikhail took his seat at the table and laughed.

"Someone strong enough to move some of those paintings for us. I'll send the second one to Ksenia as a present."

Mikhail saw red. These were men of the cloth who wreaked havoc on Russia — drinking, bingeing, gambling, and pulling him into their den to haul paintings as presents for their mistresses.

"Now listen —," Mikhail started, getting ready to grab the

servant girls and leave before he was interrupted by the third priest, who had remained silent up until this point.

"He *is* strong," the priest chortled, his voice sounding like oil and his face greasy to match. "Are you sure we can't find a better use for him?"

The priest's hand dropped below the table suggestively, and Mikhail felt his blood run cold at the insinuation. The men in the room all burst into laughter as if this was a very ordinary suggestion.

Without thinking, Mikhail grabbed the wrists of both girls and, gently as possible, pushed them towards the door. The men yelled in protest as the women fled up the stairs quickly, Mikhail blocking the door.

"You insolent little —," one of the lords sputtered, pieces of pork stuck in his beard.

"Those were the Tsarina's maids," Mikhail lied on the spot, "and she is particularly picky about her cabinet. I have a hard time believing she'd accept you," he nodded at the scene set out before him, "...pulling them from their duties."

Mikhail watched as the drunken men immediately began nodding, accepting the lies before sitting back down and resuming their game as if nothing had happened.

Mikhail turned to leave, bile rising in his chest when the original priest stopped him.

"I'd still like that painting brought upstairs," he snapped his fingers. "Take it to the carriage house and have it dispatched to my home."

Mikhail's hands curled into fists with the sudden desire to dip a match into their bottles of vodka and shut the door, burning their den of traitorous wealth — but stopped himself as he saw his mother's face in his mind, remembering his promise. They would all burn. Not today.

"Of course, sir."

3

Anastasia sat over the desk, struggling as everything in the room seemed to exist only to suffocate her. The luxurious apartments that the Tsarina kept in the Winter Palace were some of the most opulent, overly done to the point of contrition.

The tutor who was sitting next to her — Anastasia never bothered to remember their names — was holding a long switch in his hand, eyeing her with contempt as if he only lived for the moments he got to use it.

Her feet dug into the soft carpet and her back pushed into the plush chaise that she was in. She was overcome with the innate cruelty of her mother and the latest tutor's presence.

Her mother had insisted that all her tutors meet with Anastasia in the Tsarina's chambers so that she could take a *personal* interest in her daughter's education.

Anastasia had thrown a fit when it happened, knowing that it was another attempt of her mother's to keep her from spending more time with Asya. The Tsarina was envious of the gossip surrounding Asya's kitchen magic, as she had never been able to replicate anything close in her experiments.

The Tsarina was sitting in a corner, barely paying attention to the needlepoint in her hands, as she kept an eye on her daughter.

The tutors that Anastasia was subject to had a high turnover as of late, as they were fired and hired as often as the clerics were. They all had a different belief system regarding what they thought the young Grand Duchess should be educated in, and the Tsarina's opinion changed like the tides.

Anastasia's heels dug in, and she grimaced, letting out a controlled breath as she began writing down the repetitive lines the tutor had placed in front of her.

She was on the fifth attempt of completing an entire page of Latin, over and over, which she assumed was some sort of prayer. It was easy enough, but the ink was different than what she was used to. It seemed to be made of pure iron, smelling of metal, and all but burning through the paper itself.

Anastasia fought back tears as she copied the script next to her and felt a burning sensation ripple through her fingertips with every letter she managed to scratch out on the paper.

"*Again,*" the weaselly voice of the tutor came suddenly from behind her, and she shrieked when the switch came down hard on her knuckles. She jerked her hand in a sudden movement to get away from the stinging pain, the fifth strike that day, finally breaking the skin.

Anastasia watched as the ink jar spilled — no, *exploded?* — all over the desk and glass shards went flying. Her face went white, and she leaned as far away from the table as she could.

The ink spread over the papers in front of her like an ominous tide. It looked like the table was bleeding, just like her hand. Anastasia had to fight the urge to gag when she realized that it wasn't ink she had been using but blood.

She couldn't remember hitting the inkwell, didn't know what had caused it to topple over as the tutor watched it pool all over her forgotten lessons in disgust.

"What is happening?" Anastasia felt tears rushing to her eyes, overwhelmed with a sickening sensation, a cold, creeping feeling that snuck up her spine and began to twist her limbs to her sides. It was like an invisible rope was being wound around her body and pulled tight.

She began struggling violently against unseen restraints as the tutor stared at her with beady, yellowed eyes and muttered something under his breath.

Anastasia tried to gasp and turned to look at her mother, begging that she would finally put a stop to this. The Tsarina sat unmoved, like one of the many marble busts she loved so much.

"I don't know if it was enough," she explained coolly. "She should have written out the binding spell ten times in totality. It was only five."

The tutor stopped his useless sputtering and adjusted the fur cap he was wearing before pulling indignantly on his oversized robes.

"It will work! Look at her now, Tsarina. You were correct. The spell wouldn't have taken hold if she didn't have any of the Romanov curse —"

"Never say that out loud again, or I shall have you hung outside and pecked by birds," the Tsarina spat, her voice sharp and unforgiving.

Anastasia felt the telltale signs of panic threatening to sweep her up as she struggled to move her muscles. She was paralyzed in her seat and forced to watch as the blood began dripping off the table and into her lap.

There was a sudden banging noise that got everyone's attention before the doors to the Tsarina's chambers flung open.

Anastasia would've sagged in relief if she could as she watched Asya burst into the room, an expression like hellfire on her face. She watched her adoptive mother survey the room, taking in the scene as if confirming her suspicions.

"How dare you attempt these things you know *nothing*

about!" Asya's voice was a war cry, and Anastasia watched as the lady-in-waiting shook her finger in the face of the Tsarina of all of Russia.

"How dare I? I'll do whatever I see fit with my daughter, *and* you cursed whores of Satan!" The Tsarina stood up and slapped Asya across the face hard enough to make her fall without a moment's hesitation.

Anastasia watched her beloved surrogate mother fall to the ground and felt something like electricity rushing to her fingertips.

The bonds that had held her tight seemed to be loosening as the panic turned to rage, boiling over with a vengeance. She watched as the Tsarina turned around and grabbed a small butter knife from the tea set.

"Fresh blood is always best for binding spells," she hissed at the tutor, nodding in the direction of Asya. "She can finish it off with the essence of her precious *nanny.*"

"If there's any magic in her blood, it will make the spell stronger," the tutor agreed and moved towards Asya as if to hold her.

Anastasia could barely grapple with reality for another moment longer as the wicked tableau spread out in front of her. Her heart was racing, and the blood was loud against her eardrums as she watched the inevitable play out in front of her; she watched her mother move towards Asya like she was about to slit her throat.

The fear of losing the closest thing to a loved one she'd ever had gripped her tight, and she let out a wicked scream.

Three things seemed to happen all at once.

Anastasia's bonds cracked. Instead, the binding spell found the priest, locking him in place as she pulled her arms from their stationary position.

Her magic came rushing out of her fingertips with her pitiful cry, shattering every light in the room and descending the scene into darkness as the Tsarina barked commands. And as Asya had foreseen it, the spark that would dismantle the Romanov Empire was set free.

***

ANASTASIA WOKE SLOWLY AND THEN, ALL AT ONCE. HER VISION was blurry, and she struggled to sit up. She immediately was sent into a state of panic as she thought about the last moments she remembered.

As she came to, she sucked in a sharp gasp of air and pushed herself back against the headboard, coming to an understanding she wasn't alone in her room. The realization sobered her.

Anastasia's vision cleared as she sat, staring down the Tsar, the Tsarina, her tutor, and three lords whom she had often seen walking around with her father. Her heartbeat picked up as she tried and failed to get a grasp on the small crowd; they were all staring at her, unflinching. She looked around helplessly, trying to find Asya in a panic, remembering the Tsarina walking towards her with a knife mere moments ago, and a new panic gripped her. Asya wasn't there.

It was highly inappropriate for anyone other than the Tsarina to be in her rooms. The Romanovs had always upheld the strictest rules of propriety — thought that casual nuance was for the poor.

Her mother was the only person who had ever been into her chambers, other than Anastasia's own suite of chambermaids and her lady-in-waiting, Asya. It was why the selection of the cabinet maids was an incredibly coveted position; in some ways, they were more privy to you than family. The fact that now her father, a priest — and three *dvoryanstvo* — were in her bedroom was apocalyptic.

"Where is Asya?" Anastasia's voice was small, and she hated how desperate she sounded. She was hardly a teenager, but she knew that she needed to attempt a place of power in this conversation. Anastasia didn't know what had happened to her, it was something that she couldn't explain.

The Winter Palace had a problem with dark magic ebbing and flowing as political power moved around like the weather, which meant that things that could not be explained were often exterminated.

Anastasia was met with silence as one of the *dvoryanstvo* coughed quietly and clasped his hands together in his lap.

"Where is Asya?" She repeated, her voice growing more frantic. It was the Tsar who spoke first, his voice cruel and sharp.

"You killed her, Anastasia," he said her name like it was a curse. Anastasia felt her blood run cold, and the world that had been spinning around her violently stopped.

A chill began at the base of her spine, and nausea threatened to overcome her as an evil, broken shame began creeping up her back and settling in the pit of her stomach.

"N-no," she stuttered, sounding even younger now. "That's not... I didn't want to... I don't know what..."

"It's true," the Tsarina nodded, her voice somber. "You killed Asya."

"N-no, no, no, no...," Anastasia pushed herself even farther up the bed and felt that cold ball of guilt and panic in her stomach become so heavy she hardly knew how to bear it.

"Do you know what we've had to do to protect you from yourself, Grand Duchess?" One of the lords spoke up as he focused his eyes on Anastasia. She could tell from his expression alone that he was a cruel, desperate man.

She didn't answer.

"Tell her," the priest chimed in, goading him on. Anastasia clutched the sheets in a tight grip, ripping the expensive linens to keep from screaming.

"Your Asya is dead —," the lord started, and Anastasia released half of a crushed sob before clamping a hand over her mouth. He waited until she was silent and continued.

"Your Asya is dead, and we've had to send her son away. She had a son, did you know? Now he's been ripped from his world, so he cannot spread the word of what happened to his mother. That family lost two members today, and *it's your fault.*"

"NO!" Anastasia screamed, falling over and letting her sobs consume her, unable to keep them at bay any longer.

"Stop these dramatics," the Tsarina sneered. For someone who had never attempted a maternal relationship with her daughter, she found herself annoyed at the sight of Anastasia in hysterics over someone else.

"It's true," the Tsar's voice boomed as he spoke over his daughter's cries. "You are cursed, Anastasia. We had prayed for years that this devil's gift would never appear in you. It seems it was in vain. You're carrying the Romanov Curse in your blood after generations of peace."

Anastasia picked her head up in defeat, staring at her father with a confused look on her face. *Cursed?*

"Cursed," the priest confirmed as if he was reading her thoughts. "You have black magic, Anastasia. No one will ever be safe around you if you use it."

"I'll never, I'll never...," Anastasia hiccuped, sniffling out of control, "I'll never use magic! I'll never use magic!"

"You're damn right; you won't!" The Tsar erupted as if his temper had been hanging on by a thread. His voice was loud and overpowering, and the tone he used left Anastasia terrified. She crawled back to the far corner of the bed, fear and panic consuming her.

"You are never to go anywhere without a guard, Anastasia,"

the Tsar resumed his cold composure and looked over her with disgust as if he was ashamed. "Do you understand? Only those of us in this room know about your... condition," he sneered the word. "Not even your siblings."

The Tsarina nodded and continued, "Your lessons will resume with Fyodor alone," she nodded at the priest, "and His Highness is correct. We will be selecting new chambermaids for you. Your staff, schedule, and meals must be approved."

The cold sweat took over Anastasia's entire body as her vision condensed to a single point, and she felt her world crumbling around her.

She stopped hearing the words after a certain point, her mother continuing her lecture, condemning every part of Anastasia's life until she was confident she couldn't have tea without permission.

Asya, I'm so sorry. I'm so sorry. I'm so sorry. I'm so sorry...

❧ 4 ❧

Mikhail was itching for a fight. There was nothing in him at that moment that didn't seem on the edge of boiling over.

He had been on the brink ever since the priest propositioned him and was looking for an outlet; it had been a few days and the itch under his skin hadn't gone away.

He had grown up around the deranged opulence of the Romanov court; had seen the influence of their neglect to rule on the streets and knew that the priests and lords drank, gambled, and fucked their way through the palace — but seeing it and almost being entrapped in their games was another experience entirely.

He hadn't even brought himself to tell his mother about what had happened. While he figured it was a conversation that could wait until they were home, he found himself tripping over his own anger. He seemed to *vibrate* with it.

He moved silently on the edge of a wall, not entirely sure what wing of the palace that he was even in. Mikhail's brow was furrowed and he felt his hands tighten into fists, only to relax, tighten, relax, tighten... he paused when he realized the hallway had come to an end.

Mikhail looked up and was staring at an oil portrait twenty feet high that depicted some overly pompous lord, sitting on a horse that was probably worth more than Mikhail's entire existence.

He stared up at the artwork and found himself glaring. He studied each painted ring and saber that hung from the man's jacket, mentally calculating what all of it cost, fueling the anger inside of his chest. He turned on his heel, truly taking in his surroundings for the first time.

Portraits lined the wall next to an endless row of tables, each with some sort of sconce, vase, or candlestick — all priceless treasures that could feed a family for weeks — and this was a hallway that led nowhere. It was a dead end. All the wealth he could ever imagine lining the walls on the way to nothing.

His blood began to boil, and he forced himself to take a deep breath. As he sucked in air, he found himself preparing to scream — except before he could, someone screamed for him.

Mikhail stopped, hearing a sudden loud commotion coming from the other end of the hall. He heard women screaming and immediately took off towards the sound. When he reached the corner, he turned and saw the openings to a grand set of chambers.

As Mikhail tried to comprehend the scene in front of him, it nearly broke him. He was staring into the corner of a sitting room, his view partially blocked, where his mother was on the floor as the Tsarina began yelling at someone else in the room.

"If there's any magic in her blood, it will make it stronger —," he heard a male voice say. Mikhail opened his mouth, every part of him coiled and ready to run to his mother when a rough hand clamped down on his face and another grabbed hold of his shoulder.

He started kicking furiously and pushing against the constraints on him, yet he was no match for what he now realized were multiple sets of hands on his body. They continued to attempt to drag him away from the chamber, Mikhail was determined to reach his mother and fought them enough to stay in earshot.

"What are you even doing here, you useless..."

Suddenly, there was a huge bang, like a shockwave, sending them all to their knees. All of the lights in the hallway had gone out.

Mikhail tried to regain his senses and get away in the chaos, but hands wrapped around his ankles as he crawled desperately towards what he thought might be the direction of his mother. He heard the men that held him speaking in angry muffled whispers as he strained for his hearing to come back from the blast.

"That's her son," he thought he recognized the *T*sar's voice.

"I don't think..."

"He saw enough..."

Mikhail felt like he was going to vomit as he tried to stumble onto his knees, fighting against the hands still pinning him down.

"Handle it," he heard the Tsar's voice close to his head. Then there was a sudden rush of searing pain at the back of his scalp... and he heard nothing.

♣♣♣

EVERYTHING HURT.

Even with his eyes closed, Mikhail knew that he was

shrouded in darkness. He took a deep breath and blinked his eyes open, and sure enough, was met with obscurity.

Sensing pain in his lip, Mikhail coughed as he took a few shallow breaths and tried to come to grips with his surroundings. He realized that he was lying down, and seemed to be moving, maybe in a carriage from the motion he felt beneath him, and couldn't spy even a stitch of light.

His hand reached to the back of his head and he winced, feeling dried blood and matted hair. Someone had hit him — *hard* — and taken him, he had no idea which one of the men in the darkness had done it.

He slowly pulled his legs up and found something solid beside him, realizing that he didn't seem to be bound, and sat up, leaning against a wall.

He ran a mental scan and began flexing his fingers and wiggling his toes, making tiny ministrations until he was satisfied he had no other injuries.

It took an impressive amount of control for him to offset the panic that he was feeling; desperately hoping his eyes would adjust with no luck. He replayed the last few moments that he remembered in his head, trying to keep his grip on reality in the complete darkness.

His mother. Oh God... What had happened to his mother?!

There was a sudden sharp squealing that sounded like the brakes of a train car. He had never ridden one before but recognized the sound from the depot yards he had run through as a child.

The noise got louder, and Mikhail grimaced, covering his ears and lurching forward as what must be a train came to an abrupt stop.

Pushing himself back up against the wall, he listened closely to the sounds of men yelling and grumbling to one another along with footsteps that seemed to drift closer with the voices, unable to orient their direction.

Suddenly, he was blinded by the sudden influx of light as someone pushed open a door. He blinked rapidly and felt hands on him once again as they hauled him out of the darkness. It took him a few moments to take in the scene in front of him.

Mikhail realized he was being held in-between two men, both dressed in a royal guard uniform. They were standing in a train yard, the landscape around them nothing like the one he was used to in St. Petersburg.

He could smell the seawater even if he couldn't see it, and there was one solitary fortress about half a mile from where they stood near the tracks. The cliffside dropped off ominously behind the building, and Mikhail had a feeling it fell to the sea.

"Where am I?" Mikhail summoned all his courage and tried to posture so that he didn't feel as exhausted as he did. The men holding him were silent, but it was a different voice that answered.

"Welcome to the Solovetsky Monastery, Mikhail," a serpentine voice made Mikhail's skin crawl as the owner of it came into view. He fought the urge to spit at the priest in front of him, dressed in full robes that trailed behind him as he turned to face Mikhail.

"Where is my mother?!"

"Your mother is dead." The priest said the words with no inflection as if he was reporting on what he had for lunch that day.

Mikhail felt his chest seize and his heart stop, the words sinking in his stomach like a stone. He was frozen in place as he stared up at the grotesque face of the holy man in front of him, whose permanently rosy cheeks and pockmarked face reeked of overconsumption.

"You lie! You are lying!" Mikhail yelled, immediately rocking back and forth and trying to dislodge the guards who were holding him.

He fought against their cutting grips — on a normal day,

Mikhail could easily take on two versus one. Injured and disoriented, his attempts were feeble as his face turned red and he began crying in frustration.

"You lie, you lie, *you lie!*" He bellowed out the last word and dropped to his knees, his arms sagging above his head as the guards held tight. He hit the semi-frozen ground and released an earth-shattering scream, so loud and devastating that Mikhail nearly passed out from the exertion.

The guards flinched at such a desperate and unholy sound, the priest blinked twice. With a great, grunting effort that mimicked a pig, the priest got down on one knee in front of Mikhail and looked him in the eye.

"Listen here, boy," his breath smelled like fish. He leaned in and began whispering in Mikhail's ear as he quieted down to broken sobs, "The Grand Duchess Anastasia *killed your mother.* Did you know that? She used the *devil's magic.*"

"No...," Mikhail trailed off, swallowing his cries as he tried to move away.

"She did. Anastasia *killed your mother.*"

Mikhail swallowed thickly and spit on the ground, feeling like his mouth had gone dry as cotton. His head pounded so aggressively that black spots started to dance in the corners of his vision.

How could this be possible? He wanted to weep and curse his mother for her optimism, making him promise that he would protect the Romanov magic when it would be the thing that killed her.

"Why am I here?" He choked out, turning his head to stare at the priest.

"Someone's life must be given to God to atone for the death taken by Satan's dark purposes," the priest leaned in even closer and clasped a sweaty hand on Mikhail's shoulder, giving it a libidinous squeeze.

No... no, that couldn't be happening....

Mikhail's head snapped up as he looked past the priest and towards the fortress — no, the *monastery* — at the cliffside. His head began to swim again, but this time, it filled with rage as his breathing picked up, and he stared at the priest with wild eyes. The priest chuckled.

"Welcome to the priesthood, Mikhail," he waved an arm that looked like a sausage towards the monastery. "It is time that you join your brothers in God's work."

Mikhail turned and spit right in the priest's face, causing the man to rear back and topple over. He jumped up as quickly as his portly figure would allow, his face even redder as he huffed in indignation.

The priest nodded to one of the guards in a subtle movement and Mikhail felt a sharp box on his ears that made him lose his vision for a moment.

The priest leaned down again and got nose-to-nose with Mikhail, grinning wide and revealing a particularly yellow set of teeth.

"We have many ways to break converts," he sneered, slapping him on the cheek a few times in a patronizing gesture.

"I've never met a man more in bed with the devil than the ones who wear the priest's clothes," Mikhail whispered back. His eyes were alight with his own holy hatred as he stared down the reality that he would soon become what he despised most. The priest laughed.

"We'll make you cry out for God, *boy*," he stood up and grabbed a handful of Mikhail's hair, forcing his head back.

The priest fumbled for a moment and from somewhere brought out a small, crystal decanter that Mikhail recognized as being used for holding communion wine. The priest yanked his head back and threw the wine into his eyes. Mikhail cried out as the vinegary substance blinded him, sending a current of sharp pain down his spine.

"In the name of the Father, the Son, and the Holy Ghost," he could hear the priest murmuring detachedly, "We divorce thee of the name given to you by the devil. Welcome to your day of new birth... Rasputin."

☙ 5 ☙

П ятнадцать лет спустя - *Fifteen Years Later*

THE STEPS OF THE SUMMER PALACE WERE ANASTASIA'S FAVORITE
place to read, as obnoxious as it was. It was an unusual reading
place, not known for its quiet or its seclusion, but over the past
fifteen years, Anastasia had come to fear her solitude for what
she might find in it.

The back steps leading up to the Summer Palace held a
gilded fountain in the middle, with water shooting up around
the steps in a dazzling show. They were some of the most ostentatious steps in existence, designed and manicured by Catherine
the Great.

Priests with dignitaries would come to walk the steps,
showing off the gilded statues and shining archways. Men
would frequently take their mistresses, as its semi-public status
meant they needed no special permissions to see it, and could

still boast of their presence on the palace grounds making it an especially attractive spot.

It was here that the Grand Duchess had pushed herself up against a railing, her nose so far into a book that it looked like a part of her features.

Not far behind her were two members of the *leyb-gvardiya,* the Russian Imperial Forces, who were constantly assigned to her.

True to her father's threats, Anastasia had not been alone for a moment since that fateful day fifteen years ago. Her personal cabinet had all been replaced by women selected by the Tsarina and her priests; the priests often handed over the positions to their mistresses to bestow favor.

Anastasia used the knowledge that these women could be bribed only to secure her privacy in the water closet, and the chambermaids continued to report on her whereabouts as if they had been privy to that, too.

Anastasia, now at twenty - eight, was a shell of the teenager that she had once been. Her father hardly ever let her out of his sight, in addition to the constant presence of her guards.

No one knew what had transpired that night except for the priest, Tsar, Tsarina, and the three lords who had stood witness — and that boy she hadn't seen, the boy who Anastasia often reflected on and made her want to tear her hair out in grief.

I'm so sorry! She wanted to find him and scream; *I don't know what happened, you must believe me!*

She had inquired once as to his whereabouts, in hope of sending an apology or even expanding her circle by just one more person, and was rewarded immediately with a heady slap across the face by the Tsar.

One of his rings had clipped Anastasia beneath the eyebrow, where she still bore a tiny scar. She never spoke of it again.

To most of the court, it seemed as though Anastasia was her

father's favorite — a prized possession that he kept at his side at all times.

While St. Petersburg had become a den of sex, wine, and filigree for its patrons and ruling class, it wasn't surprising that a highly Orthodox man would keep his unwed daughter from the festivities. Now, close to thirty, Anastasia was the only one of her siblings unwed.

During the many masked balls and soirees, she was never allowed a dance with a single suitor or visiting nobleman. Her father's obsession with keeping her magic under wraps had molted into a reputation that had accidentally made Anastasia the most desired of all.

"The finest opulence from the Tsar's table that no one seems to be allowed to taste," a lord had sniveled in the dark recesses of a ball one evening.

A spy loyal to the Tsar had overheard him and his tongue was cut out unceremoniously left behind a velvet curtain for some unfortunate young lovers to find during the next masked soiree.

The Tsar had tried on several occasions to arrange Anastasia's marriage, but it was the one time that she was able to put her foot down against her father. She had become a quiet, timid woman, not in the way that one is shy or conserving of their time. Rather, she was perpetually on guard.

There was a fire behind Anastasia's eyes that had been dimmed, while not yet extinguished, and she had the face of a woman silenced.

When the topic of marriage was brought up, her fires roared, if only for a few fleeting moments. She argued — rather effectively — that if she was truly to eradicate herself of the curse, they must be sure it had been exorcised from her before she was sent to a marriage bed.

"A nasty surprise if it is not, don't you think?" Her gaze

would turn icy and she would often stare down whichever of her mother's priests had been granted an audience that time.

The threat that her magic would be unleashed and their secret exposed always proved a good enough reason to delay marriage. The lack of matrimony didn't keep her from learning herself, however.

Anastasia had snuck off when she was a teenager and had enough trysts with stable boys who didn't know who she was, but it behooved her greatly to push a false picture of her ignorance on her father. That worked well enough for many years, but the Tsar grew impatient after a while.

The point of hiding her magic was to keep the gossips and revolutionists at bay, instead of losing interest, the gossips seem to morph like a hydra with every year that the Grand Duchess went unwed.

Anastasia's thoughts often drifted as she read, and found that reading proved a wonderful pretense for avoiding conversation. She gripped her book tighter and flinched, the fresh cuts on her knuckles cracking.

According to the gossip, Anastasia was potentially one of the most pious women at court, due to the amount of time that she spent with religious tutors. It couldn't be further from the truth when in reality, it was a never-ending audience of the Tsarina's ever eclectic clerics who all promised new ways to test the Grand Duchess's magic and banish it.

Anastasia had no idea how to control it and never called it to the surface, so she could offer no explanation to the discussion. Unfortunately, that meant she could offer no rebuttal to each new "method" of testing her magic, often involving Anastasia enduring various stressors, as the tutors called it, to see if her magic ever clawed its way back to the surface.

Scars littered her knuckles, wrists, and back from various whips, switches, and at one time, even a mace allegedly brought back from King Richard's holy crusades.

She had unknowingly defined court fashion through the long-sleeved and high-backed gowns the Tsarina demanded upon.

She turned to tug the lace trim of her gown down a little farther as a trickle of blood appeared between her fingertips.

"Sashy!"

Anastasia looked up as she heard her younger brother, Alexei's, voice bound across the steps. While their time together was also monitored, he was one of the few joys in Anastasia's life.

Now eighteen and already two years married, he was the true pride of the Romanov family. However, whenever greatness was thrust upon him, he simply shrugged it off as if he knew that it would never be his.

She smiled, seeing his bright grin and blonde hair running towards her, "Yes, Alexei?"

"It's much too lovely a day for a book, dear sister. Will you come riding with me?"

One of the few pleasures that she was allowed — since her guard could so easily follow — Anastasia's sanity had become dependent on her rides, especially with Alexei.

"I can deny you nothing," she grinned, her voice still quiet and repressed within the earshot of her attendants. Alexei laughed and gently grabbed her elbow, the two of them descending the steps and heading towards the stables, falling into easy conversation.

♣♣♣

Anastasia and Alexei were out on the palace grounds, slowing their horses to a walk as they reached the perimeter.

This part of the gardens was surrounded by a small wood often used by hunting parties. It wasn't large enough to hold any actual game, but trapped stags were frequently set loose here for a mockery of the hunt to be enjoyed by the often drunk lords.

Alexei was deep in a story of something embarrassing that a local emissary had done as Anastasia's thoughts began to drift, staring at the edge of the dark wood. Something in it seemed to call to her, to encourage her to kick her horse and flee — just to see how far she could get.

One of the guards seemed to read her thoughts and moved his horse in between her and the tree line.

"*Nyet,*" his voice was low and angry as if he was ready for a fight. Something in his tone and the call of the land beyond her made Anastasia feel unsparingly bold, for once.

"I am the Grand Duchess Anastasia," she straightened in her saddle, old scars flaring up like a sick warning, "You are tasked to watch me, are you not? So, watch —"

Her taunt was cut off with a sharp scream, which she recognized belonged to her brother Alexei.

Anastasia turned around in her saddle and saw Alexei's horse rearing back, the young monarch gripping onto its sides with his legs to avoid sliding off. Her gaze flew past them to find a large wolf emerging from the underbrush.

She gasped and felt her blood run cold as the animal stared her down. She had never seen a wolf in person before and found herself shocked by its size, larger than a man and at chest level with Alexei's horse.

Its eyes seemed to flicker red in the sunlight, with a beastly glow that if you blinked, you might miss. The creature stalked towards Alexei and the horse, struggling in one place as though it was tied by the bit to an invisible post.

Alexei shouted desperately and tried to kick his horse into motion, but its coat grew damp with sweat, and its foam-flecked face anguished as it kicked fruitlessly.

Anastasia could barely rip her eyes from the scene as she

turned to yell at her guards for assistance, only to find that both of them wore vacant expressions.

The guards sat on their horses with their arms relaxed by their sizes, eyes glazed over as if they were toys that had suddenly been abandoned by a vengeful god.

Anastasia's heart raced as the air seemed to electrify around her and static danced between her fingertips. She gasped as it tore quietly at the new lacerations on her knuckles.

No, no, no, no... her blood went cold as she remembered the very last time she'd felt this feeling.

Another sharp cry pulled her back into the moment as she saw the wolf lunge for Alexei, its maw spread wide. The horse pivoted to the right at the last moment, working with what small range of motion it seemed to be confined to. The wolf missed and landed gracefully, spinning with an efficiency that should be impossible for an animal that large. It went to lunge again, surely, Alexei right in its path —

"ALEXEI!" Anastasia screamed, throwing out both of her hands in fear as an ice-cold sensation flooded her body and burst through her as if she was exploding.

A great pulse went hurtling over the gardens in front of her and with a loud yelp, the wolf tumbled over as if it had been hit with a battering ram.

Anastasia watched in shock as the wolf hit the ground and began convulsing, twitching like a grotesque experiment, until its cries turned to screams.

Her head spun as she watched the creature morph into the body of a naked man in front of her, writhing on the ground and cursing as if he was holding a live wire that he could not let go of.

Alexei watched on, the blood drained from his face and his expression fearful until Anastasia realized that he was looking *at her.*

She began to sway in her saddle, her hearing muffled and

her vision was beginning to condense to a single point. The icy sensation in her body turned hot as she became flushed all over.

Vaguely, she heard her guards snap into action somewhere near her, both of them galloping over the short distance towards the prince.

Not again... oh God... not again... not again... I swore... never again... they'll die...

Anastasia slumped forward against her horse's neck and descended into the blackness as it consumed her vision and rippled through her.

♔♔♔

Anastasia thought she was fairly acquainted with fear. She had made friends with it, welcomed it even. Anastasia learned the difference between fear and panic when she blinked her eyes open.

Fear had a way of being deathly quiet and stoic, sending chills and stealing breaths, but panic was loud. It was fast heart-beats and sweating palms. When Anastasia woke up in her bed, she panicked.

"ALEXEI!" she screamed before her eyes were even fully open.

"I'm right here, sister," Alexei's voice, calm as ever, appeared next to her.

Anastasia blinked her eyes a few times to adjust to the light, realizing that she was again in her chambers and had woken up to an audience.

Horrible memories came rushing back to meet her as she saw the Tsarina, the Tsar, and his ever-faithful three with him, now with Alexei.

"What happened?" She turned towards her brother and grabbed his arm. Alexei brushed his hand over her hair and kissed her forehead, squeezing her shoulder.

"You saved my life, Sashy."

"That... thing... that creature!" Her voice trailed off as she sat back in bed, leaning against the headboard, trying to rationalize what she had seen.

Anastasia was well-versed in the world of angels and demons — it came with the territory of being cursed — but seeing such a violent shapeshift was pushing the boundaries of her imagination.

After years of being sheltered from the world of her own powers and the supernatural, what else existed beyond the limits of her knowledge? What other things could only be explained by magic?

"A *khlyst*," the Tsarina's voice was sharp as glass, interrupting her children, "a zealot. Clearly, one who had made a deal with the devil. Sent here to attack the future Tsar of Russia and God's followers."

Her voice had a level of fake piousness to it that made Anastasia want to roll her eyes. She knew her mother was only outraged because none of her chamber of religious zealots had ever displayed that kind of power.

"And I...," Anastasia trailed off, looking down at her hands in her lap, her mind jumping through hoops as she thought about what reaction her family would have.

"You stopped it," it was the Tsar this time and Anastasia found her head snapping up and to attention unwittingly when he spoke.

There was a deathly quiet as she ran her gaze over the faces of the lords, their expressions betraying nothing. "It seems as if this could be an... interesting development," the Tsar paused and ran his hand across his chin.

"As you know," one of the lords spoke up, with a voice that sounded like a snake-oil salesman, "the great Romanov line is under intense persecution. Your family's enemies are hiding in plain sight and spreading lies among the people. There are many...," he paused and smacked his mouth a few times as if tasting the next word, "*political* advantages to a gift like yours."

Anastasia's eyes grew wide with shock, "Political? All this time —"

"Do not forget your place," the Tsarina snapped, her hands coming to rest over one another at her navel. "You have also *killed* someone, Anastasia, so do not get righteous now."

Cold shame flooded Anastasia, and she squirmed uncomfortably like a child, once again cornered in her chambers by a suite of people determined to wield her like a weapon, her soul being drawn and quartered in front of them all.

The Tsar coughed once and held up a hand, "You will pursue this, Anastasia." A quiet, cold command. Anastasia felt her head begin to spin at the sharp turn that her life was taking.

"I... I don't...," she stuttered, unable to meet her father's gaze even after fifteen years, "I don't know how."

"Your mother will arrange for a tutor," he snapped, taking one step closer to the bed, "and they will let us know hourly how you are progressing. We will all return to St. Petersburg. You are to be removed from court —" Alexei and Anastasia both let out sharp gasps of surprise, "— and you will dedicate your days to figuring out your curse until a time has come that we may have use for you."

"Think of what you can do for God," the Tsarina offered up a smile that was as sadistic as it was contrite. Anastasia felt sick.

"You will start tomorrow. Do not leave your rooms," the Tsar commanded once as a way of a goodbye, flicking his finger towards the door ordering everyone to depart.

Alexei was the last to leave, pausing at her door and turning to look at his sister. She knew that look — one that he had perfected over the years. It was the 'shall I talk to Father' look.

Anastasia shook her head once and nodded her chin in the direction of the door, encouraging him to go.

If I'm going to be a weapon, I'm afraid of the collateral it will require.

♣♣♣

Anastasia's life was now the picture of perfect control. After they returned to St. Petersburg, any semblance of freedom she had before in her already over-regulated life was gone.

Every movement was now monitored, each conversation recorded, and every waking hour laid out for her. Yet, not long after Anastasia had rediscovered her magic through saving her brother's life, there was one small flickering minute of hope.

Every Sunday morning, the palace emptied as people headed to the nearly day-long church services. It was as much of a place to be seen as any ball or masquerade, making it a must-attend event.

The court attendees went in one of two directions: either still wearing their outfits from the night before in a testament to their debauchery or changing in the early light of the morning to showcase their piety.

During those blessed morning hours on Sunday, Anastasia noticed very quickly that even her attendants and her father's babysitters left her alone.

It was one of those fateful Sundays that — for a moment — Anastasia might have believed in God. She found herself engrossed in watching the last of her father's attendants depart, her current priest with them.

For most of her confinement, she had been too afraid to try anything during these brief moments of reprieve.

She knew that her father had commanded her to explore her magic, but diving back into something she had been afraid of for most of her life was daunting. She didn't trust him. The last thing that she wanted was to become one more cog in the ever-turning wheel of other-worldly influences.

That fateful Sunday, something in the air had shifted and made her feel reckless. Her life couldn't shrink down any more than it already had, so what did it matter if they caught her trying?

Anastasia found herself moving quickly, changing in her bedroom into a simple shift that a lady-in-waiting had left behind. She crept towards the door, listening for any noise, and when she heard none, slid it open and peered out.

She was shocked to see that her father hadn't even bothered to place her typical rotating guards at the door; always watching even in her own chambers.

Anastasia sprinted down the hall, not bothering to look behind her. She didn't give herself a moment to react or breathe, moving on instinct and refusing to let her fear get the better of her. The halls were empty as she had assumed, not even a drunken straggler to be found.

Before too long, she found herself standing at the back door to the palace. Anastasia pushed against it once, twice... she cursed, thinking it was locked... but the heavy, forgotten door swung open on the third push.

Anastasia was taken aback by the cold air on her face, yet, she refused to let the shock stop her. Everything was moving in a blur, and before she knew it, she was exiting the palace gates and was on the streets of St. Petersburg.

Her memories of the city were few and far between, mainly from her childhood, always from the back of a moving car or carriage. She felt paranoid as she moved through the streets, stopping and pausing to stare at the most mundane of things. No one looked at her twice, allowing her freedom that she had never felt before.

She took stock of the city block, and as she surveyed her surroundings, felt the pit in her stomach begin to sink. Asya had told her years ago that things were not well in Russia. That the atmosphere in the palace was an anomaly; the country wasn't partying until dawn. They were starving. The street was overrun with people moving quickly as if they were always late, desperately clutching groceries to their chest or fighting over half-loaves of bread.

This was the first time that Anastasia had seen it and it pulled at her. The place she held in her heart for her family calcified further, and she wondered how much farther it could go until it fossilized.

It wasn't until she stopped in front of a small house, the door half-off its hinges, that she was unable to look away. Anastasia peered into the house and could see a mother, desperately fanning the embers of her fireplace.

From the looks of it, she had no money for coal or wood, and keeping a fire alive in their home would consume her. Something came over Anastasia, something she wasn't familiar with... something that caused her magic to flicker alive within her.

It startled her, for a moment, how naturally it seemed to warm in her bloodstream and flush her cheeks. She had been keeping her magic suppressed for years, and now the strength of it coming over her nearly overtook her on the spot.

What's happening to me?

The sparks danced over her fingertips and she found herself taking a few steps forward, as if on autopilot. She knocked on the door frame, startling the woman.

"*Privet,*" Anastasia smiled softly, "May I?" She pointed to the fireplace.

The woman seemed utterly confused, more than anything, but nodded. It was perhaps the shock of seeing a stranger offering to stoke the fire. She took a few steps inside, her shoulders tight as a wave of anxiety crashed over her.

Why in God's name am I going to try this?! I've killed someone with this fucking magic.

Her thoughts raced, yet there was something in her overriding it, an instinct, that drove her to abandon those fears as soon as they arose. It kept coming back like the tide and she grew nervous at the ebbing and flowing of the terror and magic within her. As she approached the fireplace, she let her mind go numb and extended her hand out.

The stranger watched on in awe as Anastasia let the magic flow through her fingers, causing the embers to glow hotter until they erupted into flames. Her cheeks grew hot and she felt herself grow weaker, as she watched on in equal awe as the woman next to her.

"My God," she muttered, before turning up and looking at Anastasia with tears in her eyes.

For the second time in her life, Anastasia had used her magic for someone else. It was unpredictable but had never come as easily.

6

"This is the definition of insanity," Anastasia muttered under her breath as she stared at her fingertips with a defeated sigh.

It had been three weeks since she saved Alexei's life and seemingly ended her own. Anastasia thought her world before that incident had been controlled, but she was unprepared for the gilded cage that her parent's acceptance of her power brought her.

Tolerance is more like it.

Anastasia fought the palpable urge to scream as loud as she could for as long as she could, avoiding the gaze of the newest tutor that had been assigned to her.

True to her father's threats, Anastasia had been removed from court. There had been no formal announcement or any decree that described her absence, which led most of the nobility to believe that she had gotten pregnant out of wedlock.

They whispered the Tsar was trying to save face. Her father doubled down on controlling her meals; someone in her father's cabinet suggested Anastasia keep a "clean mind" to pursue her curse — no, it was a *gift* now.

While the hundreds of guests and nobles in the palace gorged themselves on caviar and sturgeon, Anastasia now survived on cold oats for breakfast and buckwheat cutlets for the rest of the day.

Her mother had assigned a new priest to her side, one who was more "proficient" in the magical arts. Anastasia knew better and rightfully assumed this simply meant he had a proficiency for dark magic rituals that ultimately looked terrifying and completed nothing.

She was moved back to the Winter Palace alone while her family spent a few more warm weeks at the summer property. Even though the Winter Palace was not the court seat — court was held wherever the Tsar went— she was only allowed to leave her chambers for a walk in the gardens once the social hours ended.

The bottom of the upper class lingered around the out-of-season palace, regardless of the official royal schedule, effectively reducing Anastasia's walk schedule to the middle of the night, if that.

Daily messengers were dispatched to the Summer Palace with updates on Anastasia's progress, and to date, not a single letter held any real news.

Anastasia felt the last remnants of the fire in her soul begin to flicker out like a gas lantern on its last few drops when it would suddenly flare again for a few brief seconds. She felt like a defunct, rusted weapon, locked away in ten-room chambers, lined with precious metals that left a disgusting, metallic tang in her mouth.

She stared at her hands and couldn't decide if she wanted something or nothing to happen. The idea of using her magic still terrified her, as someone always seemed to die when she tried.

If she ever got her magic to work, that also meant she would quickly be deployed like a warhorse in her father's army, so her life was lost to her either way.

Nothing happened as she rubbed her palms together, feeling a warmth between them but nothing else; even the sparks that she used to entertain herself with as a child never appeared again.

She snapped her fingers to see what would happen and was ripped from her thoughts as a switch struck across her upper back. She hissed but swallowed her reaction as best as she could, turning around to face the tutor that never left.

"Don't do that," the priest hissed — Anastasia refused to remember his name as her sole act of defiance — and he shook his head, brandishing the switch like a broadsword. "You must *tell me* before you do something."

Anastasia grinned as she studied the look on his face. He was afraid *of her*. He had no clue that she didn't have the slightest idea how to use her magic. None of them did.

She smiled wider, mimicking the cruelty in the faces of those she had grown up around, and waved a hand in front of her. Nothing happened and the priest fell backward as he tried to scramble away from her.

Anastasia felt the last of her resolve begin to crack and she started to laugh. It was not a joyful or merry sound, but a heart-breaking one, the sound of a soul resigning itself to nothingness and expunging any sounds from their lungs that could mimic mirth.

She began to laugh louder and louder, spinning in circles and throwing her hands out wide in every which way.

"Stop that!" The priest screamed, waving the switch at Anastasia haphazardly, managing to get a few hits in, the pain dulling with every blow as she let herself slip into the delusion. She kept spinning, spinning, spinning... until she didn't even realize she had started crying, falling to her knees, and screaming for Asya for the first time in years.

Anastasia didn't know how long she had sat there in her chambers, delirious with the shambles of her life and the heart-breaking knowledge that there wasn't a single person alive who knew who she was, including her.

She tipped her head back and screamed as loud as she could... when suddenly, a wave of power burst from her fingers and sent shockwaves across the chambers. Every mirror broke and the lights were extinguished, sending glass and sparks flying around her.

Anastasia stopped immediately, her eyes wide with fear, afraid that she could hurt herself. She sat in silence, surveying the room, waiting for the cavalry to descend, but no one came. The chandeliers were still trembling in the aftershocks and she hugged her knees to her chest, watching. Waiting.

It was not until she saw the dusk descending that she realized the priest had gone, and she was alone.

♣♣♣

"This is your fault," the Tsarina's voice was flustered and high-pitched as though she had just stopped running. The priest was on his knees in front of her and the Tsar, in a private audience, far away from the listening ears of the policy rooms.

"She is the devil's daughter, I'm sure of it," the priest wheezed. He had left Anastasia in the midst of her breakdown, convinced that he would be killed, unaware of the explosion that had shaken her rooms, "There is no harnessing her magic! It's only controlled by the —" he was cut off as the Tsar waved his hand, two guards stepping in and hauling the man away.

Anyone who had been brought in to help Anastasia control her magic had been killed shortly after they'd failed, this priest would be no different.

"What do we do?" The Tsarina dropped back in the over-stuffed chair that she lounged in. "We should just marry her off.

Send her to Siberia or Crimea and give her to some lord as a war prize."

She waved her hand passively as if she was discussing wallpaper samples that she didn't like instead of her daughter.

The Tsar turned to face her, his expression growing even stonier as he picked up a vase and threw it at the wall. It exploded behind the Tsarina and she shrieked, covering her head with her hands to protect herself.

"Do you know what she could *do* for me?" he yelled, "What that kind of power could do? Have any of your charlatans even come close to replicating it? Even that khlyst in the gardens had more power than anyone you've managed to find!"

The Tsar's face was swollen-red and spit got caught in his mustache as he bellowed. The Tsarina rolled her eyes, used to her husband's tirades, which had only gotten worse as their grip on the court and country had been weakening.

"What do you suppose we do?"

The Tsar was quiet for a moment before he stopped and looked at his wife. "That boy. The one we sent away...," he snapped his fingers. "That woman. Her nanny. She had magic."

"She had *kitchen* magic," the Tsarina scoffed, downplaying it in an attempt to self-soothe the fact that she couldn't headhunt the magic practitioners that she truly fancied.

"It worked and that boy already knows about Anastasia. We won't risk another person knowing about her curse. If he fails... There were enough rumors about his mother. We pass the blame. Label him as a heretic. Jail him. Move on."

The Tsarina sighed, not wanting to admit that it was a better plan than throwing another failed Orthodox priest at their daughter.

"Fine. Send for the boy."

♛♛♛

Russia was known for its cold winds; they were somewhat famous for it. The wind that blew off the water and over Solovetsky Monastery seemed to carry a bitterness that was all their own.

The monastery was fortified by an outer wall with three separate turrets, making it look more like a castle than a house of prayer... or a house of prayer for a very angry god. Beyond the external wall were three steeples that rose from the ground, the onion-shaped *lúkovichnaya glava* domes visible from miles away.

Over the years, Rasputin had grown to hate those domes that always seemed to watch him. Whenever he left the monastery walls to fetch food, run errands, or haul the bags of traveling religious emissaries, he was able to find a few, brief moments of freedom.

He was never able to escape the towers, their bulbous appearance staring after him and constantly reminding him of every overinflated priest that he had to deal with.

The chapel of the monastery was covered in stained glass windows, gilded arches, and silver incense burners.

Upon first glance, it was a holy testament to the wonder of man's greed, not God. Once you had spent a few minutes in the chapel, its facade began to slip.

The benches were threadbare and the altar set of silver and gold pieces were mysteriously flecking off paint. There were cracks in the stained glass that left the chapel prone to leaks and blasts of cold air. At one point in his tenure, Rasputin had been forced to kneel in prayer in front of a particularly cracked window until his fingers turned blue.

One cannot compare the pain of those who are broken, but it was safe to say the past fifteen years had been equally as hard on Rasputin as they had been on Anastasia.

After he had been tossed to the predators of the monastery,

it was at least five years before he had surrendered enough to their whims to make his daily life digestible.

The first few weeks and months saw Rasputin refusing to accept his new name, missing prayers, neglecting lessons, and generally being more than willing to start fights with the other novitiates.

The other men who had been brought to the monastery were a mixed group of those who had volunteered and those who had been sent there as an alternative to imprisonment or death.

For weeks after his arrival, Rasputin had refused to succumb to any of the whims of the priest, Andrei, who had renamed him. He had not been assigned living quarters, instead dragged to an abandoned wine cellar, stripped naked, and left in irons.

The Reverend Father Andrei had visited him thrice a day, whenever it was mealtime, and commanded that Rasputin say the Lord's Prayer a hundred times before he would be allowed to eat.

Rasputin refused for a week until a different hieromonk had brought him some bread and water to keep their game of "priest and acolyte" going.

After his continued refusal of the Lord's Prayer, the hieromonk had brought him a stack of theological texts and he was instructed to begin his course of study.

The Reverend Father continued to make his visits daily and would attempt to test Rasputin on the knowledge. Rasputin refused to open a book and the sick game continued.

"If you will not read of the works of God," the priest arrived one day, "then perhaps you shall feel His might."

He pulled a golden and gem-encrusted crosier from his robes, only pausing for a moment before swinging it like a club and hitting Rasputin in his side.

In his already weakened state, he barely cried out but

managed to look up at the man with the same contempt he only shared for one other person: the murderess, Anastasia.

Rasputin ended up staying in the wine cellar for almost six months, to which time was lost to him entirely. His body had deteriorated to almost nothing, his beard had grown out, and his hair hung in dirty shambles to his shoulders.

It was only when the priest had grown tired of their game that he allowed Rasputin to be given a small room near the other novitiates.

In the end, all it took was for Rasputin to respond to the name for the priest to tire. He refused to open a text or transcribe a word of Latin in that cell where they held him, and he kept it up as they tried to force him to study and take his vows.

After five years of wreaking havoc and suffering through enough beatings to drive him to the point of near-death, both sides seemed to call a ceasefire. Rasputin was moved into a separate shed on the outskirts of the property and began working as a handyman for the monastery.

The Reverend Father still accosted him whenever he had the chance and had propositioned him on more than one occasion when he was drunk.

For the next ten years, Rasputin listened, watched, and waited for every opportunity to learn about what was happening in St. Petersburg.

He became well-versed in the way that the clergy seemed to operate, how they hid and manifested their sins, their gambling dens, and their drunken orgies. He even began to recognize the telltale signs of when acolytes would be preparing to perform dark rituals in the tunnels underneath the monastery.

He watched and he waited, his youth stolen from him day by day at Solovetsky until he was a bitter, angry man who had one goal in mind: revenge.

Rasputin was monitoring the movements of some of the

priests on the grounds, watching as they chatted with an emissary who had arrived in a royal carriage.

Glancing at the crest on the side, he tightened his grip on the ax he had been holding, praying that God had finally made himself known and he could take his revenge right here, right now.

His blood ran cold as he saw the priests turn towards him, waving Rasputin over. He froze for a second and wondered if a god had truly heard his thoughts.

"Rasputin," one of the priests nodded his head in greeting, "it seems that the time has come for you to leave us."

As much as he tried to keep his composure, Rasputin dropped the ax he was holding and it made a dull thud against the semi-frozen ground. He stared at the priest in disbelief, who merely nodded and continued.

"You're being beckoned back to the palace to return to the Tsar's service. It seems that God has a plan for you after all. The Tsar is requesting you specifically to tutor the Grand Duchess Anastasia."

Rasputin paused, unable to comprehend the words that he was hearing. He hadn't been able to leave Solovetsky for fifteen years and now, he was being ushered back to serve the Grand Duchess herself, as if they had forgotten what he knew.

Selfish pigs, he thought, *must have been drunk for over a decade.*

He was ripped from his thoughts as he felt the priest clap a sturdy hand on his shoulder.

"God speed."

Rasputin nodded in response and slowly brought a hand up to rub the stubble on his chin, his mind beginning to move at a dangerous pace.

He watched as the priests began walking back to the monastery; the carriage awaited him to grab his things and depart.

To pick up the last fifteen years of his life like it had been a short tenure and return to their chandeliers and sturgeon.

I'm going to kill the Grand Duchess Anastasia.

D eparting from the monastery was vastly different
from arriving. Mikhail took one last look around the
apartments he lived in for the past fifteen years,
tossed a few spare pairs of pants in a duffle bag, and purposefully left behind the bibles and rosaries pushed upon him over
the years.

There was no reason to stay and get sentimental over a
prison that he hadn't deserved and had been forced to shuffle
through. He was ready to leave the years behind.

One of the hieromonks appeared in his door and alerted him
to the departing coach, which had a seat for him in it. On his
way out of the door, Mikhail paused, feeling a rising rage at the
thought of everything he'd been through at the monastery.

He turned with a sharp conviction and grabbed the crucifix
on the wall, ripping it down with his bare hand, bringing
chunks of plaster with it.

Brandishing it like a sword, he swung it against the thick
walls of the room until it snapped in half. Mikhail dropped it
with a massive exhale, his chest heaving and sweat dripping
down his arms from the exertion.

The hieromonk stood and stared at him with wide eyes but did not attempt to try and stop him - as if he could. Mikhail stood a good foot above him and had now spent well over a decade working hard labor to avoid saying his prayers.

Mikhail kicked the broken cross with his boot, turned his head and spit before he walked out the door and headed for the royal carriage, revenge on his mind.

♛ ♛ ♛

Anastasia sat at the desk in her sitting room, another iron pen firmly in hand. She was simply grateful that this time the ink wasn't blood.

She knew better than to say anything, but the iron always made her hands go numb. If she said anything about how her magic was affected, she knew the circus she'd be subject to.

For that reason, she had never reacted to anything and even kept herself in the dark when it came to her abilities. Sometimes, when it was dark and she was alone in her bed, she'd release the magic at her fingertips just to see what would happen.

Nothing ever did, besides a light show that she never let grow too large for fear of being caught — and she was terrified that the same spark had flickered out in her soul. The only time she let it out was when she escaped to St. Petersburg on Sunday mornings.

Maybe it's a devil's curse after all. A cursed life.

The door to the sitting room opened quietly, the familiar sound cutting through the silence. Anastasia barely bothered to look up, expecting another iteration of the same priest her mother always sent.

Instead, she met *his* eyes. The room became stifling as they stared at one another — as if the oxygen had been replaced by something simmering and heavy. She thought she had seen everything over the years, but nothing prepared her for the man blocking the doorway.

He wasn't dressed like a priest.

His clothes were simple, which seemed out of place in such a gilded box, but it was the air around him that had Anastasia forgetting how to breathe.

Every man that she had ever met had tried to emulate it. In their words, their clothing, their violence... power. Now, seeing him, she knew beyond a dark shadow of a doubt that they were all charlatans.

The man in front of her wasn't mimicking or pretending... he *embodied* it. They sized each other up as opponents, and she was ignorant to the sparks that began flickering between her fingers.

Palpable, unadulterated authority flowed off of him before he even opened his mouth.

When he finally spoke, it was a voice that Anastasia would never forget, slow like honey, as if he was trying out how her name tasted.

"It's been a while, *Anastasia.*"

Anastasia couldn't move, the pen dropping from her hand onto the desk, "I don't believe we know each other. Although, your manners are dreadfully casual."

He felt her icy gaze rake down his body, and it was his turn to suppress a shudder, although his heartbeat was in his throat. He had spent the last fifteen years doing hard labor at a frozen monastery, and it showed, down to the hair he refused to cut and kept in a low bun.

After all this time, he was sitting in the rooms of the Grand Duchess Anastasia — he had been ready to murder her the first night she slept, but her fiery gaze made him wonder what fuel was stoking that flame. What could such a spoiled duchess be angry about?

The tension was broken by a servant who stepped in behind the man, nodding in acknowledgment.

"Your Grace," the servant bowed low, "This is Mikhail —," the man stopped. He held up his hand in apology, "Forgive me. We knew each other when we were children. Your Grace, this is Father Rasputin."

"Just Rasputin," his voice was cutting. The man looked at him in surprise, and he shrugged, "I never took the vows." The man nodded as if that was a simple answer that didn't beget a million more questions.

"My mother won't be pleased to know that she's sent someone who didn't take his vows," Anastasia found her voice and was surprised at how steady she sounded.

The man turned on his heel and left quickly, sensing the explosive atmosphere between the two. Mikhail laughed.

"Your mother has certainly hired worse."

"I can't imagine what knowledge you would have of that."

"I have much knowledge about what happens in your rooms, *Duchess.*"

Anastasia sucked in a surprised breath, shocked at how direct he was being with her — and resenting how refreshing that she thought it was.

Each fool and acolyte that her mother had paraded in front of her to encourage her to use her magic was cruel, abusive even, but they were always somewhat afraid of her. No one had spoken to Anastasia candidly in years.

"You can address me using 'Your Grace,' Mikhail."

"You can address me as Rasputin, *Your Grace.*"

"Why? That's an awful name. A terrible one. It frightens me even to say it."

"Maybe that's best, Your Grace," his face curled up in a smirk as he leaned against the doorframe. Anastasia sat back in the chaise that she was sitting in, Mikhail's eyes going directly towards the papers in front of her.

"How often do they have you transcribing pointless spells?" He nodded in her direction and Anastasia cursed her heart for skipping a beat.

"How do you even know what this is? I can't make heads or tails of it," she shrugged and wrote out a few more lines. "It's just easier to give them what they want sometimes."

"Do you give everyone what they want, Your Grace?" Mikhail pushed himself off of the doorframe and took a few more steps towards Anastasia, squaring off.

Anastasia caught the sarcasm dripping off of his tone and subconsciously began rubbing her fingers together, causing more sparks. Mikhail's eyes went directly to them and started mentally logging away every tick, every reaction, and how her magic responded.

"You have no idea what people ask of me, *Mikhail*," her voice was still as she stared up at him.

He chuckled darkly, a sound that sent Anastasia's pulse fluttering on command and the magic between her hands buzzing. She tried to act subtly as she pulled her hands from the desk and slid them into her lap, out of view.

"I've asked you once not to call me that."

"I will refuse. I don't know why you'd want to go by a name that some priest gave you."

"You don't care for priests, do you?" Mikhail grinned. "Good thing I'm not one."

"You don't go by the name they gave you?"

"I have my reasons."

"Why wouldn't you want the name your mother gave you, Mikhail?" Anastasia quipped, getting more frustrated with this man's presence in her apartments.

There was an immediate change in Mikhail, whose good-natured grin vanished, replaced by a stone-cold expression that froze over his face. The transformation made Anastasia's eyes widen.

Mikhail sat there and fought the sudden urge to take out his revenge at that moment, to leave the room and burn down the entire Winter Palace and everyone in it.

Her family must have told them that he was Asya's son — and this spoiled brat was *mocking* him. Anastasia knew no such thing and had assumed anyone would prefer their family name over one-handed to them in a pompous, overinflated religious ceremony.

"Do not call me by that name," his voice was low and threatening. "You speak of things that you do not know, *Your Grace*. Do not mistake me as a pawn of the Tsarina's or someone who gives a fuck about the golden cage you've grown up in."

Anastasia's magic sparked between her fingers, and she stood up for the first time, only coming to Mikhail's shoulder.

"*You* speak of things you do not know!" Anastasia's cover broke, and fifteen years of pent-up anger came to the surface. "How dare you assume anything about the life I lead — the life I've been imprisoned in."

"What could you know about imprisonment?!" Mikhail roared, turning around and waving at the settings around them. "It certainly looks like you're struggling, *Duchess!* Tell me, are you cold at night? Is your little belly full?"

Anastasia bit down on her lip and crossed her arms, burying her hands close to herself to keep her magic at bay.

"You know why they sent you then," she shrugged, matching him in tone. "Am I cold at night? Only when they force the windows open to see if the weather affects my magic. Am I full? I haven't been, not for fifteen years, in case hunger drives its potency. I've been caged, kept, and pushed to the edge of desperation and back to see what makes me tick — and fuck you, *Mikhail,* if you think I'll listen to a word you have to say!"

Anastasia spun on her heel and stormed off to the door leading into her bedroom, slamming it for good measure. She leaned back against it and sank to the floor, burying her head in her hands, beginning to sob.

She had stayed calm and kept her cool for fifteen years, and in fifteen minutes, this strange man had ripped her limb from limb... and left her wanting more.

♣♣♣

Mikhail stood on the other side of the bedroom door, shocked. He had spent the past fifteen years imagining what Anastasia would be like... and she had shattered every preconceived notion that he had.

He had been expecting a Grand Duchess that was spoiled, with her every whim catered to in order not to invoke the wrath of her magic. He'd assumed that the palace had decided to hide her gifts as a weapon — or as part of another convoluted religious plot of the Tsarina — and she wreaked havoc on the Winter Palace as a result.

In reality, she had been forced into captivity, which sparked a flicker of something in his chest that he didn't want to react to. He sat down in Anastasia's chaise, inhaling the scent... violets and something heavier, darker, smokier... magic.

He peered over the spells that they had her writing and scoffed at the idiocy of everyone in the palace.

Mikhail had learned a good deal from his mother growing up; while he could tell Anastasia's magic was much more potent than hers, the basic mechanics were the same. That meant that he understood the ins and outs of controlling and manipulating the gift.

He stared down at the parchment, noticing how haphazardly her lines had been drawn — almost like her hand had been cramping.

If I could just find the... ahh. There it is. Iron. Idiots.

Sure enough, the iron pen would bother Anastasia's magic

like a thorn in her side, but without any counterspells on it, it was useless to inhibit her.

Rasputin correctly assumed they had no idea it affected her at all. He dipped his finger in the inkwell and rubbed them together, giving it a cursory sniff.

His mother had taught him to look for dark magic in the most benign places because only there could it thrive. It would never stand against goodness.

Mikhail sighed and leaned back in his chair, his thoughts drifting to Asya and some of his rage against Anastasia returning.

She knows that Asya is my mother. Why else would she mock me so? What a self-righteous... his thoughts trailed off, and he cursed himself for not being able to finish them and give over to the rage entirely.

He had seen in their brief — but explosive — meeting how much she had been trapped and a puppet to the Tsar and Tsarina's will. If she was telling the truth.

No matter what he felt about Anastasia, it made him hate the monarchs even more than he already did, which he didn't think was possible.

The idea that they could abandon their daughter so fully, so entirely, and subject her to the will of these lecherous men, all aching for a hit of her power... Mikhail stopped himself before he tossed the ink well against the wall, partially out of the self-hatred that began to tangle in his chest when he realized how protective he was of her already.

It has nothing to do with her. It's only because it's wrong. It has nothing to do with her; it's the situation.

Mikhail ran a hand through his dark hair and leaned back in the chaise, one hand resting behind his head. He needed a plan.

Anastasia was going to get under his skin if he wasn't careful. She had killed his mother. That's all he needed to remember.

When he called upon the memory of Asya's kind face, all he could hear was her promise to help protect the Romanov magic. It seemed that even Asya's ghost wanted him to protect her... to help Anastasia.

He scoffed in a turmoil of self-hatred and anger, unable to diffuse, and began wondering which door was his.

Upon arrival, he was told that Anastasia's rooms were ten in total, most of them sitting empty as she wasn't allowed private maids anymore.

There was her main sitting room, where she was forced under the tutelage of crackpots and charlatans, her bedroom, and one room set up for the current tutor.

Mikhail felt something sink in his gut when he thought about how these men were allowed to sleep in her rooms... a new feeling entirely swelled in his chest when his mind dwelled on how baseless these men could be and how many had probably tried to breach Anastasia's door at night. She had likely not fallen asleep feeling safe in years.

A feeling I can relate to, dear Duchess.

8

After their explosive meeting, the next two days felt like a minefield. Mikhail and Anastasia managed to keep away from each other as best as possible, but living in the same rooms made it difficult.

Anastasia resigned herself to her bedroom most days, only emerging for meals — the only time they saw each other. The first time the heavy, silver cloche was lifted to reveal the Duchess's diet, Mikhail was repulsed.

He knew from her outburst the first night that her meals were heavily controlled, but he didn't think it was as bad as she said it was. Breakfast was cold oats, no sugar, fruit, or dressings of any kind; for lunch and dinner, she was only served buckwheat cutlets.

The portions always seemed ridiculously small, which caused Mikhail to notice how frail Anastasia was. He hadn't seen it in the dim light of the evening during their first meeting, and it was hidden with how bountifully she dressed.

The sleeves of her dresses went past her knuckles, and multiple layers of skirts hide a dangerously small frame.

Mikhail watched her eat her dinner at the end of the first day, unable to keep himself from asking.

"When was the last time you had hot food, Anastasia?"

She looked up from her dinner with wide eyes, shocked by both his breaking of the silence and the nature of his question.

"I don't remember," she said quietly, with no emotion in her voice, leaving nothing to betray her feelings on the matter. Mikhail's mind spun dangerously as he grappled with the intense shattering of his preconceived notions of Anastasia.

He had spent the last fifteen years hating her, despising her very name and image, and swearing revenge for killing his mother. The person in front of him was someone else entirely.

Yes, her cage was a ten-room suite with heavily decorated golden walls, but she resembled someone who's been kept in a bare room and starved.

The pair had spent most of their time apart, he'd imagined that she was taking advantage of the fact that he had not demanded any lessons yet.

He'd pulled some information from the messenger on the way to the palace; most of Anastasia's schedule was set by her tutors. If they commanded her to be up at six in the morning and recite lessons until nine in the evening, then that's what she would do.

The Tsar and Tsarina had remained mainly detached from their daughter's schedule, preferring to commune daily with the priests assigned to her and nothing else.

The Tsar had issued the order that pulled her from the court and was the one who dictated her meals, but they had minimal contact with their daughter.

Even Alexei was increasingly distraught over how removed his sister had become over the years, but he looked up to his father too much in the matters of ruling an empire to question how he ruled his children. His blind faith was a danger to them all.

Anastasia finished what was left of her meager dinner before she stood and gathered her skirts.

"What time shall I escort you to services tomorrow, *Your Grace?*" Mikhail found himself taunting her just to see an emotion — any emotion — on her face and cursed himself for it.

"I do not attend the Orthodox services with the boyars and the court," Anastasia said quietly, refusing to meet Mikhail's gaze. Something about his presence deeply unsettled her in a very different way from how she was used to feeling about her various tutors.

Mikhail scoffed, "How, pray tell, did you get out of that one?"

"Ten years ago, I convinced my family that I would take services privately with my tutors," she shrugged, "I said that I thought it would be best, God forbid that I be overcome by the Lord and release my magic during a service with nearly three hundred members of the nobility. A few months ago, I told my tutors I'd take services alone."

Her voice lifted near the end, and Mikhail saw the beginnings of a smirk on her face. He peered up and saw her eyes, that piercing blue fire, begin to flicker alight once more. The very sight made him want to push her harder, to fan the flame.

"Did that ever happen?" He grinned, leaning back in the chaise and sliding an arm behind his head.

"Did *what* ever happen, Mikhail?"

He chuckled at her stubborn use of his name, "Were you ever *overcome* by the Lord during time with your priests?"

Anastasia felt heat rush to her cheeks as she stared at him, shocked at the unabashed way he talked to her. It took her only a moment to regain her composure.

"Not once," she raised an eyebrow, "I guess none of them were very proficient."

"That's a damn shame, Your Grace."

"The stable master, on the other hand, proved well taught."

Mikhail sputtered audibly, sitting up and nearly falling out of his chair. Anastasia laughed, throwing her head back in an unrivaled gaiety, a sound that immediately transfixed Mikhail and made him feel like a man starving with a thirst for more.

He chuckled, shaking his head and looking up at the Grand Duchess. She was still smiling, and Mikhail began to scold himself internally for how much he loved that smile. The realization flooded over him like a bucket of cold water.

The smile quickly dropped from his face, sobering up immediately as he was caught in an intense wave of self-hatred and shame for finding even the smallest of joys in the company of his mother's murderer.

Anastasia noticed the abrupt change in his expression and figured she had gone too far. Soon, the tutor would surely emerge from within him.

"Well," she broke the silence, smoothing her skirts, "We leave tomorrow at dawn."

"I'm sorry?" Mikhail looked up at her in confusion. "I thought you said you didn't go to services."

"I don't. I have my own things to attend to. I'll need an escort." Anastasia turned and began walking towards her room.

"Is the stable master indisposed?" he snapped, suddenly and simultaneously full of ire at himself and the idea of Anastasia spending any time with someone who likely didn't want to understand that fire in her eyes.

"No," she said quietly, opening the door to her rooms, "My last tutor had him killed."

♣♣♣

The next morning, Mikhail was ready at dawn and prepared for anything.

It had been barely thirty-six hours since he had come crashing back into Anastasia's orbit and found himself perplexed. She was a woman who had layers to her; that much was apparent.

After her family had diminished her, she must have hidden the last precious bits of her soul so they couldn't be stolen.

The door to Anastasia's room swung open, and she stepped out in a plain sarafan, betraying her underweight figure.

Mikhail couldn't keep the surprise from showing on his face as he studied her, his fists tightening at the thought of the Tsar demanding his daughter be underfed... just to see if it would spark her bloody magic, for fuck's sake.

"You'll have to change," she said quietly, nodding towards the habit that Mikhail was wearing. "Although if you didn't take your vows, I'm not sure why you're wearing that at all."

He scoffed, "It seems to be the only thing the Tsarina keeps stocked for your tutors." He held out his arms, the sleeves riding up.

Anastasia shook her head, avoiding his good-natured probe, "I'm serious. Please. This is important to me." Her voice got quieter when she said it as if it was a great secret that she hadn't shared with anyone before. He felt his chest seize when he realized that there was a good chance that she very well hadn't.

"One moment, Your Grace," he nodded, all of the informality between them slipping away, as little of it as there was, to begin with. When he emerged, wearing the only clothes he had brought with him from the monastery, Anastasia nodded in approval at the rough shirt and canvas pants. With that, she turned and walked towards the door.

"You'll need to go first," she said without turning around. "If anyone sees us, they'll assume it's some sort of penance."

Mikhail nodded, sliding in front of her and placing his hand on the door, "Where are we going?"

"Out the East Wing, straight out of the palace grounds. We shouldn't see anyone since Mass has started. If we do, they were likely too drunk to go to service and won't notice."

"Keep your head down," he said in warning, pushing the door open and leading Anastasia out of the room.

They wound their way through the never-ending hallways, the obscene amount of wealth plastered to the walls and hanging from the ceiling bringing back a familiar nausea in Mikhail that he fought to keep off of his face.

He was grateful that Anastasia was behind him and unable to see his expression as he grappled with an onslaught of emotions navigating through the palace for the first time in fifteen years. When he had arrived two days prior, he had been brought straight to her chamber.

Anastasia's predictions about the castle activity were apt, and they didn't see a single soul on their way out. Mikhail was shocked as they made it to the exit in the East Wing, a surprisingly common door with no guard.

"No one can see it from the front gate," Anastasia whispered from behind him as if she was reading his thoughts, "so no one uses it. See and be seen, of course."

"Of course," Mikhail scoffed and pushed it open.

As soon as they left the courtyard, Anastasia overtook him and began leading him through a series of alleys in the city of St. Petersburg.

He was once again grateful that she couldn't see his face, as he was bereft with the sights and sounds of his home city after so long.

A day hadn't gone by when he hadn't worried about the life he left behind, the tiny neighborhood where they had lived — which they had called 'the Village' after their ancestral farmland before a *boyar* snapped it up.

He was so pulled into his thoughts; he didn't realize where they were until Anastasia turned on another side street, and Mikhail stopped, staring at the crowded slum in front of him.

"Where are we?" His voice cracked, as he recognized every slanted roof, doorframe, and broken window.

Anastasia turned to face him, her voice deadly quiet as her eyes lit up. "If you tell anyone about this, it will harm them more than it ever harms me," her voice was foreboding. "Do you understand? No one knows about this, but you... well, you're hardly a priest."

"Hardly," Mikhail nodded, wondering why Anastasia brought them to the street that he had grown up on. She let out a shaky breath, and Mikhail leaned closer to her, his mind spinning a million miles a minute.

"I'm sure you were told a myriad of things when you were hired," she pulled them to the side of the street to get out of the way. "The first time my magic... exploded," she chewed over the word as if they didn't feel right, "I killed someone."

Mikhail stopped, unable to move, unable to think, unable to breathe.

"It was my lady-in-waiting," Anastasia's voice cracked, and she bit her lip hard. "Her name was Asya. She was the only person I loved in the whole world. And it was during another one of my mother's fucking lessons!"

Anastasia released half a sob and choked the rest down like rotten food, her hand going to cover her face as she looked anywhere but Mikhail's gaze.

"The priest had put some sort of binding spell on me, I don't know... it all happened so fast. Asya broke into the room and tried to help me all while my mother went after her with a knife. I screamed; I was so scared... then it all went dark."

She doesn't know Asya was my mother, he thought as he watched her tremble.

Anastasia wiped at her eyes, breathing shakily and Mikhail eyed a tremor in her hands, still frozen to the spot in front of her. He couldn't believe what she was saying after fifteen years of holding onto one singular notion of how that fateful night had gone.

"When I woke up, my whole life changed. They told me that

I had killed Asya, or, I suppose, my magic did. I have been cursed by the Devil himself. The only woman who ever showed me kindness... it was an accident. And I killed her."

"Anastasia...," Mikhail reached for her, but she stepped back.

"It gets worse," she hiccuped and began wringing her hands together. "She had a son, you know. They had to send him away, ship him off. He saw it happen. I ruined his life. I tried, over the years, to get them to bring him back..."

Mikhail paled, unable to breathe as his world unraveled in front of him.

She... she had no idea. It was an accident? An accident? Did she send for me? She sent for me!

"I know," he said, looking up at her and trying to catch her gaze. When she refused to look him in the eye, he leaned forward and captured her chin with his thumb. "Anastasia," he said again, "I know."

They stared at one another, so close now that they were almost touching, as realization dawned over Anastasia — this man had Asya's eyes. She shook her head repeatedly, choking the words out as tears began running freely down her face.

"No, no, no, no...," she gasped, her hands going to his wrist near her face. "It can't be."

He nodded, "I think we've both been living in our own prisons for a very long time, Your Grace." His voice was dangerously detached and calm as he stared at her, unable to stop thinking about how utterly captivating she was when she cried.

"Could... could you ever forgive me?" Anastasia's voice was quiet and sad, a demure quality to it that didn't suit her. Mikhail hated it.

"I don't know if forgiveness is the word for it," he shook his head, abandoning himself to fate at that moment and unable to process. "Maybe the best we can ask for is acceptance."

Anastasia nodded, "It was bold of me to ask. You must hate

me." She stepped back, and they released their holds on one another.

"I thought I did," he said quietly, so low that she could barely hear it. She knew not to press him on the statement. "Answer me this, Anastasia. What are we doing here?" He waved his hand around them, looking at the streets.

"I come here every week. I have been for the past few months," she said quietly. "The *dvorovye* return to their families on Sunday, if they're lucky, before going back to the fields and their lords."

Mikhail looked around and got a sick feeling in his stomach as he saw, for the first time, the serf boys running around wearing *rogatka;* spiked, iron collars that would ensure they returned to the farms to have them taken off.

"I give them all the money I can. I'll smuggle a few trinkets out of the palace," she shrugged quietly. "I can use the littlest amounts of magic, sometimes, if it works. Help their families with their chores before they say goodbye to their sons. It's... horrid. This system, Mikhail. You must know."

"I do," his voice was somber, yet filled with confused awe, as he found himself completely at a loss for how to respond to this version of the woman he thought he had hated.

"I need to stop it," she said quietly, and Mikhail's attention snapped to her immediately. "I don't know how."

He suddenly remembered his mother's vision, the last of the oracle gifts she had given him, to *protect the Romanov magic.*

"I can teach you, Your Grace," he gave her a soft smile, "...if you require a tutor."

❦ 9 ❦

The next morning, a quiet calm had settled over Anastasia's rooms. The first two days together had challenged all of Anastasia and Mikhail's perceptions — and both of them struggled with the revelation of the other.

Mikhail was awake early, a habit from spending the last fifteen years in a monastery, unable to sleep in once the sun was up. He was pacing his bedroom, hands behind his back.

The overly done furnishings of the room made him dreadfully uncomfortable, and he had half a mind to hock it to make Anastasia mad before reconsidering.

She has no loyalty to her family... She even wants to see their cruelty abolished.

Mikhail's mind was turning like a cog on wheels without coolant, throwing sparks and threatening to explode. He had spent over a decade with one singular version of Anastasia in his mind. Now, he was face to face with her, and she was exactly the opposite.

Seeing her family's cruelty end doesn't mean she necessarily wants a revolution... he wagered with himself, wondering how deep her loyalties ran.

When his mind drifted to her controlled diet and how thin she'd become, how trapped she was in these rooms, forced to sit through an endless barrage of useless acolytes poking her for her magic...

How did she not destroy the whole place as soon as she could? As soon as she had a chance?

Maybe she wanted to. She hadn't known who Mikhail was when he arrived and he could see during her confession how deeply Asya's death bothered her. It had been an accident, that much he could see was true.

He knew what it looked like to carry a burden for that long, a lump of hot coal turning in your stomach, how those lines took shape on a person's face. It didn't matter that it had only been two days, the circumstances under which their lives had come together were a crashing force, like tectonic plates battling it out against one another.

Now, only time would tell if they would be able to recognize each other's matching scars or if the animosity of things out of their control would drive them apart.

Protect the Romanov magic. Rasputin heard his mother's voice in his head, her *last* oracle message... but how could he forsake his love for her to help her murderer?

An accident. An accident! She was a child... you've seen how she's been taught to feel about her magic.

His thoughts were at war with one another when he heard a knock on the chamber's main door. Mikhail quickly moved to go answer it, feeling like the noise was a disruption of the uneasy truce that had settled between the two of them.

When he swung the heavy door open, one of the servants was there with a serving tray full of chargers and cloches.

"Set it on the table," Rasputin's voice was quiet and he realized that he didn't want anything to wake Anastasia.

He groaned internally, the dichotomy of his heart threatening to drive his brain in two. The servant quickly dispatched the food and was gone moments later.

Mikhail filtered through his options before settling on one — going over and knocking gently on Anastasia's door. She swung it open nearly a second later, betraying that she had been awake for quite some time, too.

Anastasia fought to keep the expression off her face as she soaked in the sight that was early morning Mikhail; his canvas shirt and trousers rumpled from sleep, hair pulled onto the top of his head, and his smile shockingly warm.

"I didn't want to disturb you," he grinned easily, "I wanted to wake you before the food got cold."

"The — before what?" Anastasia's eyes went wide as her gaze shifted to behind Mikhail. She gasped and her hand flew up to her mouth, as the tops of the cloches had been removed and a full breakfast was spread out in her sitting room.

"Oh my *God*," her voice was reverent as she descended on it, sitting down and grabbing the first piece of pheasant that she could get her hands on.

Anastasia sunk her teeth into it and collapsed back in her chair. She began to gorge herself on the hot food while Mikhail watched on with a smile on his face as a warm feeling expanded in his chest.

Once she finished the piece of meat, she reached for something else and then — paused. Anastasia's eyes rolled over the table as she seemed almost overwhelmed, tears beginning to shine in her eyes.

Mikhail was hammered with the realization of how long she had gone without.

He was next to her side in an instant, gently putting his hand on her arm, "Here, let me."

Anastasia nodded and leaned back a little in her chair, resigning and letting Mikhail fix her a plate.

In an incredibly ironic twist, after living her entire life in the Winter Palace surrounded by feasts, Anastasia had no idea what half of the dishes were and didn't know how to serve them to herself.

Mikhail handed her the heavy, silver plate, loaded with food for the first time in years... Anastasia accepted it and looked up at him, sniffling quietly.

"I... I don't...," she stopped and stared down at it, "I don't know what to say. You should hate me, Mikhail; you really should."

He shrugged, leaning away from her as the physical proximity was beginning to make him twitch.

"Maybe I still do," he shrugged, now unable to meet her gaze. "I don't know. I really don't... you need to eat, especially if we're going to work on your magic."

She nodded and fell back onto the plate. Mikhail watched her eat for a few moments, his heartbeat clanging at the joy on her face before he forced himself to turn away.

When she was finished, Mikhail shook his head, grabbed the plate, filled it for a second time, and handed it back to her.

"Eat, Anastasia," his voice left no room for argument, and she accepted the plate. She stared at it for a few moments before Mikhail raised an eyebrow at her, silently conveying his confusion.

"I don't...," Anastasia's voice was quiet, as though this was suddenly the most uncomfortable she had been around him. "I'm already full."

Mikhail stopped, a sick realization settling over him. As much as Anastasia was fighting against a starving man's mentality, pushing back against the urge to eat everything in sight, her stomach was small from years of neglect. He turned away from her.

"I have no intention of letting them starve you like that again." Mikhail's voice was stoic, speaking the gentle reminder out loud to ease Anastasia's panic. She nodded once, changing the subject.

"What was it like for you?" She asked quietly, popping another bite into her mouth, keeping her eyes downcast. Mikhail stiffened and looked at her, his eyes going wide.

"Are you sure that you want to know?" He sighed, wondering if it would be better for the both of them to leave the past buried. Anastasia nodded.

"I need to know. It was... my fault."

Mikhail didn't say anything before shrugging, "It wasn't pleasant. I fought with the priests often. The first six months, they held me naked in a wine cellar and beat me until they realized I'd never accept the priesthood."

The way it fell out of his mouth so casually made Anastasia nearly drop the bite that she had been holding. Her face paled, and a heavy sense of shame sank in her gut, a red flush rising to her ears.

"I... I am sorry."

"I was more upset over the loss of my mother," and as soon as Mikhail said it, he realized how much of a barb that it was. Anastasia put her fork down and stared at him, the both of them easing back into their emotional corners, a tense atmosphere settling over the room.

"I loved her, too, Mikhail," she said, her throat tight as she fought the sensation of wanting to run and hide. "You weren't the only person who lost her that day —"

"Because you killed her!" Mikhail's voice had a reverberation to it that sent chills down Anastasia's spine, and both of them jumped to their feet.

"It was an accident! Why can't you understand that? I don't know even know how —"

"You did. You did! *Fuck*, Anastasia, did you truly have no idea what you were doing?"

"I was a *child!*" Anastasia screeched, her face flushing as the two squared off, their posture going cold and hostile; any truce between them earlier in the morning evaporated.

"You're a murderer!"

"You don't think I know that? I've lived every day —"

"— You've *lived*!"

"Do you call this living? I lost the only person who ever —"

"Don't you *dare* say that she loved you!" Mikhail's voice shook the chandelier; his face was red and his chest heaving, his hair beginning to slip out of its knot.

Anastasia's hand flew to her face and her teeth began to grind, feeling an intense wave of melancholy wash over her as if he was trying to steal the only happy memories she had.

"You have no idea what she meant to me. I know she was your mother, Mikhail —"

"MY NAME IS RASPUTIN!"

"Fuck you and *fuck that name!*" Anastasia screamed, her voice matching his in power as sparks began to flicker between her fingertips.

She cursed, clasping her hands together and rubbing her fingers across her knuckles to get the magic to die down.

"What, are you going to light me up, too?" Mikhail taunted her, tugging at his shirt and loosening it from where it had been tucked in.

Anastasia stopped, all of the blood leaving her face as that awful day came rushing back to her — the shame, the guilt, the leering looks, and the day her freedom ended.

Without thinking, she picked up the lid of a cloche, reeled back and threw it at Mikhail's head. It narrowly missed him as he ducked to the side, crashing into the wall with an echoing, metallic clang.

Mikhail turned to look at her, his eyebrows raising, all of the hatred he had struggled with towards her rushing back to the surface.

He turned and stalked towards her, Anastasia backing up until she was standing against the wall. Mikhail moved across the room and was towering over her, his massive frame boxing her in.

"Go on," Mikhail teased her with a sneer that she hadn't ever seen on his face before, "Try something. What's the worst that can happen... You'll kill me too?"

Anastasia let out a strangled cry, the tears finally slipping down her cheeks as she screamed in frustration. She raised her hands in front of her face, hardly able to see through her tears as they came harder, holding her palms out in front of Mikhail's chest to try and summon her magic... but nothing happened.

She let out a scream of frustration and slammed both of her hands down on his chest, railing against him with fifteen years of caged emotion.

Mikhail grunted, grabbing her wrists and raising them above her head in one rapid motion. She pushed her back off the wall, refusing to be subdued until he moved his leg between hers and pinned her there.

Anastasia gasped and tried to wiggle free as his hands tightened around her, not enough to hurt but enough to convey that she wasn't going anywhere.

He leaned in impossibly close until their bodies were flush, heat radiating off of one another. They stood there for a moment, neither of them able to make a sound as they worked to catch their breath.

Anastasia tried to twist out of his grip again, once, twice — to no avail. Her eyes went wide as she felt his anger beginning to melt off of him, a dark chuckle vibrating along her skin and forcing her to glance up at his face.

"Tsk, tsk, tsk," Mikhail muttered, shaking his head in mock sincerity. "You would need magic to get out of this, *Your Grace.*"

"Fuck you."

Anastasia cursed internally as her tone betrayed her, now utterly bereft of any malice.

"I think, despite everything... you'd like to," he winked, "You do look rather torn up about it, though."

Mikhail gave her a saccharine smile and released her wrists, letting her push off the wall and shove past him — forcing the thoughts of his weight pressed against her out of her mind. She reached the door to her bedroom when his voice stopped her in her tracks.

"Lessons are at noon."

"Excuse me?" Anastasia spat indignantly, turning on her heel and staring at him, her eyes livid and full of fire.

Beautiful. Mikhail thought. *She's a murderer with no control of her magic... but she's stunning when she's alight.*

"Lessons," he cleared his throat and nodded at the destroyed breakfast in front of them. "Your mother will want some sort of report from me. And, I'd rather prefer it if you got a grip on whatever... power," he rolled his eyes at the word, "you do possess."

Anastasia felt something cold wash over her as if she had jumped in freezing water. As volatile as their relationship was, he wasn't like anyone her mother had ever sent before. That something different had given her brief glimpses of hope.

If he was hellbent on being another tutor... he wanted something. Riches from her parents, a title, land, maybe. Whatever the past three days had been, she thought it at least had been real.

He's been trying to get under my skin this whole time to get a rise out of me, hasn't he? It's all a show to be the man who unleashed Anastasia's magic.

"I'll let you calm down," Mikhail winked at her, settling back down next to the spilled food as if he didn't have a care in the world. "We'll try in a few hours."

Anastasia stood in her doorframe, shaking her head. "When a tutor fails, my father has them killed," she opened the door to her room. "If my magic doesn't kill you, the fact that it won't appear, will."

10

A nastasia disappeared into the bedroom, slamming the door behind her and running her hands through her hair. She took several deep breaths, trying to calm down and regain her composure.

Her thoughts ran wild as she tried to reconcile the man who had brought her breakfast with the man who still blamed her for Asya's murder.

I was a child. I didn't know...

Anastasia slid down the wall and buried her head in her hands, beginning to cry quietly as she cursed the tears that sprang to her eyes.

No, no, no... I can't let him hear me.

She was torn over the quickly discarded belief that he would be someone different, someone who might break her from this cage — and the realization that he was just like every other priest before him.

Except he wasn't even a priest, and he probably wanted her dead for what she'd done.

She pulled her knees up to her chest and rested her head there, letting the tears fall. The crushing weight of her past, of a childhood devoid of love and full of judgment, went sweeping through her, making her feel as if she was being pulled apart at the seams.

She let out a stuttered breath and forced herself to put a lid back on her emotions, wiping the tears away with the back of her hand and standing up. She smoothed her skirts, looking at the clock and realizing that it was barely past daybreak.

There were a few hours to go until her lessons began... and she prayed she wouldn't spend the whole time thinking about Mikhail's body pressed against hers and how his grip felt on her wrists. He had seemed even more massive as he had held her against that wall...

Stop it! Christ, Anastasia. That man would love to see you hang. It would help if he weren't so... domineering.

She let out a grunt of frustration and tossed herself on the bed, unable to decide if she was nervous or excited for this to truly begin.

❦❦❦

Mikhail watched as Anastasia stormed off, the threat hanging in the air between them. What were they doing? He knew that her loyalties were fragmented at best, and she wanted to change things. They couldn't seem to get past their personal hurts enough to have more than a few minutes of conversation.

We've spent the past fifteen years orbiting one another in our own ways... neither of us has seen the sun.

Both Mikhail and Anastasia were victims of a system that had wounded them grievously and brought them to their knees.

They were each so blinded by their obsession to cover their scars that they couldn't see their injuries were the same.

Mikhail grunted as he stood, letting his hair down and running a hand through it as if he could shake out the tension. His whole body felt tight.

That damn woman.

With a glance and a thought towards her door, Mikhail stood up and headed into his room. He shut the door behind him and felt like he could breathe, if only for a second, with two walls between them. He laid down on the bed, unable to shake the strain from his muscles.

"*Proklyataya baba,*" he cursed under his breath, sitting up and leaning against the headboard. Since their argument, he had been painfully hard feeling Anastasia twist underneath him had nearly driven him mad. It would have been so easy to close the gap between them, to grab her face and pull her into an angry kiss.

Despite his fury towards their past, he had spent the first few days of their time together aggressively fighting the urge to imagine what she would feel like underneath him; having her pinned against the wall had given him everything and nothing.

"For *fuck's* sake," he hissed, giving up.

Mikhail's hand went straight to the band of his canvas pants, losing all sense of hesitation and pushing them down until his cock sprang free. He wrapped a hand around himself, immediately beginning to stroke as his head rolled back against the headboard.

He tried to force himself to think of something else — anything other than Anastasia. Her eyes, that blonde hair, those perfect, pouting lips... His breath picked up until it was ragged, sweat breaking out on his forehead as he fought back angry grunts. God forbid she hears him.

"*Yebat,*" his control shattered, and he forced out a guttural sound that was almost inhuman. He stroked himself faster and faster, trying his hardest to keep his mind on someone else.

He finally found a rhythm while imagining some faceless woman to occupy his dangerously possessive thoughts. The closer he brought himself to finishing, the more his mind flickered back to Anastasia, to her body pressed against his, that angry fire in her eyes, her blonde hair.

He twisted his hand just the way he liked, finally discarding the suffocating need to ignore his thoughts of her. He let images of her flood his mind, tension coiling at the base of his spine as he stroked faster, his lips drawing in a ragged breath to keep from making too much noise.

He clenched his teeth, imagining what it would feel like to touch her skin, to slide his hand between her legs and bury himself deep inside of her.

The thought of it broke him, his release rushing through him so violently he bit down on his fist as hard as he could to keep from shouting, coming as hard as he ever had to the thought of the woman he'd sworn he hated.

♔♔♔

Anastasia waited until it was approximately five minutes past his commanded lesson schedule before she emerged from the bedroom, purposefully late.

Mikhail was sitting down, his ankle resting on his knee and a curious look on his face that she couldn't quite place.

"Sit," his voice left no room for argument.

Anastasia eyed him cautiously as he couldn't seem to look her in the eye when she took her seat. He was rifling through a stack of papers that she had inscribed spell after spell on.

Occasionally, he'd lift one to his face and smell it, analyzing either the ink or the paper; she couldn't tell. It was an agonizing five minutes before Anastasia broke the silence.

"Well? Are you going to say something? Or are you just going to keep me here all day for no reason?"

"You aren't really in a position to be making demands, Your Grace." His voice was heavy, and Anastasia raised an eyebrow, growing frustrated.

"What is your game here, Mikhail?" She said his name in the same tone that he used as if she was trying to get under his skin. She was. Mikhail stopped and put the papers down, looking down from where he towered above her, even as he sat.

"We don't have to like each other for this to work," his voice took on a deadly quiet tone. "We need to at least respect each other. Can you agree to that?"

Anastasia didn't know what to think as she stared at the man sitting across from her. They had shared some moments that she had cherished greatly, and she'd trusted him enough to bring him to the slums the day before. Their argument at breakfast had shattered any illusion she might have had that he might be different from most of the acolytes her mother had brought before.

He was, of course, very different looking... None of the tutors that she had been forced to study under had made her wonder what it would be like to be, well, *under them.*

They stood on shakier ground with even shakier hearts, both of them recoiling from the sudden impact of their pasts colliding with their present. He did, at least, seem eager to teach her about the use of her magic, whatever the situation. If anyone could teach her anything, it was surely Asya's son.

Anastasia's eyes fluttered, and she looked up at Mikhail, making his heart stop in his chest.

A man could die happy being on the other end of a look like that.

"I can agree to that," she folded her hands in her lap, "For Asya."

Mikhail's gaze snapped up, staring at Anastasia and finding his breath becoming erratic again at the mention of his mother's name. This woman was going to be the death of him if she continued to remind him of their past.

"Don't —"

"Stop it," Anastasia held up her hand. "We can't pretend like she didn't matter to the both of us. We can't. We do not have to like each other, I agree. We can respect each other. It doesn't feel respectful to your mother's memory to ignore what she meant to us."

Anastasia cursed the tears in her eyes, wondering why being around this man had unlocked a gate that she had kept around her emotions for years. She subconsciously began tugging her sleeves down over her knuckles.

Mikhail made note of the tick but said nothing. He had noticed how she had deferred to referring to Asya as his mother instead of using her name. He noted the respect on her features and the ache in her voice, plain as day, scattered across her words.

The duality of his emotions was enough to make him consider going back to the monastery. Mikhail felt like kicking himself again every time he came face-to-face with how much pain she had shouldered alone for years.

Fifteen years. Fifteen years where he had been doing the same. Both of them sequestered from the events of one night that left them with scars they were too afraid to show anyone.

"Alright," he sighed, finding his resolve cracking every time that he was around Anastasia. "We can respect each other. For Asya."

Anastasia nodded in response, and the silence dragged on for a few more moments. Nothing could fill such an intimate silence dragging with remnants of their wounds. Mikhail cleared his throat, pausing to take his hair down and refasten the knot.

"So, from what I've gathered," he leaned closer to her and showed her some of her old spell sheets, "Your tutors had no idea what they were dealing with."

Anastasia couldn't help it and burst out laughing at the remark. Mikhail recoiled, a little surprised by the sound.

Dear God, I love that sound. I wonder how much this woman has laughed in the last fifteen years. Not enough. Fuck. Stop it.

He cleared his throat, and Anastasia's hand went to cover her mouth, stifling back a few giggles as she thought of all of the priests that had promised they held an understanding of the gift she hardly knew herself.

"So," Mikhail started again, "from what I gather, they really did think you were cursed."

"I'm not?"

"No. Well, 'cursed' is a relative term. I don't think you are cursed —"

"What makes you say that?"

"Anastasia," his voice took on a disciplinary tone that made Anastasia blush, "Can you please stop interrupting me?" Anastasia nodded and beckoned for him to continue.

"Anyway," Mikhail flipped a few of the sheets, "No, I wouldn't say that you're cursed. A curse is typically inflicted *on* someone throughout their life. You have hereditary gifts. By definition, it doesn't fit a curse."

"They did say it was in my father's bloodline."

Mikhail nodded, "Yes, it's Romanov. I dug around in your family's library. From what I found, it looks like your mother was chosen to wed your father specifically based on the lack of magic in her bloodline to help dilute his."

"That worked well," Anastasia rolled her eyes, "She's *obsessed* with it."

Mikhail shrugged, "She's obsessed with control. Your family is waning in popularity politically, but people remain highly loyal to the Orthodox Church. If they can keep enough mystics and clerics performing *miracles* —"

"They stay in power simply due to the religious fervor," Anastasia finished for him and Mikhail gave her a reprimanding look for cutting him off again. She blushed.

A woman could die satisfied being on the other end of a look like that.

"Yes, that's essentially it. As you already know, your mother seems to have a talent for crackpots more than anyone with authentic magic. They've forced those people into hiding when they suppress gifts like yours. People already gossip about your tutors."

"They do?"

"Yes. You aren't the secret that your family thinks you are. People whisper, especially the devout ones, about the demon princes that have to mentor Anastasia. Why do you think they're always killed?"

"I figured my mother was upset."

Mikhail waved a hand dismissively, "Your mother doesn't care. Your father does it to keep people at bay. It's all a political show to make him look like a good, Orthodox man, executing the tutors that he discovers are using black magic."

"That's all of them..." Anastasia's face paled as she realized how far her father was willing to go to have his cake and eat it, too.

It was a vicious cycle, hiring priests who practiced the dark arts only to have them executed publicly for their magic as a political move when they failed him.

She always knew that she was a pawn but the gravity of her situation seemed to slowly pour over her, freezing her blood like ice in her veins.

"How do you know all this?"

Mikhail shrugged, "Some I learned from my mother, but you'd be surprised how much monks gossip even when they're hundreds of miles away. The books I found in the library bridged the gaps."

"Do you think... Do you think he would kill me, too?" Anastasia looked up at Mikhail. He unsuccessfully attempted to squash down the protective feeling that rose in his chest.

"Anastasia," his hand going to cover hers, "I don't... I don't know how we're going to move forward. I don't. I will promise you this — I will not let the Tsar hurt you."

"You wouldn't mind seeing me dead!" Anastasia removed her hand from his grip, her brow furrowing.

Mikhail let out a grunt and picked up the spell sheets again, "I already told you. I'm not going to promise anything about us working together."

"Well, that won't work for me!" Anastasia jumped to her feet and scoffed, "I'm just supposed to trust you blindly, *respect* you, while you might be planning my demise. Do you think I'm stupid?"

"No," Mikhail kept rifling through the papers as if he was dealing with someone throwing a tantrum that he had no patience to sort through. "I think you're sheltered, and you have no idea how to use your magic. Honestly, the biggest threat to you right now is *you.*"

Anastasia sputtered, looking around the room in frustration before sinking back down in her seat. "I don't like it."

"You don't have to," he shrugged. "I don't like it, either. Is your tantrum over?" His voice was antagonistic as he looked up at her, chewing on his lip, shamelessly eyeing her flustered cheeks.

Anastasia settled in her chair, plastering a perfect smile on her face that Mikhail already knew to fear. "It is. You'll have to forgive me. It sounds like I'm a little more *pent up* than the present company." She arched an eyebrow, and it was Mikhail's turn to freeze.

Fuck. Did she hear me?

"The walls are thin," Anastasia smirked, "Do remember that next time."

He swallowed thickly and recovered swiftly, "I wouldn't be surprised if you're a little more *tightly wound.* Judging by your magic — you have no idea how to *release.*" He cocked a brow, making his tone unmissable.

"You are an insufferable —"

"Stop," Mikhail's tone was firm as he cut her off, "Your

magic." Anastasia let out a long breath and glanced down at her sparking hands; the conversation pivoted before they ended up at each other's throats once more.

"Go on."

"It's hereditary. My mother was an oracle, but that's clearly not what you possess," he said, analyzing the magic swirling around her hands." It's much more powerful than that. You're an amplifier."

"I'm a *what?*"

"Essentially, you can manipulate energy down to an atomic level. You can speed them up, slow them down, make energy and matter respond to you. It's why you could explode gas lights that night — you made them react to your magic and amplified the flame until it burst."

"What about with Alexei... the... whatever he was."

"A khlyst priest," he nodded, "I heard about that. You did the same thing with air instead of fire. You turned it into a weapon."

Anastasia's mind began to spin at the implications. *This* was true power and it scared her. Her heart rate began to pick up at the thought of what would happen if her family discovered the full extent of what she could do.

"They'll turn me into a weapon," she said, her voice going quiet.

"You need to learn to control your magic so that doesn't happen." There was a tone to Mikhail's voice that made Anastasia's blood boil, as though she had willfully neglected her magic all these years - as if it had been a choice.

"Don't blame me for this," she snapped. "I've used my magic twice in my life, and both times were enough to make me want to cut my hands off."

"You need to lean into who you are, Anastasia," Mikhail felt his temper going hot at how willing she was to pass off her gift. "You're right. If you don't get a hold of this, they will make you a weapon. You have to figure it out so you can fight them off."

"Why are you acting like I haven't tried?"

"Have you?" Mikhail pushed, wanting to see what happened.

"Well... how could I?! I've had nothing but priests sleeping a door away from me my entire life. They've all just been waiting for the opportunity to tell my parents that my magic has reappeared again."

"It's not reappearing. It never left you."

"It's unreliable!"

"You use it when you go out on Sundays," he stared at her, his eyes challenging her. Anastasia felt her blood begin to boil in a way that only seemed to happen when she was around this man.

"I use the smallest amounts, and it is barely useful, at best. I've never been able to recreate the results of... what happened," she muttered. It was true. She could make small things happen, and she was hardly ever without her faithful sparks, but she had never been able to make the great pulses of power come flooding out of her body.

"It's because you don't want it," Mikhail shrugged, putting the papers down and clasping his hands in front of him. Anastasia turned to face him, gritting her teeth.

"How could I want to kill someone!" She screamed, her resolve cracking.

"You're *afraid*."

"How dare you —"

"You're afraid of who you could be. You're afraid of who you already know you are."

"CAN YOU BLAME ME?" Anastasia shrieked, throwing her hands in the air and releasing the truth about her fears surrounding magic for the first time. Mikhail stopped, the both of them staring at one another — Anastasia flushed and Mikhail frustratingly stoic.

The silence stretched between them, moving them farther and farther apart until he physically reached across the gap, grabbing Anastasia's face with his hands and pulling her into a vicious kiss.

There was nothing tender or exploring about it, both of them meeting in a crushing embrace that was more fight than finesse.

Mikhail paused for a moment, shocked by his lack of control. Anastasia fisted his shirt and brought him back to her. In one smooth move, Mikhail rolled Anastasia over until she was under him.

She squirmed in response, and he bit at her lip, hard and punishing as if he was trying to pull the fear from her.

Anastasia let out a noise that sounded foreign to her as she felt Mikhail's large hand moving up her side. He cupped the side of her breast, and Anastasia tossed her head back, giving Mikhail access to her neck.

Her breath hitched as he moved down, placing kisses along her jaw and neck. She tugged on his shirt, desperate to get it off of him as he moved back up to capture her mouth with his.

His hand moved again and gave her breast a firm squeeze, sending shockwaves through Anastasia — which sent Mikhail flying off her.

The moment was shattered, Anastasia's magic exploding out of her in response and leaving her wanton and breathless on the chair. She stared wide-eyed at Mikhail, now kneeling at her feet.

Both of them sat there for a moment, once again on a precipice where they had no idea what to do with their reactions to one another. Mikhail broke out into laughter.

"That was one way to get you to use your magic. I was right."

"Right about what?" Anastasia snapped, sitting up straighter and attempting to straighten her skirts.

"You have no idea how to *release* your magic," his voice was dripping with innuendo that made Anastasia feel light-headed all over again.

"I have my magic, though," she offered a lame rebuttal.

"You have uncontrolled magic that is released by... extreme emotion," Mikhail chuckled and stood, running his hand over the stubble on his jaw. He sat down quickly again, and Anastasia rolled her eyes at his feeble attempt to hide his hard-on.

"Hatred is still a very extreme emotion, Mikhail."

Mikhail grinned, tossing a hand behind his head in a picture of male arrogance that made Anastasia want to hit him and beg him to climb on top of her again.

"Hate me all you'd like, *Your Grace*," he licked his lips, "It seems I'll get what I want either way."

"And what is that, Mikhail?"

"I want your magic to burn this palace to the ground."

11

"Hold it, hold it…," Mikhail's voice was steady as he watched Anastasia grow a sphere of light between her fingers. He stood behind her, keeping a safe distance between them. It had been a few weeks since their explosive first attempt at uncovering Anastasia's magic.

"*Gav-no*," Anastasia hissed, the light between her hands expanding in a great burst and showering them both in sparks.

"It's okay," Mikhail nodded. "You'll get there."

"When?!" Anastasia hissed, turning around and staring up at him. He couldn't help but suppress a grin. He loved it when she got flustered.

As much as he enjoyed their repartee these past few weeks, neither of them could get comfortable with one another. They fought like cats and dogs one minute and had to force themselves to their separate bedrooms the next.

"When it happens," Mikhail shrugged easily, the picture of nonchalance as if the world wasn't threatening to fall around them.

Amidst their uneasy truce, the political restlessness in the

Winter Palace had been growing and hurtling towards a fever pitch.

The divide between the serfs and the boyars was at an all-time high, and the rolling religious fervor with it. People of all backgrounds flocked to the Orthodox Church to find reprieve from what ailed them.

A rise in witch-hunts and acolyte trials filled the streets, with the Tsar publicly executing more "false idols" every day in political theatre.

The Tsar and Tsarina continually pestered Mikhail for updates on Anastasia's magic, eager to begin utilizing her as a pawn in their games amongst the turmoil. Every day, they summoned Anastasia and Mikhail to show off Anastasia's gifts, and every day, the two refused.

Mikhail always managed to tell them that she wasn't ready; the excuse that her gifts were still a danger to others — even just to show her parents — worked. Both of them knew their time would run out.

Anastasia had grown increasingly anxious about her parents executing *her* as a testament to their dedication to the Orthodox cause if she couldn't produce results. It was something that drove the two of them to arguments at every turn.

Anastasia was ready to run, and Mikhail insisted that she could bring about real change if she just *tried.*

"When I finally gain control of my powers," Anastasia scoffed, waving him off and sitting down to lunch. Mikhail had insisted that Anastasia be fed properly. "You're learning," he nodded, sitting down opposite her. "You already know how to use it. You just don't know your limitations."

Meals were the only time that they both agreed to put their proverbial weapons aside. Whenever they sat down to eat with one another — which was three times a day — the energy shifted, and they seemed to be able to relax, conversation flowing naturally.

Anastasia helped herself to a piece of fish, and her smile widened, still not used to eating food she actually *enjoyed*. Mikhail felt his chest inflate. Every time he noticed her figure filling out, a sense of possessiveness and satisfaction rose in him.

You're going to have to stop that. What is this? You're not trying to prove you can provide for her, you fool.

"Mikhail," Anastasia wiped a bit of food off of her lip and stared at him. "We've been at this for... what? Three weeks?"

"Yes. It can take a lifetime to master magic, Anya."

"Stop calling me that," she shook her head, her cheeks flushing when she heard the nickname fall from his lips.

"It's either that or 'Your Grace.'"

"You could call me by my name."

"You could call me by mine."

"Your name is Mikhail."

"It's Rasputin," Mikhail's tone went sharp.

Anastasia bit her lip and looked away, letting out a quiet sigh and returning to her food.

She knew that he was sensitive about his name but couldn't seem to let it go. That name held something heavy, something rotten. She didn't like associating him with it.

Mikhail watched as she deflated and felt like kicking himself. He knew he had to be careful around Anastasia. She seemed to either go to arms or shrink away much too easily.

It was a common enough response for someone who had only ever known pain and betrayal by those closest to them. She had no confidence in herself, and it drove Mikhail crazy.

Most days, he went back and forth from wanting to walk out the door and never seeing her again to never letting her out of his sight for the rest of his life.

"Anyway," Mikhail cleared his throat, "It's going to be like a light switch. I promise. Once you figure out how to control it, what your limitations are, then it'll come easy. You might even think it's fun."

"I don't see that happening."

"Will you just trust me for once?"

"Trust *you!*" Anastasia put her fork down. Mikhail groaned when he saw the look in her eyes. There went their peaceful lunch. "For all I know, you're going to turn me over to my parents!"

"I wouldn't be that stupid," Mikhail rolled his eyes. "You're too afraid of yourself. I get it; I would be too —"

Anastasia's face turned bright red as she felt him cut to the quick of her. She *was* afraid. She was terrified. She was dealing with forces within her that she didn't know how to control.

It was like operating machinery without a manual. The gears worked, the output occurred, but it was unpredictable. She had no idea who she was.

How could she even discover what was within her? Anastasia had learned from a very young age that the only way to deflect all of the trauma around her was to be bigger, bolder, and more terrifying.

She portrayed an ice queen facade that exuded fake confidence. A fear that she instilled in others, that she had no idea how to back up. She was all bark, no bite. Her entire existence had been carved out in survival mode. And it had left her broken.

Here was this man, this failed priest — a direct result of her actions as a child — sent to her by her parents. She had no idea if she could trust him. Yet, he looked at her and saw to the heart of her. It made Anastasia want to run and hide. Since that wasn't an option, she fought.

"I'm not afraid!" She snarled, moving away from him, turning to run into her bedroom just to get a wall between them.

"Anya," he said again, this time in a soft, coaxing voice.

Gentle even. Anastasia could count on one hand how many times someone had spoken like that to her in her life. "Please. You're running right now."

Anastasia stopped, feeling the blush on her cheeks intensify.

"You've got me there," she admitted quietly, still not able to turn around and face him. Mikhail moved towards her. His footsteps echoed in the sitting room, sounding heavy, making Anastasia tense.

He was behind her suddenly, the presence of his massive frame apparent as he moved closer to her.

This man doesn't even need to touch you, does he? And you lose your mind.

She sucked in a deep breath when Mikhail put his hand on her back, so large that it nearly covered her corset.

"Come with me," he said quietly, electing to diffuse the situation. "I think we should try something new."

Anastasia quietly looked up and over her shoulder at him, turning ever so slightly to face Mikhail. His face was impassable as he raged internally over their constant game of quickdraw.

It exhausted them; revealing their scars would have been so much simpler. The impenetrable wall they had both built around their hearts felt impossible to dismantle. It drove them both in constant predatory circles around each other. Both looked for weaknesses in the other's defenses when they simply could've handed over a key.

Mikhail knew that it was best to try and find another avenue to get Anastasia to tap into her power, to find some confidence and purpose.

What she needed was to brush aside the idea that her magic was cursed and worthless. He just didn't know if this game between them would kill them both as they hunted for the intimacy they craved but refused to ask for.

"What do you have in mind?" Anastasia asked.

"It is Sunday, isn't it?" Mikhail watched as Anastasia's grin spread over her face, genuine and as bright as the dawn.

♛♛♛

This time, Anastasia followed Mikhail as they moved through the streets. They hadn't come back to visit since their first trip together, and she was surprised to see several faces that seemed to recognize her.

People glanced at her as she walked by with cautious smiles on their faces. She was shocked when she noticed that they were receptive to her — that they had missed her, even.

"Do you see?" Mikhail turned around to look at her. "They aren't afraid of your gift."

"They don't know what I've done."

Mikhail opened his mouth to say something and stopped. It's true. They didn't know. He still didn't know how he felt about it. Their delicate truce depended entirely on no one bringing up the past, an impossible feat when both of them were determined to be defined by it.

The pair walked in silence until they approached a front door that Anastasia recognized. She had stopped by this house a few times when she used to sneak out. The family had three daughters and one son; their son worked as a farmhand, which was brutal work.

On Sundays, he was allowed to return home to attend church with his family; the iron collar was always thick around his neck. On the boyar's land, he was forced to sleep in irons next to a dozen others. They were always locked up at night like cattle, ensuring that they couldn't get away.

Anastasia knew their family struggled — like every serf family did these days — with daughters who couldn't make as much money as their son.

She had several conversations with their mother, who

seemed to struggle with an intense self-loathing that stemmed from her inability to keep her son from his forced, laborious servitude.

The door opened just a crack, one of the daughters poking her head out. She looked skeptical, evaluating Anastasia and Mikhail's attire. Even when they came in the simplest clothes that they had, they still stuck out sorely.

"Mama!" The girl disappeared, slamming the door. A moment later, the kind face of the matriarch appeared.

"Darling, Anastasia," she grinned, throwing the door open and wrapping Anastasia in a hug.

"*She* calls me the right name," Anastasia grinned, tossing a glare at Mikhail over her shoulder.

"Come in, come in," the woman smiled, ushering both of them into the small home. It almost felt colder inside than it did outside. There was a broken furnace, a small kitchen, and several sleeping mats pushed off to the side.

Anastasia figured that all five family members lived in the small space, six when their son was home.

"Anastasia is here to help," Mikhail grinned, gently pushing Anastasia forward.

"Yes, yes, we know," the woman ushered them even further into the room. "Whatever you can do." She had seen Anastasia's small efforts before and knew that amplifying magic could do anything from multiplying bread loaves to filling their oil lamps.

Anastasia smiled — a genuine one that wasn't just covering up fear — and the sight made Mikhail realize this was the right way to get her out of her head. She knew what to do here.

Outside of the Winter Palace walls, without the dead eyes of oil paintings staring at her, choked by everything the Romanov Empire had come to represent, she was more at peace with herself.

When she had first pulled herself out of it and had begun

sneaking here on her own, she knew instinctively what to do. He just needed to remind her.

Mikhail watched the transformation as Anastasia began using her magic without hesitation. It flowed from her effortlessly. She followed the woman around the kitchen, gently grasping bread loaves and jars of pickled herring, amplifying them like Christ until the kitchen was full - a true miracle.

The rest of the family was now crowded by the door in awe. Some of the siblings ran outside, grabbing neighbors, people on the street, friends, family members. Soon, a small crowd had gathered in the impossibly small doorway to watch Anastasia work. The transformation in her face left Mikhail breathless.

It was as though her layers were peeled away from her, revealing a woman who walked in total faith in herself with the support of the world at her back.

She laughed and chatted easily with the matriarch, the magic flowing between her fingers as though it was an extension of her — and it was. Mikhail looked upon her face with a proud adoration, feeling a sharp pang of regret as he realized how stifled and trapped Anastasia lived daily.

He wasn't much better; living at the monastery had changed him forever. He still harbored conflicting feelings for Anastasia.

Everything about his existence had been centered around the idea of revenge on *Grand Duchess Anastasia*. It had defined him, drove him through all of the abuse at the monastery, swearing that he would get justice for his mother's death.

Asya. The woman who had made him swear to protect the Romanov magic. The woman whose death was a chasm between them. Mikhail felt himself cursing under his breath, wondering how Asya had managed to bring them together and, at the same time, keep them apart.

Because you two won't drop your pride. Mikhail heard his mother's voice in his head. *You're too afraid you won't accept each other once the scars are out.*

There was an outburst of laughter, and Mikhail looked up. Anastasia entertained a small group of children with dancing sparks, making shapes of animals in the air.

He realized that he was staring, his jaw nearly down to the floor. Anastasia looked so full of life it paralyzed him. There was a love for her gift that he saw in her eyes when she used magic here as if she felt the purpose behind it.

It wasn't this terrifying thing that was pent up inside of her, driving her mad, but something that could better someone else's life. Her magic confused her — and at this moment, she loved it.

I thought I knew captivity, Mikhail thought to himself, *but at least I had sunshine. I even ate better than she did. I went outdoors. It wasn't so bad once they accepted I wouldn't take the vows.*

"Mikhail!" Anastasia *giggled.* He looked up at the sound, utterly enraptured, as he struggled with the inability to release his hatreds and heal.

It was a conflict that both he and Anastasia were dealing with and had made little progress in over the weeks.

"Yes, Anya?" He smiled, pushing off the wall where he had been leaning with one foot, and walked over to her. Anastasia's breath caught in her throat. She often forgot how *big* he was until he moved closer to her, the bun piled on his head nearly brushing the top of the low ceiling.

"Duck!" Her smile was bright like her magic as she tossed a ball of sparks in Mikhail's face. They exploded all over him like dandelion seeds. He started sneezing uncontrollably, the magic tickling his face as he waved the last of the sparks away.

"Anya!" Mikhail couldn't stop himself from grinning — he couldn't even begin to be bothered when Anastasia was in front of him, *smiling. Laughing. Joking.*

When his vision cleared a second later, she was crouched on the floor with several of the children. They all exploded in giggles and ran to hide behind the kitchen counter.

Mikhail opened his mouth to let Anastasia know they

needed to leave soon when the door to the small home shuttered open with a bang.

It got everyone's attention, and the small crowd turned, seeing the family's oldest son standing in the doorway.

He was wearing the iron collar from the boyar, with large spikes sticking out to prevent him from lying down or sitting comfortably.

It was a cruel practice. The sight of it made Mikhail sick to his stomach as it always did — he had seen a lot of the practice at the monastery. The boy offered a small smile, embarrassed that he had accidentally drawn so much attention to himself.

"Come here," Anastasia's voice broke the tension, and Mikhail turned to look at her. She stood from where she had been sitting with the children and held out a hand to the young boy.

He walked toward her without fear, which was more than Mikhail could say for himself when he had first met Anastasia.

He studied her face and tried to decipher the emotion that was on it. Her brow was furrowed, and she tossed her long, blonde braid over one shoulder. She laid a delicate hand on the boy's shoulder; her sleeves always pulled down over her knuckles.

Mikhail watched as she closed her eyes and began to focus, her expression contorting as if she was deep in thought.

The atmosphere in the room changed as the air was electrified. With a sudden gust of wind, half of the lights went out, causing the crowd in the room to gasp and huddle closer to one another.

Anastasia didn't seem to notice; her eyes still screwed shut as a sheen of sweat began to break out across her forehead.

A small whirlwind began to circulate around Anastasia, trapping her in a vortex as her skirts whipped around her ankles. The boy just stared at her, transfixed, with a small smile on his face. Whatever she was doing didn't seem to affect him in the slightest.

All of a sudden, the iron color began to glow. The cracks in the craftsmanship began to show as it shone red like it had a molten core. It grew brighter and brighter until it looked like the entire piece of metal was hot, aflame, and straight from the blacksmith's fire. The boy remained unaffected.

Whatever was happening, it wasn't burning his skin or even seemingly giving off any heat. Mikhail watched, transfixed as he realized what Anastasia was doing. She was changing the energy, manipulating the metal.

Her magic seemed to work best with more organic forms, such as amplifying the food, water, or using air. He had never seen her change metal before.

There was a great flash that covered the whole room in bright, white light. As soon as Mikhail's eyes adjusted, he gasped. The collar had disintegrated completely, pieces of it flying up into the air and floating down like ash.

The whole room was silent until the boy reached up and realized that the awful device was well and truly gone. He started crying, overwhelmed as he ran to the safety of his mother's arms.

Mikhail looked around and realized the whole family was crying. He couldn't even begin to describe what he felt, but his eyes immediately turned to Anastasia.

She looked incredibly pale, the sweat still sticking to her forehead, as using that much magic untrained likely drained her entirely.

Mikhail didn't even think as he ran to her, wrapping an arm around her waist and pulling him to his side to support her.

"I'm alright," she offered a lame protest while simultaneously sinking into his embrace. Mikhail's expression was stunned as Anastasia looked up at him.

"Anastasia...," he started, his eyes wide. She didn't know her limits or the ins and outs of her magic, apparently, but when there were stakes she cared about on the table — she knew what to do.

Anastasia felt cold after such an outpouring of her magic and found herself unable to turn from the strength of his warm grasp. She reached up and undid both of her earrings — still leaning into Mikhail's side — and motioned for the mother to come to her.

"Take these," she pressed them into the woman's hands, "You can sell them for a good price. Leave St. Petersburg with your family, so the *boyar* doesn't come for your son."

The woman began to sob, looking up at Anastasia in awe.

"You are not like the other Romanovs, Anastasia."

12

Anastasia smiled politely, not knowing how to respond. There was no love lost between her and her family. She was afraid of them if she was honest with herself. It made her uncomfortable whenever someone spoke about them, as if they were always hiding somewhere around the corner and waiting.

Mikhail tightened his arm around her, and she couldn't help herself as she leaned back into him. "It's late, Anastasia," he said quietly, nodding towards the door.

"Oh God," her face paled as she looked up at him. "How long have we been here?"

Mikhail shrugged, "I'm not sure... Why?"

Their conversation was interrupted by the sound of church bells, causing the remaining blood to leave Anastasia's face. Mikhail's brow furrowed. He saw fear on her face and didn't like what it did to him.

"The services ended," Anastasia groaned, burying her head in her hands for a moment before she covered her expression of dismay with a grin to hide her emotions from the neighbors.

She moved away from Mikhail and waved for him to follow her into the corner.

"What is it? Why does it matter that church is out?"

"Because," Anastasia hissed, "We can't *sneak back in* if everyone isn't in church!" The realization dawned over Mikhail, and he sucked in a sharp breath through his teeth.

"Surely, there has to be some way that we can get back?"

"No," Anastasia shook her head. "I've been at this for fifteen years, Mikhail. I know every door of that palace, and it's the only time that's safe to sneak out of."

"Well, we can't stay here until next Sunday — so we're just going to have to figure something else out."

"Most people are afraid of being labeled as heretics," Anastasia began chewing on the inside of her cheek. "So they'll all go to services."

Mikhail shrugged, "Then that's when we'll have to go back."

"And what's your grand plan between now and then?" Anastasia looked at him with an exasperated look, trying to figure out why he wasn't taking this as seriously as she was.

"I'm sorry," another woman took a few steps towards them, "I overheard. I have a boarding house down the road. It's small, but you could stay there until tomorrow morning."

"Perfect," Mikhail smiled, clapping his hands together and looking at Anastasia. "Isn't that a lovely offer, *Your Grace?*"

Anastasia stared up at him, and he watched her, seeing the anger rolling under her skin like a storm about to break. He knew that he had to break her of this fear of living, of existing — she had so much more in her life than her family, if only she would stop being afraid of who she was.

If it happened to work out that they had more time outside of the Winter Palace now, then it would only be good for her. Once she got over being mad at him, of course.

"Yes," Anastasia forced a grin and turned back to the innkeeper. "I would be touched to stay at your home." The woman smiled and grabbed Anastasia, pulling her into a warm embrace.

Anastasia froze, her eyes going wide. Mikhail watched with a smirk on his face — until he realized that Anastasia was likely so unaccustomed to warmth and affection that she was overwhelmed by that simple gesture.

The innkeeper released her and encouraged the both of them to spend the rest of the day with the neighbors, and she would have dinner ready for them at nightfall.

The pair thanked her again and stepped outside, making their way up the street. The word of Anastasia's gift had spread quickly and people were waiting for her in the streets.

She felt overwhelmed, seeing how many people were here for her, but Mikhail kept his hand on her back in reassurance, afraid that she was going to use up too much of her energy.

Anastasia didn't seem concerned, grabbing the hand of the nearest person and listening to their worries as she'd done a hundred times before.

Mikhail was struck by how gracefully she stepped into the role of a public servant; how eager she was to *help*. She didn't feel like a Romanov once she left the palace walls; she came alive as Mikhail had never seen her within them.

Would her family even come to this street? Mikhail was unable to keep his eyes off of her. *Probably not. They'd destroy the whole block if they wanted to put new stables in.*

He shook himself from his thoughts, following Anastasia down the street as she disappeared into another home.

The rest of the day proceeded like that, with the Grand Duchess following the crowd from house to house. She went into homes, filled pantries, and amplified jars of oil for gas lanterns.

Mikhail stood quietly beside her, watching as her eyes filled with warmth and her shell started to crack. She didn't seem like the woman who was afraid of her own gifts anymore.

Anastasia walked into every home with an eagerness about her magic, ready to use it and ready to help.

She has no idea how powerful she is, Mikhail thought. *Her family could never contain her if she sets herself free.*

Every time that he found himself thinking something about Anastasia, a cold sensation ran down the back of his spine, and thoughts of his mother crept into his mind.

She had killed the one woman who could have spent her whole life teaching her how to use her magic better than Mikhail ever could.

It was the reason that when he lost himself in her, even only for a moment, and his pride left a sick taste in his mouth. He couldn't seem to let go of his mother's death, no matter how it happened.

Because as soon as you let that go, you'd be open to her. His mother's voice seemed to be in his head again. *How do you think that would go? Do you think she could love a man like you? You can barely look at each other for a few hours without fighting.*

Mikhail was pulled from his thoughts by Anastasia's voice — cutting through the noise of the crowd like a bell, clear and resonant, a honing beacon that his body reacted to even as his mind protested.

"Mikhail," her voice was tired, and she walked away from where she had been fixing some broken tools. "Can we go now?" Her voice was sheepish, embarrassed.

Without thinking, Mikhail put his hands on her shoulders and squeezed gently.

"Are you alright?" He scanned her face and looked at her to confirm that she wasn't injured.

"I'm tired," her voice was quiet, and he noticed how withdrawn she looked. Using that much magic all day must have drained her completely — he cursed himself for not noticing sooner. "I don't want to tell anyone no…"

"You're no good to anyone if you hurt yourself and can't help *anyone.*"

"I'm no good to anyone if I can't —"

"Stop," Mikhail's voice was firm as he ducked down to her eye level. "Your worth isn't defined by what you can do for others, either. You are *not* a weapon or a tool. You want to help. So we will. We'll help everyone. We can't do it all today."

Anastasia's eyes got wide as she listened to Mikhail, his impassioned words making her skin flush. He had never talked to her that way before, and she had to bite her lip to fight the tension it created in her body.

She nodded, and Mikhail straightened up, smiling gently at the crowd. He excused them both — Anastasia was too far gone, staring at his profile to hear what he said. He put his hand on her back, gently directing her towards the boarding house.

It was a short journey, and the pair walked in silence. It couldn't quite be described as uncomfortable or easy silence: it simply was.

Anastasia walked a few steps behind him, letting Mikhail lead the way and escort them through the crowded city streets. She was tired. She had never used so much magic, and she didn't know what had compelled her to do so today. She did know that it had never come so effortlessly.

She looked around as they walked towards the boarding house, seeing the appalling conditions spreading out around them. It was all a result of her father, her family... she felt sick to her stomach when her mind reeled with the wealth sitting in the palace, collecting dust.

She was lost in her thoughts when she ran into Mikhail, who had suddenly stopped, bumping into his back. He turned around with a small smile on his face.

"Are you alright there, *Your Grace?*" He always used the nickname when he wanted to bring some of the fire back to her expression.

Anastasia rolled her eyes, and Mikhail nodded towards the front door that they had stopped in front of.

"After you."

The pair was quiet as they stepped inside the door, immediately greeted by the innkeeper's warm face. She ushered the both of them through a warm sitting room, plain but cozy, and up a slanted set of steps.

Mikhail and the innkeeper chatted easily back and forth; Anastasia watched on, studying his face. He was kind and attentive to the innkeeper, listening to the tales about her family, but she couldn't place the other emotion on his face when his eyes flickered to hers.

"Here we are," the innkeeper's voice got a little louder as she pulled out of the conversation with Mikhail to address them both, "It's small, hopefully, it will be comfortable. I've had some food brought up."

"I'm sure it's wonderful," Mikhail grinned. "We need to leave before dawn anyway. Thank you for your hospitality."

"Thank you," the innkeeper had turned to Anastasia, grabbing her hands. "You have no idea what you did today. People are whispering. You bring *hope*." She squeezed Anastasia's fingers and handed Mikhail the key to the room, then jogged off down the stairs, wiping tears from her eyes.

Anastasia stood there, paralyzed, not sure what to do with the praise. Mikhail studied her, noticing how uncomfortable she got when someone complimented her.

"Let's go," he leaned over and put his hand on her arm, nodding towards the door. "You need to eat to replenish the magic you used today."

Anastasia nodded silently, following Mikhail as he unlocked the room and let them both inside. Anastasia stepped in front of him, studying the small room.

"Mikhail," she hissed, turning to him as he shut the door behind them. "What were you *thinking?*"

"What?" He looked at her, confused, as he took in the small space. "This is much nicer than most people in the city could ever hope to achieve, Anastasia," his voice got stern. "If you think that this isn't —"

"No!" Anastasia cut him off, crossing her arms over her chest. "Mikhail. There's *only one bed.*" He stopped, standing up straighter and looking over at the bed as if it was the first time he saw it.

An awkward silence fell between them, Mikhail stopping to let his hair down and retying it.

"We can't do anything about it," Mikhail finally shrugged. He went to sit down at the small table at the foot of the bed, unwrapping a basket of bread. "Come eat."

"We can't *do* anything about it?" Anastasia snapped, careful to keep her voice down so the innkeeper wouldn't overhear. "We can't stay here!"

Mikhail ripped off a piece of bread and dipped it in a pot of stew, gnawing on the end. "Where else do you suppose we go? Unless you want to sneak back into the palace tonight."

"We can't do that, but, Mikhail, this is —," Anastasia blushed furiously and waved towards the general direction of the bed. "It's improper!"

Mikhail looked at her, a deadpan expression on his face. "Really? You care about court etiquette right now?"

"I just think —"

"I'll sleep on the floor if you're scared of me," Mikhail smirked, raising his eyebrows once more before chuckling darkly to himself and digging back into the food.

"Scared of you?" Anastasia hissed, sitting down across from him in a huff. "You're impossible."

"Eat," Mikhail nodded towards the food, "I wasn't kidding. You used up a lot of energy today; I was worried you were going to overexert yourself."

"You were worried about me? Touching," Anastasia quipped

back, the small space feeling even smaller around the both of them. The air seemed to get thicker, and she took a deep breath. If only she weren't wearing so many damned layers.

"Of course," Mikhail shrugged, looking up at her, "We can't have you losing control."

Anastasia stopped, her food halfway to her mouth, "What the fuck is that supposed to mean?"

"Oh, stop it," Mikhail groaned, leaning back in his chair and letting his head drop back, "Everything isn't an insult."

"That sure sounded like one."

"It's the truth!" He sat up, "You can't control your magic, Anastasia. That's it. Stop acting like I'm attacking you every time I mention that."

"Well, maybe if you were a better tutor...," she rolled her eyes, digging back into her food.

"I'm going to let that pass for the sake of finishing my dinner in peace," Mikhail grunted, both of them refusing to meet each other's gaze, wondering how their camaraderie had descended so quickly. It never took long. Anytime they seemed to be getting along, one of them would perceive a slight, and fireworks followed.

"Eat this last piece," Mikhail broke the silence several minutes later.

Anastasia nodded, reaching for it from across the table and grabbing it off of his plate. Except Mikhail had other ideas — he dropped the spoon he was holding and grabbed her wrist.

"Mikhail!" She squeaked, trying to pull away from him. Mikhail stood up and leaned over the table, his other hand going and tugging the sleeve of her dress up higher. "Stop it!"

Anastasia writhed to try and escape his grip, but he held firm. She felt her face flush with heat and embarrassment, tears springing to her eyes.

"*Please,*" she hissed while Mikhail stood stoically above her. He finally released her wrist, and she retracted her hand, cradling it against her chest. One heartbeat. Two. "Don't say anything."

"Anastasia," Mikhail's voice was cold, sharp — a tone she had never heard before. "Who *the fuck* did that to you?"

Anastasia's arms were riddled with scars, going down to her knuckles, which had taken the brunt of the force. They had been hit with switches, rulers, or even pens so many times over the years... she'd lost count.

She despised looking at them. Every single mark that had been left by one of her mother's tutors over the years made her relive the moments of pain over and over again. She had broken the mirror in her bathroom years ago.

"Anastasia," Mikhail said again, pulling her from her wretched memories, "I asked you a question." He sat down at the table, his gaze searing through her.

"I forget who started it," she shrugged, turning away from his eyes. "It was from all of my *lessons* over the years."

Mikhail let out a heavy sigh, rubbing a hand over his stubbled jaw. He stared at her, neither of them able to speak.

"I'm sorry," he finally said, reaching a hand across the table and holding it out to her, palm up. "It shouldn't have happened to you, Anya."

Anastasia blinked a few of her tears away, sliding her hands into his. "It's in the past," she shrugged. "I'm just glad I don't have to stare at the ones on my back. They're worse, but at least I can't see them." She watched her hand in Mikhail's, how his palm completely enveloped hers.

"...What?" Mikhail's voice had dropped an octave and made her shiver as if a single word could lick her skin. Anastasia glanced up, seeing the fury had returned to his eyes, an unrivaled expression that made her believe he might kill anyone who tried to even glance at her sideways.

"Fuck," Anastasia cursed, quickly pulling her hand from his. "Forget I said anything."

"Forget?" Mikhail hissed.

"They're all dead now; it doesn't matter," Anastasia looked away and waved her hand dismissively.

"If they weren't, I'd kill them."

Anastasia's eyes went wide, and her gaze snapped back to him — both of them flushed now, the tension settling over the room in a palpable way that made her want to throw open a window for a reprieve.

Every muscle in his body was tense. Anastasia said nothing and absentmindedly ran her thumb over some of the scars underneath her sleeve.

"Let me see them," Mikhail said quietly, his voice coaxing. "All of them."

"What?" Anastasia's voice was muted, her heart beating in her chest as she looked up at him in an intense exchange across the table.

"You heard me," he said, standing up — his head nearly brushing the ceiling of the cramped room. She stood up, shaking her head and backing away from him.

"No, you can't — they're not...," she shook her head, stepping backward until she hit the wall. "They're ugly."

"Like these?" Mikhail crossed the room in a few steps, diminishing the distance between them until it was nonexistent. He stared at her for a second before reaching down and grabbing his shirt, tugging it off over his head.

Anastasia couldn't stifle a gasp at the sight in front of her. He was riddled with scars that wrapped around his ribs, his shoulders, his torso... God, *he was beautiful.*

Every inch of his body seemed to have been carved from stone, and Anastasia couldn't help herself as she reached her hand towards him.

Mikhail closed the distance between them, grabbing her hand and pulling it to his chest. She almost recoiled at how hot his skin felt underneath her palm.

"Touch them," he growled, leaning down and brushing his lips against the top of her head. "Go on. Do they feel *ugly* to you?"

Anastasia sucked in a sharp breath, bringing her other hand up, running her hands over his chest and down his sides, feeling her pulse pounding in her cheeks.

"N-no," she stuttered, pulling herself back from him and leaning back against the wall.

"Your scars aren't ugly, Anya," he leaned in and put his arms on either side of her, caging her in with his body.

He leaned down once more and whispered in her ear, his lips brushing against her and making her go weak in the knees.

"I promise. You've seen my scars, Anya... why won't you let me see yours?"

She knew that he wasn't talking about the ones on her back.

"Stop it," she hissed, turning her head away from him and slipping out from underneath his grip. "Don't say things like that, Mikhail!" She snapped at him, crossing her arms over her chest in frustration.

"Say things like what?" He turned around to face her. "Say things I mean? Do you think I'm still lying to you?"

"I don't know what I think," Anastasia hissed, "We need to keep our distance from one another."

"Keep our *distance?*" Mikhail scoffed, looking at her in disbelief as he beckoned from the tiny room to his discarded shirt on the floor. "How do you think that's been going for us?"

"It doesn't matter —"

"No, I'm curious," he said, stepping close enough to wrap an arm around her waist and tug her to his naked chest. "What's the distance like between us, Anya?" He leaned down, whispering in her ear. "Do you think about me when you touch yourself at night? Does that *distance* between our rooms get to you?" Anastasia sucked in a sharp gasp, writhing in his hold.

"I think about you," Mikhail's voice was a sin. Anastasia let out a rushed breath, her chest heaving as if she wasn't able to get enough air.

"You're a bastard."

"I am a bastard," he agreed, licking a hot stripe up her neck, "You want me. I want you. It doesn't have to be anything more than that."

"Pig," she hissed, slapping her hand against his chest, "And you were the one asking me about my *scars.*"

"I'll kiss them all *malyshka* if you let me. You want to keep the distance between us... so I'll take what I can get."

"This hardly feels like distance," Anastasia snapped, turning and grinding her hips against him, stuttering back her cry when she felt his erection hot and heavy against her. Mikhail groaned and tossed his head back.

"Tell me that you want this," he murmured, "Or I'll walk out that door right now." Anastasia looked up at him. Both of them barely held onto their restraint, eyeing each other with fury and aggression they seemed to reserve only for each other.

"Say it," he demanded again, "Or I'm leaving."

"Fuck you!"

"I will — say it."

"Fuck... I want it!" Anastasia hissed, throwing her arms around his neck as she jumped up and wrapped her legs around his waist. Mikhail caught her, crushing them together in a vicious embrace and walking them both over towards the bed.

He dropped Anastasia down onto the edge of the mattress, immediately rucking all of the skirts up around her waist and pulling her undergarments down.

She sat up, chest heaving, pulling at the strings of her corset until her breasts were free. She fussed with the back of it, making sure it stayed on and to cover her scars. Mikhail made a guttural noise, pushing her back onto the bed and biting down on her nipple.

"*Oh God,*" Anastasia moaned, falling back onto the mattress and wrapping her legs around his torso as he switched back and forth between her breasts relentlessly.

He paid attention to her like a man truly possessed — each bite and sting followed by a hot and soothing glide of his tongue. Her hands flew to his hair, tugging it out of the knot and raking her fingers across his scalp.

"*Anya,*" Mikhail moaned, coming up for air and leaving a trail of kisses up her neck. "What do you want?" His hands started moving up her thighs dangerously slowly, teasing her.

"I want you to touch me, *you fool,*" she hissed, tossing her head back as he resumed his leisurely pace, getting closer and closer to where she really wanted him.

"Fine," he shook his head, nipping at her jaw. "We'll do it your way then." Anastasia gasped at the sudden departure of Mikhail's body as he backed up off the bed and stood over her. He had a smirk on his face that sent heat straight to her core.

Mikhail kneeled and hooked his arms around Anastasia's legs, tossing them over his shoulders, scooting her to the edge of the bed.

She gasped, the air feeling heavy around her as she thought about how none of her previous trysts compared — quick, hurried affairs that had never left her as breathless as the sight of Mikhail between her legs.

He dropped his head to taste her, the stubble burning against her thighs in a delicious heat that threatened to rip Anastasia apart at the seams.

She was slick and ready against him, her hands sliding back in his hair, tugging roughly. He devoured her like a man crazed, latching on to her clit and savoring it.

"*Fuck, Mikhail,*" Anastasia nearly screamed, her back arching off the bed, her lifted hips allowing Mikhail to slide two fingers inside of her.

"Watch that mouth, Anya," he chuckled, the reverberations

of his voice against her nearly sending Anastasia over the edge. "It is still technically the Lord's day."

"Oh God," she moaned again as he crooked his fingers inside of her in a way that had Anastasia's legs locking around him. His other hand came up to her hip, anchoring her down as he dipped his head back and delivered another long lick up her center.

"Does it feel *this* good when you do it, Anya?" he laughed, enjoying the blissed-out expression on her face with a quiet, male satisfaction — as he was trying to ignore how painfully hard the taste of her made him.

"You bastard," she hissed again, her insult getting cut off as Mikhail gently slipped a third finger into her and began to move them at a devastating rhythm. She couldn't help but join him, rocking her hips against his mouth.

"Answer me," he murmured again, pulling his head up from her and licking his lip obscenely, her wetness shining in his beard. "Does it feel this good when you do it?" His fingers kept going, his thumb replacing his lips on her clit.

"Oh — oh," she fisted the sheets and struggled to catch her breath, "Touch me, please —"

"Answer me first, Anya. Be a good girl and answer the question."

"You fucking —" She was cut off when he leaned down and bit her hipbone, making her squirm against the pain.

"I'm just being a good tutor," he murmured against her skin. "Answer the question, *malyshka*." His fingers had slowed to a dangerous place that was balancing Anastasia on the edge.

"Fine!" She screamed, nearly shaking off of the bed, "No, no, it doesn't feel as good when I do it — now *touch me,* you mother fucker!"

Mikhail leaned up and crashed into her, a kiss that was possessive and biting, "Yes, *Your Grace,*" he chuckled before kneeling back at the edge of the bed and resuming sucking on her clit and picking up the speed of his fingers.

It didn't take long for Anastasia to come fast and hard, her vision nearly going out as her legs locked around Mikhail. He gripped her thigh and kept fingering her through the throes of her orgasm — watching her fall back on the bed.

He gently removed himself from her and stood up, staring at her from the end of the bed as he licked his fingers, savoring the taste of her.

"Well?" Anastasia looked up at him, panting and flushed, waiting for him. Mikhail shook his head.

"That's all for tonight," his voice took on a dark tone as Anastasia looked up at him in shock. She could clearly see the outline of his heavy cock against his thigh, hard and ready. Mikhail shrugged.

"You want to keep your distance," he sneered, arching a brow. "And if I fuck you, Anastasia," the words sent a shiver up Anastasia's spine, "I won't be able to stay away."

Anastasia stared after him, unable to say a word — as he grabbed his shirt off the floor, tied up his hair, and left the room.

She heard his heavy footsteps down the stairs until the sound faded completely — leaving her alone and half-dressed, lying on the bed and wondering how they were going to survive each other.

＃ I ʒ ＃

Anastasia didn't know how long she stared after Mikhail. His absence struck her all at once, the warmth dissipating from her body and leaving her cold.

His sudden departure hit her like a freezing blast of air. It took her a moment before she was able to release a deep breath, sit up, and fix her dress.

What in God's name was that? I mean... It was amazing... What happened? He can't possibly mean what he said. He couldn't. Right? I'm still a Romanov. He wouldn't care if I was dead.

She looked around the room, noticing the dishes from dinner had fallen off the table, standing in disarray at the foot of the bed.

Anastasia finally stood and walked around to the desolate scene. She muttered under her breath as she began to clean it up, wiping up remnants of their food and cursing when she saw some of the dishes had cracked.

The poor innkeeper will lose wages trying to replace these.

Even though she had been using her magic all day, something about Mikhail's sudden departure had left her feeling raw. They had been at each other's throats for weeks, but it didn't change the ache in her chest and the emptiness she felt when he'd left so abruptly.

The idea of using her magic to fix the dishes made her feel nauseous. The idea of the innkeeper scraping by to replace them hurt more.

So she bent down and picked up one of the plates, closing her eyes and taking a deep breath. To her surprise, her magic flooded her hands, a cloud of gold dust erupting all around her. The magic responded openly and willingly to her, the plate lifting into the air and beginning to spin. It drifted back down gently, all of its cracks having mended themselves.

Anastasia let herself smile, her chest warming slightly at the idea of being able to help, but the heat banked itself almost immediately.

With a wave of her hand, she repaired the rest of the dishes and made up the table. It was hardly nightfall, but the day's effort — and an unexpected orgasm— had left her tired. She looked once more at the door as if she could summon Mikhail to walk right back through it and climbed into bed.

♣♣♣

Mikhail had no plan when he stepped into the cold street. It had taken everything in him to leave that room, no part of him wanting to.

Forget the fact that the taste of that woman nearly made him finish in his pants like an adolescent... just being near her was starting to cloud his senses. The more he saw her growing confidence in her abilities, the more it drove him mad.

Everyone in her life, particularly the men, was afraid of her. He was drawn to her power like a moth to a flame. Not to use it, harness it, or keep it, but to fan it. He wanted to stoke the fires of her magic and watch as everything burned down around them.

Every time they got close to each other, one of them backed out at the last second. They were dancing around one another's insecurities, waiting for the other to strike. It was maddening foreplay that forced them both to the edge and threatened to break them in half if they couldn't get over their pride.

Mikhail walked the streets for hours. There was nowhere that he needed to go. He had no family left and, after fifteen years away, didn't remember any of his friends. He simply put his hands in his pockets and headed off in a random direction.

It wasn't until it was well past dark that he figured he could return to the boarding house, hoping he'd wasted enough time for Anastasia to have fallen asleep.

The innkeeper gave him a small smile when he returned but didn't make any mention of the disruption he was sure their argument had caused. He took the steps to double-time to get to their room —

The room. Not our room. Just the room.

He couldn't fight it — he wanted to see Anastasia.

Mikhail was almost halfway up the stairs when he heard an ear-piercing scream coming straight from the room. He caught himself as he started to trip and sprinted up the remaining steps. He wasn't prepared for what he saw when he pushed the door open.

Anastasia was tangled in the middle of the bed, her legs caught in the sheets as though in restraints. He could hear her sobs, a wretched sound, cutting off her screams, making Mikhail feel sick.

She rolled over on her back, her face contorting in some phantom remembered pain. He stood immobile in the door, frozen by the idea that she wouldn't want him anywhere near her, even as the impossible urge to pull her close and take her from her nightmares built in his chest. He didn't want to know what in her life could haunt Anastasia so terribly.

Then she made a soft noise, a subtler one. It was a pathetic, mewling sound, barely above a whimper. It was so much worse than when she screamed. It was a surrender, and it broke him.

Mikhail threw caution to the wind and rushed towards the bed, asking for forgiveness under his breath. He climbed into it with her, kneeling by her side, gently removing her from the tangled web of sheets.

"Anastasia," he coaxed gently as his hands slipped onto her shoulders lightly while straddling her, taking care to keep his body weight off of her. She let out another strangled sound, and it felt like a punch to his gut.

Mikhail leaned down, brushing the sweaty hair off of her forehead and cradling her jaw in his hands.

"Anya, Anya," he tried again, his voice a little louder but keeping its soothing tone. "Anya. Wake up."

Anastasia's eyes flung open, a loud gasp escaping her as she sucked in air, her whole body jerking. She let out a frail cry as she looked around, her vision unfocused and blurry with tears.

Mikhail moved off of her and sat next to her on the bed, giving her some space even though no part of him wanted to.

Anastasia blinked rapidly, her chest heaving as she struggled for composure.

"Mikhail?" Her voice cracked, and she looked confused to see him there.

"It's me," he gave her a soft smile, afraid to reach across the distance between them. They were both sitting up in the bed, but there might as well be a chasm between them.

He fought the instinct to crush her to his chest and lay them both down, the instinct to try and take the pain away.

"You left," her voice was distant and small, sounding like a wounded child. "You left... I don't...," she trailed off as she realized she was in no place to be making demands of him. She buried her face in her hands, "Everyone leaves, Mikhail!"

Her frame was wracked with sobs. The way it contorted her body made Mikhail want to jump in front of a train to stop her from feeling any of the pain that she was feeling.

"What do you mean?" He nudged her gently, and she looked up at him with blotchy cheeks.

"Everyone leaves. My parents don't care. Even the tutors don't last. Alexei stopped coming to see me years ago... everyone leaves."

When was the last time someone deliberately took care of this woman? Mikhail wondered, aghast. *And then when she let me close to her, I said it wasn't enough and left. Fuck. Fuck!*

Mikhail sighed. Anastasia stared at him, and the last of his resistance melted away when he met her bright blue eyes. He leaned forward and pulled her into him, lying both of them down on the bed.

Mikhail gently shifted her until her head rested on his chest, wrapping his arms around her tightly. He barely breathed as he waited for her reaction, waiting for her to scream and push away from him. To declare that she was fine and didn't need this from him. He waited, preparing his apologies.

A moment passed, and Anastasia sniffled, her head moving back and forth in the smallest of mannerisms as she burrowed closer to him. Her arms went around his neck and her legs tangled with his, pressing them up against one another until they couldn't tell where one started or the other ended.

They were quiet for a moment, and Anastasia's soft cries started up again. Mikhail rubbed her back gently, pressing soft kisses to her hairline.

"What do you need, Anya?" He murmured gently. "Tell me what you need."

"Hold me tighter," she whispered, looking up at him. "And please don't let go."

Mikhail nodded, sensing how her plea extended far past just their embrace. He obliged, momentarily using his hand to pull the blankets up around them.

"Sleep, *malyshka*," his voice was slow and lingering, sending pleasant shivers down Anastasia's spine, "I'll wake you up before dawn. We'll go back to the palace."

"Together?"

"Together."

TRUE TO HIS WORD, MIKHAIL WOKE ANASTASIA BEFORE DAWN. They had no extra clothes but quietly fixed their garments, smoothing down stray hairs in an attempt to look as presentable as possible.

Mikhail could tell from looking at Anastasia that she was embarrassed. He had caught her in a moment where she was at her most vulnerable, ripped from sleep with terrors from her past chasing her into a bottomless panic.

The past keeps getting in our way. Mikhail chewed on his lip as Anastasia tied up her shoes. *We can't seem to let it go.*

You won't heal from it, is what you mean. Asya's voice rang in Mikhail's head. Sometimes, he heard her so clearly that he was convinced she spoke to him from beyond the grave. Knowing his mother, he wasn't entirely convinced that wasn't what truly was happening.

The walk to the palace was just as silent as the rest of the morning had been. The streets were empty with the rising sun. They made their way through the sleepy town and to the side of the Winter Palace, whose gate was much less guarded than the front entrance.

The Romanovs were so convinced that the palace servants

would be happy to have a job that they wouldn't do anything to jeopardize it. The door remained unwatched and unguarded for anyone to sneak in a cousin or a friend. Or, in this case, the Grand Duchess.

Anastasia and Mikhail made their way through the abandoned hallways. When they finally saw the door to Anastasia's rooms, Mikhail released a satisfied sigh.

As much as he had tried to keep a calm facade around Anastasia the night before, he was worried that they would be discovered. Mikhail stepped in front of Anastasia politely, holding the door to her chambers open for her.

She smiled demurely as she passed him, turning to go into her rooms — but froze on the spot. The color drained from her face, and she sucked in a sharp gasp. Mikhail's brow furrowed, and he flung the door open wider to see what had caused her reaction.

In the middle of Anastasia's sitting rooms sat the Tsar and Tsarina, accompanied as always by the same three *dvoryanstvo* standing behind him. All of them stared expectantly as if Mikhail and Anastasia were late to a prearranged meeting.

Mikhail gently put his hand on Anastasia's back, moving her forward and shutting the door behind him. He felt himself edge in front of her subconsciously, an overwhelming desire taking over him to protect her from this family. Her *own* family.

"Hello, Anastasia," the Tsar's voice was calm and stoic as if it was a business meeting and not his daughter. The Tsarina could barely look at Anastasia, picking at the gold threads on her dress.

Mikhail eyed her with particular disgust; she wore a pair of diamond earrings so heavy, wiring looped over her ears to help support them.

Whatever this fucking setup is, his thoughts were violent, *I hope the Tsarina chose jewelry she doesn't mind losing.*

"Your Imperial Majesty," Anastasia's voice rang out clear and strong. Whatever fear she felt, she hid it well. She used the formal address for the Tsar, and Mikhail was overcome with the impulse to throw her over his shoulder and run far, far away.

"You have been missing for a day, Anastasia." The Tsar seemed to finish every sentence with her name, as if he sought to punish her with it, to remind her that she was one of them. "Please do let us know where you've been. The streets are full of rioters these days. It's a dangerous time. You can imagine how distraught we were when we discovered you were gone." His voice was foreboding and full of thinly-veiled threats.

"I was with the tutor." Anastasia's voice was detached. She spoke of him like that's all he was to her — the tutor. The latest in a line of them, soon to likely be executed like the rest of his successors.

Mikhail had faith in Anastasia, but this cold remembrance dripped down his spine, and he recollected what a dangerous game they were playing.

"The tutor, yes...," the Tsar's voice was cold, calculating. "Do you understand that's highly improper?"

Anastasia fought back the impulse to roll her eyes at her father. He had forced her to share her chambers with hand-selected maids and tutors for years. "I'm always alone with my tutors," she made the double entendre clear.

"You are alone with your tutors in private," the Tsar snapped, his control slipping ever so slightly. "Not where other people can see you."

"So it doesn't matter what they might have done to me, as long as it didn't spin the rumor mill?" Anastasia's voice rose, and Mikhail couldn't help but be proud of her. Standing up to an abusive father was one thing; it was another entirely when your father was the Tsar to all of Russia.

"We have enough to worry about without having to worry

about *you*," the Tsar barked, his facade cracking. He took a deep breath, rearranging one of the broaches on the grandiose sash that he insisted on wearing at all times.

"Perhaps," one of the *dvoryanstvo* spoke up from behind him, "We would feel better if we knew how your magic was progressing."

"It's magic now?" Anastasia laughed darkly, staring daggers at the overinflated old man. "Because I distinctly remember you sitting in this room when I was thirteen while everyone talked about what a curse I was."

"Anastasia," the Tsarina glanced up, finally looking interested enough to take part in the conversation, "That's inappropriate."

"Inappropriate?!" Anastasia scoffed. "That's *rich* coming from you." Anastasia always shrank in front of her parents, but something in her had shifted.

The opportunity to use her magic, help people, right some of the inequities that she was raised in... It had rocked her sense of purpose to the core. What that meant - she couldn't be sure. She wouldn't spend another minute listening to her parents conspire.

"I don't care if you're fucking the priest," the Tsar's voice was like crude oil, "Anastasia, you must use your gifts for the family. You have no idea what we are up against."

"For the family?" Anastasia threw her hands up in the air. "You have no idea what that word even means. You don't even know what I can do —"

"You do know?" Another one of the *dvoryanstvo* perked up, catching the implication in her voice.

"Tell us everything, Anastasia," the Tsar went still. "Tell us now."

The silence that settled over the room was deadly. Mikhail felt his hands pull into fists, ready to fight anyone in the room — including the Tsar himself — if it meant pulling Anastasia out of there.

"No." Anastasia's voice matched his in contempt, drawing a line in the sand. It was the first time that she had ever stood up to her father directly. She was directly refusing an order from the Romanov Tsar.

"Do not ask me again," she continued, her voice full of iron, "Or I will show you what I can do. Is that understood?"

Mikhail couldn't help but turn and look at her in awe. This woman had completely risen from the ashes of an imprisoned life.

Her family had attempted to crush her under the wheel of their dynasty and political games, yet here she was, giving *them* orders. He didn't know what she would be able to control but the threat was likely enough.

The Tsar waved once, and the *dvoryanstvo* quickly got up and filed out of the room. One look from the Tsar and the Tsarina followed, leaving with a passing glance at Anastasia that looked more bored than anything.

"Anastasia… Rasputin," the Tsar looked at them both, an unholy fire lighting in his eyes. The cracked facade of this great man in front of them made him look like he was ready to erupt.

"You will come to see the magnitude of what you have refused to do here today. With God as my witness, *daughter*," he said the word like it was a curse.

"You will extend your servitude to me as your father and as your Tsar, or I will have your magic bound, and you will be married off. Am I clear?"

Mikhail felt his blood pressure rise, ready to clear the gap between him and the Tsar - to send him falling to the floor. It was Anastasia's hand on his back that made him stand down, as she took a step towards her father.

"Best of luck finding someone more powerful than me to accomplish that," she said primly. "You are dismissed from *my* chambers."

Mikhail's jaw dropped as he watched Tsar Nicholas the II

stare down his daughter — and relent. He simply adjusted another brooch, dropped his hands to his side, and walked towards the door. Before he shut it behind him, he turned to look at his daughter.

"This is war, *doch.*"

❧ 14 ❧

"I can feel your anxiety from out here," Mikhail groaned, leaning back in his chair. He was sitting in an overstuffed chaise in the salon of Anastasia's suite.

She had barricaded herself in her bedroom, fetching for one of her lady's maids — who was shocked to have been called for — to help get her dressed. Tonight was one of the infamous Romanov masked balls, and they were making an appearance.

After her father had declared war upon them both, they had entered a deadly stalemate. The Tsar and Tsarina were afraid to go after Anastasia and Mikhail directly while the extent of her power was unknown to them.

Likewise, neither Anastasia nor Mikhail had a plan for going after the Tsar of all Russia, understandably. It was clear there was now no love lost between them. The whole situation was rushing towards a head that Mikhail knew would end in bloodshed.

Over the past few years, the Tsar had executed over three thousand people labeled as terrorists, and their religious fervor had only grown.

Mikhail could sense the dark magic in the palace's halls at night whenever he left Anastasia's rooms, hooded figures perpetually slipping in and out from behind paintings, processions with lit candelabras and incense burners... all of which put Mikhail on edge.

He and Anastasia had decided that their next move was to find allies. The two of them couldn't possibly begin to go up against her parents — or the entire Romanov dynasty — by themselves.

They stood a better chance if they could move some of the boyars and *dvoryanstvo* to Anastasia's cause. Anastasia complained that they didn't even *have* a cause yet, but Mikhail pushed back on the semantics, saying that's what the politicians could figure out.

The important thing was seeing the iron grip on the country end, through whatever means: be it revolution or reform. To find allies at court, they needed to be *at* court.

Anastasia hadn't made an official court appearance in fifteen years, the rumor mill around her existence still as alive as ever. The pair had decided that it would be best to wait until one of the more grandiose weekly events, the masquerade ball held every Tuesday.

They would arrive unannounced, giving her parents no time to plant any seeds of propaganda around her whereabouts, which brought Anastasia to call on her lady's maid to help her dress for such an event.

Despite never being at court, Anastasia's closet was stuffed to the brim with appropriate attire — all outcasts from the Tsarina's tailor when he had run out of storage.

Mikhail waited for them to finish, all but feeling the nervous energy radiating off of Anastasia. He was flipping through a book when the lights flickered like they were confirming his thoughts.

"Your magic, Anastasia!" He called out through the bedroom door, knowing it slipped when she felt out of control.

Mikhail had decided that he wouldn't go in priest robes. He hated them. He also wasn't a priest, something he always had to remind Anastasia of.

'There's enough religious fervor in the court,' he had suggested. *'We'll get cooler heads to prevail if I present simply as your tutor.'*

He wore a light-blue silk shirt, a corded golden belt, dark-blue velvet trousers, and leather boots. He had put on two large, golden cuffs, both of them carved with the Romanov double-eagle, and had tied his hair up in a tight knot, keeping it tactile.

He ran his finger over the golden cuff, getting lost in his thoughts as he waited for the Grand Duchess, despising being out of his own clothes.

The lady-in-waiting appeared and cleared her throat softly, getting Mikhail's attention. He looked up, glancing at the clock on the wall.

They had a short window to arrive while the coachman was still announcing names, but most of the guests had already entered. It had been selected for the most dramatic effect.

"Are we ready then?" Mikhail groaned again, getting impatient. "I don't see what could be taking... so long..." Mikhail trailed off as Anastasia entered the sitting room. Her hair had been done up in an elaborate braided crown around her head, flecked with diamond pins.

The dress that she was wearing had silver brocade, trimmed with ermine and gold thread. There was a diamond-studded bodice, that when she moved, made her look like fire and starlight.

Mikhail's heart stopped.

"Well, I don't enjoy this," Anastasia snapped, flustered and misreading his expression, "Appearances are *everything* to these people. We have a part to play."

"And what part is mine, exactly?" Mikhail crossed his arms and raised an eyebrow. Anastasia tried to keep her pulse steady as she observed him in court attire… her mind stuck on the gold cuffs at his wrist.

"My tutor, of course," her voice was shaky as she picked up a fan her lady-in-waiting offered to her.

"The tutor. *Right,*" Mikhail rolled his eyes. "Really? That's how you want to play this?"

"Yes," Anastasia's voice was sharp, "What would you go as? My *lover?*"

"It would be more accurate."

"Technically, we never got to that part."

"You got to your part."

"You left."

"You didn't want me to stay." Mikhail's tone of voice was final, and Anastasia swallowed thickly, adjusting one of the pins in her hair.

"I never said that." Anastasia raised a brow before blushing and turning towards the door, refusing to look him in the eye. "We should go; we're late."

"Anastasia," he stopped her, grabbing hold of her elbow gently, "Is that…?" He looked down at the dress that she was wearing in more detail. "Is that the Tsarina's coronation dress?"

Anastasia chuckled, before looking up at Mikhail and giving him a wink, "I had the train shortened, so it didn't need eight damn attendants to carry, but yes," she grinned, "It sends a message."

Mikhail couldn't help the smirk that slid over his face. Some moments they could barely stand one another, but he loved how her mind worked. "That message is?"

"Move aside."

♔♔♔

The masquerade was almost in full swing by the time that Anastasia and Mikhail arrived. As they approached the steward, Mikhail had to fight against his natural appalled reaction to the ostentatious surroundings.

There were almost four hundred people in attendance. An equal number of servants whipped around the ballroom, chasing party-goers with trays of caviar, sturgeon, and ice cream.

Vodka and champagne were flowing like water. Guests were dressed in clothes that, if sold, would feed families for months.

The grand ballroom was a sight to be seen with gilded filigree, marble pillars, and elaborate oil paintings of Tsars — present and past — looming larger than life over the party.

The entire scene was so out of touch with what was happening right outside the palace doors; it felt as though they had walled themselves in a gold coffin.

He could sense the turmoil amongst them, the angst, the fear, the fervor. The energy in the room felt like gasoline, ready to explode with the smallest of sparks.

Mikhail spotted priests and clerics intermingling with the guests draped in jewel-encrusted crucifixes and gold-threaded robes.

Mikhail could sense Anastasia's anxiety as the steward beckoned them forward. He felt a sharp urge to slide his arm around her waist for support but fought against it.

She didn't want him in that way. He wasn't sure she wanted him at all.

Tonight, he was the tutor, another religious cleric selected by the Tsarina, eager to meet the other lords and seek an advisor role.

The steward didn't recognize Anastasia and his face balked when she gave him their names to pronounce. He stuttered for a moment as if he was afraid to do it.

Somewhat wisely, he was afraid the Tsar had not sanctioned this, but Anastasia leveled him with one look, and he turned around.

"Presenting... The Grand Duchess Anastasia Nikolaevna Romanova, and her royal tutor, Grigori Yefimovich Rasputin..."

The hush that fell over the entire ballroom was immediate and heart-stopping as nearly eight hundred combined guests and servants stopped where they stood.

Even the band faltered. Masks flew off, and people jostled closer to the grand staircase to get their first look at the long-missing Grand Duchess.

Through the stillness, Anastasia and Mikhail were able to find the Tsar and Tsarina. Nicholas looked as though he was ready to put a bullet through them both.

In contrast, the Tsarina's shocked expression quickly faded to one of annoyance when she recognized Anastasia's dress.

A few more moments passed of appalling silence, and Mikhail felt Anastasia move a hair's breadth closer to him. Then, just as suddenly as the party had stopped, it resumed.

Anastasia let out a controlled, sharp breath and they descended the grand staircase, immediately accosted by guests coveting the attention of the Grand Duchess.

Though she had been sheltered for the majority of her adult life, keeping up with court was still mandated for Anastasia. Her father had instructed it.

She had frequently been quizzed on the who's who of St. Petersburg, even if she had never been allowed to meet them in person. That way, in her father's mind, she would be prepared to emerge as soon as her magic was under control. His control, of course.

Anastasia wasted no time ignoring the ladies who approached her about her dress as she descended on the lords themselves. It wasn't long before they were separated, Anastasia falling into her own and beginning to flirt and schmooze the boyars.

Mikhail watched her for a moment as he tried to keep himself from thinking too fondly about how much she had evolved since returning to her magic.

A strategist, no matter the setting, Mikhail thought to himself. *Admirable.* Mikhail had no court experience and was desperately out of touch with the mannerisms and intricacies of the required etiquette. He politely excused himself to stand on the periphery.

However, a handsome man amongst a crowd of overinflated, red-faced calvary men was never alone at a party for long. Hardly a minute had passed before women began to descend and circle like sharks, their fans either open wide or held in front of their faces. Mikhail nodded politely to each one, blissfully unaware.

Across the ballroom, Anastasia was barely listening to a boyar, her eyes narrowing as she watched woman after woman present themselves to Mikhail.

He clearly had no idea what was going on, but in terms of body language and use of their fans, the women were publicly announcing their intentions to seduce him.

Anastasia felt something hot like jealousy rise in her chest, making her grip her own fan so tightly that a pearl popped off.

"I'm sorry," she turned to the lord speaking to her. "I am needed elsewhere. Would you mind saving me a waltz?" The nameless face nodded enthusiastically, and Anastasia rolled her eyes internally before giving him a graceful smile and walking away. She crossed the dance floor, shrugging off two other men, before storming over to Mikhail.

Anastasia looked up at one of the women who was circling particularly close, her fan sliding graciously up to her left ear.

The woman recoiled with a look of shock on her face before scoffing and promptly stomping off with a very bruised ego.

"What was that?" Mikhail grabbed Anastasia's arm and tugged her behind a column. "We're supposed to be making allies, Anya. Why are you stomping around like a child and scaring people off? She could've been useful."

"You have no idea how useful," Anastasia rolled her eyes. "And don't call me Anya."

"What's that supposed to mean?" Mikhail gave her a once over. "Did someone say something to you? What is your problem?"

"Look," Anastasia peered out from behind the column, "Do you see that woman?" She pointed at a blonde woman in a black Venetian mask.

"Yes," he shrugged, "What's your point?"

"Her *fan*, Mikhail," Anastasia hissed, stepping out back in full view of the party.

"Okay? Maybe she's warm?"

"Mikhail," her voice snapped, "She's looking right at you with her fan at her mouth. She's telling you and this whole party she wants to fuck you."

His eyes went wide, and his cheeks tinged. "She *what?*"

"And that one," Anastasia muttered, pointing to another woman, "She's the daughter of a Swiss dignitary. She's engaged, but she'd apparently like you to know they'd accept a third this evening."

Mikhail blinked rapidly before turning to look at Anastasia and bursting into laughter upon seeing the expression on her face. "Oh, Anya," he crooned, "Are you jealous? You look ready to tear them apart."

"I am most certainly not jealous!" Anastasia's magic flared at her fingertips, sending sparks to the floor — which only caused Mikhail's laughter to drop an octave as he stared down at her.

"Calm down," he said, a smirk slowly spreading over his face. "Your magic, Anastasia. Tonight isn't the time for people to discover it. Now, use your fan and tell me what's wrong...," he couldn't help but bite his lip to keep from laughing at his joke.

Anastasia sputtered, her temper attempting to take over before Mikhail wrapped an arm around her waist and spun them swiftly back behind the column. He pressed her up against it, his hand going to her forearm and tracing the barest of touches across her skin.

"Keep it under control, *Your Grace*," he grinned. Anastasia's eyes went wide at the feel of his skin against hers, causing her hands to spark into a brief, shining ball of light before dissipating.

Mikhail rolled his eyes playfully and shook his head as he leaned down towards her ear, dropping his voice to ensure only she could hear him.

"You're so beautiful when you respond to me, Anya." Anastasia gasped, sinking against the wall and dropping her whole weight against it.

Mikhail was off of her in a moment, swiftly turning on his heel and disappearing into the party crowd — leaving Anastasia infuriated and breathless on the sidelines.

"I should've made him play the part of a damn *mute*," she hissed before standing up and shaking her shoulders gently to clear her head.

Two can play that game, Mikhail. I will make you suffer.

For the rest of the evening, Anastasia and Mikhail kept an eye on the other. They swept through waltzes, drinks, and dinner with separate partners — both of them attempting to curry favor with nobility while simultaneously making the other jealous. Neither one of them would admit it, but they were both doing a splendid job.

Mikhail watched with a careful eye as she reintroduced herself to nearly every man in the room, finding himself drawn closer to her whenever he sensed her father was near.

The Tsar and Tsarina were too image-obsessed to try

anything in the middle of the ball, but it didn't keep Mikhail from searching for Anastasia's face whenever he felt like her father swayed a little too close to her.

Anastasia, blissfully unaware of her father, eyed every fan in the room aimed at Mikhail at not-so-subtly using hers to tell them to fuck off. It served a dual purpose — people could assume whatever they wanted about their relationship, but they talked about them.

While the masquerade balls usually went well into Wednesday morning, Anastasia felt herself beginning to fade after midnight. Most of the conversations past midnight would be futile as patrons got too drunk to care or remember.

She'd only hoped that she had made enough of a good impression with those she had met earlier in the night. Her eyes began searching the room, wondering if she should even wait for Mikhail or try to find him.

We arrived together. That was the purpose. We didn't say anything about leaving together... Anastasia's thoughts were a muddled mess as she refused to sort through her feelings.

It was a simple enough question, but she found herself paralyzed with it. She looked around the crowded ballroom and finally found him. A beautiful brunette — holding a small dog — was attempting to cuddle up next to him on a settee.

He doesn't seem... bothered by her at all, does he? No, of course not. You're the only one he despises, no matter how many excuses he makes to touch you.

Anastasia turned around as quickly as her heavy gown would allow her, rushing out of the ballroom and into the dark of the night, wondering why hot tears pricked at her face.

On the other side of the dance floor, the sparkling lights of Anastasia's gown caught Mikhail's attention like a shooting star. Maybe no one else could see it, but behind the composure on her face, he swore he saw the threat of tears.

Without thinking twice or letting himself debate over his

heart and head, he stood up — excusing himself from the brunette and rushing through the crowds of guests after Anastasia.

He finally caught up with her down the hall, Anastasia purposefully not looking at him as he kept pace beside her.

"Anya, stop," Mikhail's brow was furrowed as he got in front of her and grabbed her shoulders. "What's wrong? Did your father say something?" He scanned her face.

"What did I say about calling me that?" Anastasia rolled her eyes, pushing his hands off of her and pushing past him toward her rooms. "I'm surprised you even saw me leave."

"What does *that* mean?" Mikhail stood still for a moment with a confused look on his face before shaking his head and following.

"You seemed perfectly content where you were."

"That's what this is about?" Mikhail scoffed. "Are you jealous?"

"No!" Anastasia's denial was much too adamant. They had reached the doors to her suite, and she tossed them open, Mikhail following her inside angrily.

Anastasia suddenly felt like a girlish fool, embarrassed by whatever thoughts she had about Mikhail. She kicked off her shoes and began ripping her hairpins out furiously.

"Whoa, whoa, whoa," Mikhail rushed over to her, grabbing her wrists. "Stop that! What has gotten into you? You're the one who said that I should go as your *tutor.*" He said the last word like it was a curse.

"You're the one who can't stop living in the past!" Anastasia screamed, fighting to get her wrists free.

"Oh right," Mikhail backed Anastasia up until her legs met the couch, forcing her to sit while he towered over her. "Excuse the fuck out of me for not being over the fact that my mother died." He didn't have the heart anymore to accuse her directly.

"You don't even trust me!" Anastasia hissed, bringing her foot up to kick him in the groin and missing narrowly.

"For fuck's sake, Anastasia!" Mikhail grunted, releasing her wrists and taking a few steps back. "For... fuck's... sake..."

Anastasia watched in horror as the color started to drain from Mikhail's face. His breathing got shallower as his hands clutched at his stomach, letting out a low grunting noise.

"Mikhail?!" Anastasia stood up and ran to him, her arms guiding him to take her place on the couch. He sat down with a massive moan of pain. His face was turning red, and sweat was gathering on his brow.

"Anya...," his voice sounded parched. "The ball..."

Anastasia gasped as her hands covered her mouth, realization dawning on her. Poison was a favorite of the court, a close second to political hangings.

"What do I do?! What should I do?" She dropped to her knees as her hands went to Mikhail's face, holding his head up and wiping at the sweat on his brow.

"Anya..." His voice croaked again as he leaned into her touch. Mikhail's eyes started to flutter closed, his breath slowing down until she could barely see any movement in his chest.

"NO!" Anastasia screamed, letting go of his head. "No, no, no..." She began beating on his chest with her fists as he took one last shuddered breath and his eyes shut.

At that moment, Anastasia could see nothing but Mikhail, ignoring the sound of her cries or the tears that were making it hard to see.

She wiped at them angrily and sent her fists crashing down on his shirt, the gems sewn into her sleeves snagging on the threads on his shirt.

"Don't *leave* me!" Anastasia wept, her scream a haunted, broken sound. "I don't know how to do this without you, Mikhail!" She dropped her head on his chest, her hands going to the golden cuffs on his arms and ripping them off, unable to stare at the double-headed eagle. "I don't *want* to do it without you... how *dare* you leave, too!" She screamed, throwing her body over his as golden light flooded her fingertips.

It exploded out of her as potent as she had ever seen it; all of the lights exploded in the room as the fireplace leaped even higher. The flames threatened to spill out of the brick and up the walls.

Anastasia's magic poured out of her and covered Mikhail's body as she watched from the floor next to him, shocked. It circled him once, twice... wrapping around his stomach. It undulated over him, and suddenly, Mikhail seemed to come back to life with a massive grunt.

His body twitched as he came up to a half-sitting position before falling backward again, heavy breaths shaking his chest. There was sweat beading on his forehead, and his fancy clothes were almost soaked through.

"Mikhail?" Anastasia gasped, her face pale as her hands went to cover her face. She held her breath, afraid to believe for even a moment that he was alive. She was nervous to touch him or look at him for too long.

Mikhail sat up once more and began blinking, his breath beginning to even out only slightly. He leaned over the side of the couch and began dry-heaving.

As soon as it subsided, he had sat up and rested back against the chair, and she jumped up on the couch next to him.

Anastasia sat in between his legs, still wiping at her tears, and grabbed his arms. Without thinking, she began to rub the back of his hand.

"Oh my God," she gasped, her chest heaving with the remnants of her sobs. The anger between them had dissipated entirely.

Mikhail's face was pale as he stared up at her, while they both tried to understand what exactly had happened. Anastasia's magic had never *quite* manifested in that way before. Neither of them paid any attention to the intimacy ebbing between them.

"Well," Mikhail leaned back against the couch with a thud, struggling to recover his breath. "It seems that you can save a life, Anastasia."

A nastasia collapsed against Mikhail, weeping quietly with a sense of relief that she'd never felt before.

Without thinking, both of them fell into an easy embrace that was too comfortable for either of them to accept.

Mikhail's hand came up and cradled the back of her head, waiting a few moments to catch his breath. Neither of them said anything.

They were terrified that words would shatter the illusion hanging between them that they had found sanctuary in one another's arms, that it would only take one misspoken sentiment for them to back at each other's throat.

Mikhail struggled to keep his thoughts straight. He couldn't deny the instincts that threatened to overtake him and keep Anastasia pressed against him forever. He wanted to destroy her family and anyone who had ever made her feel like she was lesser than or had tried to diminish her power.

At the same time, he still battled moving on from the past and letting go of the hatred he had nurtured for so long. He knew that she needed to accept her gifts and abandon the cage she had been raised in to get over her past.

Until they both did that, he knew that they'd continue to tear each other apart. How could he think of anything other than keeping her in his arms when he had tasted death, and it was her magic that breathed him back to life?

It had felt like her; it was unmistakably *Anastasia* when the magic had gripped him like a lifeline. He always wanted that essence to consume him.

Anastasia sniffled and shifted on top of him, her hand coming up to caress his cheek. Mikhail let out a deep sigh and felt his heart clench. He knew he had to stop them before they went somewhere they couldn't return from.

He covered her hand with his and gave it a small squeeze, before gently rolling out from underneath her and straightening up. Anastasia looked at him, the tears still drying on her face, hurt and confusion contorting her features.

Mikhail stood and shook his head silently, trying to do the best thing for both of them.

"I think we both should get some sleep after... tonight. Your Grace." He nodded his head to her in an abruptly formal manner and all but ran back to his room.

Anastasia stared after him, too shocked to move, as she felt her heart breaking. The beginning threads of trust she had towards him snapped.

Fools. Asya muttered disapprovingly, from the ether, always.

♛♛♛

Anastasia was awake for the rest of the night, unable to keep her mind from attempting to cave in on itself. When she saw Mikhail dying, she'd experienced a fear that was new to her, different from anything she had ever experienced.

The idea of waking up the following day without him in her rooms, across the hall, circulating her... facing that reality had made her want to follow him into death.

After he recovered enough, Mikhail had left her for a second time; he had made his choice. His actions made it clear that he didn't want to be near her in the way she craved.

The fragile foundation of trust that she had begun to lay for him now lay fractured.

She never returned to her rooms. She was still sitting on the couch, hoping against her better judgment that Mikhail would come back.

He's probably still sleeping... It's early. He did die last night... I think. He was usually an early riser; her rational mind was trying to convince her that he wasn't, in fact, hiding from her in there, that he hated her.

Her thoughts were interrupted by a loud banging on her doors, startling Anastasia out of her anxious rumination. She was about to stand when the doors flew open with a massive bang.

In walked the Tsar, the Tsarina, and his three *dvoryanstvo* behind them. Anastasia stood, her heart beginning to race at the sight of her family as she braced herself.

She fought the temptation to look over her shoulder at Mikhail's rooms and found herself desperate for him beside her. Despite their aggressive entrance, the group almost looked remorseful.

"Darling Anastasia," the Tsarina began, her face contorting in what could be described as sadness that looked and felt fraudulent. "We've heard what happened. How traumatic for you."

Anastasia froze. It didn't take long for her to realize that they expected Mikhail to have died the night before.

Oh, God. Mikhail. They're assuming the poison was successful... they're betting that it happened at the ball, and there were witnesses. They probably saw us both leaving in a hurry... They don't know what I can do... They're bluffing.

"I'm sorry?" Anastasia cocked her head in a mocking sense of confusion. "I don't know what you could have heard." The

Tsar and Tsarina's facades flickered for a moment but didn't go out.

"Oh," the Tsarina chuckled awkwardly, "We didn't want to be the ones to tell you..."

Incredible. Are they so blind to see that this plan didn't work? They didn't even bother to confirm it with anyone before bursting in here.

"It seems that your tutor met an unfortunate end last night," the Tsar stepped forward, his political chagrin in full swing. "I'm terribly sorry. It seemed you two were close. Maybe it is for the best."

Anastasia gritted her teeth, wondering how far they were going to take this charade. She found herself sitting down on the couch in shock, staring at her parents with a confused expression on her face.

They were here, once again in her rooms with their lap-dog *dvoryanstvo*, attempting to manipulate her. Her parents looked at Anastasia, assuming her disbelief was at Mikhail's death and not their floundering attempt to gaslight her.

She sat back for a moment and attempted not to be over-whelmed by the realization of how many times her father must have tried to manipulate her like this in her past.

"It seemed I had a very eventful evening."

Every head in the room turned as Mikhail stepped out of his apartment and into the sitting room. As much as she wanted to see her parent's reaction, Anastasia was unable to keep her eyes off Mikhail.

He looked well-rested, even if his hair was half-up and his shirt was rumpled from sleep. She couldn't fight the desire to push them both back into his room and abandon the outside world forever.

Mikhail stood there defiantly, crossing his arms over his broad chest and staring down at her parents.

Her parents... the Tsar and Tsarina of all Russia. Anastasia, feeling emboldened by Mikhail's presence at her back, turned to face them and stood.

Her mother looked terrified as if she was staring at a ghost, more inclined to believe that he had been resurrected than that their attempt had misfired.

The Tsar's face darkened for just a moment before evening out into a twisted stoicism, a gift he had honed over the years as a tyrant.

The *dvoryanstvo* immediately began whispering to each other — and one slipped out the door, the story of Rasputin's *dark magic resurrection* on his loose lips to anyone who would listen.

"Your affinity for political assassinations is as strong as ever," Anastasia stared at her father, refusing to back down under his unholy stare. "It seems as if your efficacy may be slipping, though. I do hope it is not the sign of a frail mind." Her voice descended into a hiss — and even Anastasia couldn't believe the way she was taking on her father.

The Tsar's answering voice was cold. It did not shake with anger, frustration, or malice; it was foreboding and iron-clad in its resolution. The sound of it had made men weep at its finality. He stared down at his daughter with the face that he had taken against his own enemies.

Mikhail moved like water upon seeing that glance, silently slipping around the couch and standing behind Anastasia.

"You will be wed," the Tsar was emotionless, "to Nikolai Ruzsky. I have a suspicion that my general has become rather nearsighted on our goals as of late."

Anastasia felt a cold pit sinking in her stomach, but she swallowed thickly and let her flames lick up higher.

"What? Am I to be some distracting new toy for him?"

"You're going to kill him," the Tsar's voice was like a whip, Anastasia felt it smacking across her face.

"I... I will do no such thing." Anastasia's voice wavered but did not falter. She felt herself digging her heels into the ground as if she was preparing for a physical attack.

"You will," the Tsar commanded again. "I've had enough of your games. You chose to reappear at court. The people demand to know what is to be done with you —"

"*Done* with her?" Mikhail snapped, his hand going up and gently pressing against Anastasia's back. "She's a woman, not an object."

"She is a weapon!" The Tsar hissed. "She will be used as such." Composure flittered over the Tsar's face as he bounced back and forth between rage and deathly calm.

"What do you suppose I do?" Anastasia laughed darkly. "I don't want to kill anyone... I won't do it. You don't even — *I* don't even — know what I can do."

Anastasia fumbled weakly for an excuse, desperate to make her parents believe her magic had limits. They hadn't seen her use it recently.

"You can kill," the Tsar raised an eyebrow. "Or have you forgotten?"

Anastasia's hands pulled into fists, and she let out a controlled breath.

She took a step backward, expecting Mikhail to abandon her side and rejoin her parents at the reminder. He stood firm, his hand warm around her waist.

Anastasia felt her heart begin to race... *Is he choosing this right now? Us?*

"Touching," the Tsar rolled his eyes at the display. "This is not a request. You *will* marry Ruzsky, and you will kill him."

"How am I supposed to kill someone?!" Anastasia's voice was equal parts angry and skeptical. "You are seemingly skipping over the fact that even if you manage to marry me off to some rival of yours, I can't... and I *won't*... kill him."

"Your Grace," one of the *doryantsvo's* voices interrupted — it had a greasy sound to it that reminded Anastasia of rotten fish.

He had a jilted way of speaking as though he had to summon the courage for the following words.

"It should be quite easy... magic or no... if you are so inclined... for a woman of your... standing... to incapacitate a man when he is otherwise... distracted."

There was a tense silence that settled over the room. Mikhail felt his body stiffen as his grip on Anastasia tightened, feeling righteous anger begin to roll and burn in his chest.

He had already been holding back against the Tsar as they threatened to move Anastasia around like a weapon, a pawn — and his control was beginning to slip as he tried to estimate the prowess of his opponents.

If this man opens his mouth one more time and elaborates on this idea... He better not even be picturing this right now, or I will rip his spine from his back.

A lecherous grin slid over the noble's face while both the Tsar and the Tsarina remained impassive, hardly bothered by the perverted instructions.

"Excuse me?" Anastasia raised an eyebrow, her voice challenging.

Even from behind her, Mikhail knew the fire that had just flared in her blue eyes based on her tone. He had to fight to keep the smirk off of his face.

That's my Anya. You don't even need me here, do you?

"Your Grace," the old man coughed, shrugging as his eyebrows waggled mockingly, "I'm simply suggesting that if you do not have the power to kill him outright, you might need to fuck your new husband... for the *element of surprise*, of course."

The Tsarina flinched at the description but made no noise; the Tsar dared to look bored.

Anastasia looked at the man in shock, surprised that he had enough courage to spell it out for her. Her father turned his head in the subtleness of nods, urging the man to continue and seemingly permitting him to speak further.

"If you are unwilling or, perhaps, frightened by the idea," the smile that spread across his face was like snake oil, "There are always ways to… practice, Your Grace."

Mikhail's reaction was immediate.

He burst past Anastasia, grabbing the man by his collar. He held on tight to the smaller man, looming over the lord by a head.

Mikhail lifted the man by his shirt and slammed him against the wall. The *doryantsvo's* eyes went wide, and he began shaking, kicking his feet as they came off of the ground.

"Address her one more time," Mikhail growled, "And I will personally tear you limb from limb for *practice.*" He slammed the *doryantsvo* again, driving the point home. Near them, a painting fell to the floor with the force of Mikhail shoving his body against the wall.

The Tsarina shrieked and moved over to a corner, clearing the path between the Tsar and Mikhail.

The *doryantsvo* was a small, older man, but the Tsar was still in relatively good shape for all of his overconsumption. His perceived control over the situation snapped, and the man's rage came bubbling up towards the surface.

The Tsar turned on Mikhail, pulling a pistol from the depths of his jacket while Mikhail was distracted with the *doryantsvo*. It took Anastasia only mere moments to react. She turned on her father, throwing her body weight against him as the shot rang out… and missed.

The sound ricocheting off the walls broke Mikhail's focus as he dropped the man, who hit the ground like a bag of sand and spun around on his heel.

"*You stupid girl,*" the Tsar hissed, turning around and striking Anastasia across the cheek. "You will learn to obey me yet!"

Mikhail saw red. He crossed the room in two steps, coiled his hand back, and pummeled the Tsar in the face. The man sputtered — never having been struck before in his life — and recoiled before falling on his ass, blinking rapidly as his nose started to bleed.

Mikhail stood above him, his chest heaving and knuckles split, his broad shoulders tensed in a challenge.

"You touch her again," Mikhail's voice sounded like fire and brimstone, "and you'll die."

"Mikhail," Anastasia's voice was quiet as she stood a few steps away. "I'm okay." Her voice snapped him out of his haze, and he turned to face her. Her cheek was red, her hair mussed, and he noticed the slight tremble in her hands.

"Anya," his voice changed into something deep and soft that made Anastasia's shoulders relax — and other parts of her tense — all at the same time. He walked over to her and gently cradled her face in his hands, cringing when his thumbs smeared some blood on her cheek.

He chuckled quietly and wiped it off with a devilish wink that made Anastasia forget about the chaos that they were standing in. "Are you okay?"

Anastasia nodded, the adrenaline beginning to fade as she surveyed the room behind him. The *doryantsvo* lay passed out on the floor while the other one and her mother had fled in the chaos.

The Tsar was beginning to stand shakily, all parts of her father gone and a furious ruler rising in his place.

🎋 16 🎋

"You have lived a sheltered life, *doch*," the Tsar's voice was rough, spitting blood. He began waving his hands around manically. "You have no idea what we are dealing with! If you think you do, you have been severely misled by... by this... priest."

"I'm not a priest," Mikhail's voice had turned again when he looked at the Tsar, "But I will lead a holy war against you if that's what it will take."

His arm slid down to Anastasia's waist and pulled her closer to him. Somewhere in the corner, the *doryantsvo* stirred, slowly rising to his feet.

"He's a cursed man," he spat. His voice sounded cracked and hoarse, the bruising already beginning around his throat from where Mikhail had held him up against a wall. "Cursed!"

He began fumbling around in his overcoat as the Tsar wiped the blood from his lip, again leveling the pistol at the both of them. A few seconds later, the *doryantsvo* did the same — Anastasia and Mikhail pushed up against one another, each staring down the barrel of a gun.

"This won't get you what you want," Anastasia hissed,

looking at her father. "Do you really want this? If you kill us now, you'll get nothing."

"I'll have a threat eliminated." The Tsar's eyes were almost entirely black as he stared them down, looking like the commander in chief that he was. The last semblances of a fatherly facade had been ripped away.

"*Moi Tsar,*" the *doryantsvo's* voice broke the staredown between father and daughter, "Let me take out this one," he nodded the pistol at Mikhail, "and then we can still use the Grand Duchess to eliminate Ruzsky."

"What makes you think I will do anything for you?" Anastasia yelled, turning to look at the *doryantsvo.* "Do you have a plan? Oh, that's right. You just wanted me to *fuck* him. A master strategy!"

"Shoot him," the Tsar rolled his eyes, pocketing his pistol, clearly intent on sorting out Anastasia once they were rid of Mikhail.

The command broke something inside Anastasia, her blood running cold and then hot. She was consumed with the idea and was almost violently sick at how it made her chest clench.

The *doryantsvo* grinned like a leech, raising a shaky hand. All at once, Anastasia threw herself in front of Mikhail and tossed her hands up in front of them.

The lights went out again in the apartments as the fire went out. The weak will of the dawn was no match for the heavy, opaque velvet curtains as the rooms were plunged into darkness.

Anastasia's magic came whirling out of her fingertips, the telltale gold dust spreading around her fingers and up her arms. The Tsar watched on as his eyes widened, witnessing his first glimpse of Anastasia's magic in action. The expression on his face flickered in awe… and then turned to jealousy… and, the most terrifying of all, greed for power.

The vases, candelabras, and plates in the room began to rise and vibrate, suspended in midair. Mikhail looked around, frozen at the sight of Anastasia using her magic to such a powerful extent.

It was as though the oxygen had been sucked out of the room entirely. The *doryantsvo* gasped before leveling his gun once more and cocking the pistol.

"Don't you *dare!*" Anastasia yelled, followed by a horrendous scream as she tossed her hands forward. The suspended objects went hurtling towards the wall, crashing against it and exploding in a spray of shattered glass.

She took another step forward, staring at the *doryantsvo's* eyes and flicking her wrist to send another wave of magic his way. He was knocked to the ground, his eyes wide as he started clawing at his throat.

The Tsar watched — stunned — as Anastasia had the man gasping for air on the floor with a mere twitch of her fingers.

"Is this what you wanted?" She stepped forward, looking like she was possessed.

Mikhail stood behind her in awe, staring at the woman who was standing up to her father and his lackeys after decades of being under their thumb.

"You wanted me to get that man into bed and do something like... what? This?" She twisted her wrist again, and the *doryantsvo's* back arched as the rest of his air was cut off. Mikhail watched and quietly stepped forward, squeezing Anastasia's gently.

"You have every right to kill him, Anya," his voice had that warm, gentle tone that he only took when speaking to her, "I think you'll regret this."

"They spent *years* shaping me for this," she muttered, her magic spinning around them like a golden vortex.

"I know they did," he said quietly. "I'll kill them all with you if you asked me to...," he leaned down and kissed her shoulder, "I know you. You're better than them. You'll regret this."

"No!" She shrieked, contorting her magic again and making the *doryantsvo* flail while tears began streaming down her cheeks. "They turned me into *this!*"

"Don't be afraid of who you are. Don't be afraid of magic. Don't use it for this."

Anastasia grit her teeth, the internal struggle apparent on her face as she wrestled with her magic.

Fifteen years of feeling minimized, ashamed, made to be afraid of herself... all boiled down to this moment. Yet, she stopped. The magic went out like a light.

Anastasia sagged against Mikhail, the sudden outburst of her power leaving her exhausted.

The *doryantsvo* gasped for air, standing up and stumbling out of the room. By the time he had regained his breath, he had begun ranting madly about what happened when he had tried to kill *Rasputin*. And so, the rumor mill started again. No one moved to go after him.

The lights found their way back on as Anastasia's magic crept back over the room in tendrils, recoiling into her.

The pair slowly turned over to look at the Tsar, who was staring at the both of them with a wild look on his face. He'd never had someone resist him in his life.

Everything had always been done according to his whims, wishes, and wants. People fought to give in to his desires, to make them happen. He had his dissenters like any royal — namely Ruzsky — but those were distant threats. They were often handled for him.

Now, he was staring down the first two people who had ever stood up to him directly; the daughter that he should have dealt with years ago and the priest he had brought back into his home.

"Anastasia," he gritted the words out, as though her name tasted bitter. "Do you think your little light show has frightened me?"

Mikhail almost growled, unable to keep the anger off his face as he helped Anastasia stay on her feet. He knew what these exertions did to her and was desperate to pull her to safety. If her father figured out how quickly her magic could deplete, the Tsar would lock her in irons right now.

"I frighten you," Anastasia said, her voice sounding as clear as a bell despite the exhaustion threatening to overtake her. "I frighten you simply because you can't control me anymore. You're scared of anything that you don't have under your thumb."

The Tsar's eyes flickered before he was able to course-correct his expression. "I will *end* you, Anastasia," he bellowed, the blood from a broken nose drying on his face. "No matter what it takes!" His voice grew louder at the end until he was almost yelling.

"Your empire will fall," Anastasia said clearly, feeling like she had discovered herself for the first time in her life. "I will push it over the edge."

"If I fall," the Tsar sneered, "I will take every Romanov down with me... and that means you." With that threat hanging in the air mingling the remnants of Anastasia's magic, he spun on his heel and left.

As soon as the door was closed firmly behind him, Anastasia let out a gasp. She sank the rest of her weight against Mikhail. He shifted her gently until they were face to face.

"Talk to me, *Your Grace*," he used the nickname to inspire a flicker of annoyance on her face. "Talk to me."

He leaned down and scooped Anastasia up, clutching her tight to his chest and walking them into her rooms. He put her down on the bed and began rubbing his hands over her arms, trying to massage some life back into her.

She looked incredibly pale, and her arms felt cold. Anastasia let a small smile creep onto her face while shaking her head.

"I'm okay," she shook her head, laughing as his hands moved to her ribs and tickled her sides. "Oh, stop it!"

"I'll do anything to hear you laugh," Mikhail chuckled, sitting up on the bed next to her and kissing her forehead softly. "Are you sure you're alright?"

"It's just the magic. I need a nap."

Mikhail nodded, silence settling over the both of them as if they were afraid to acknowledge what had just happened. Anastasia had started a war with her family — they had seen her magic.

The Tsar now knew what she could do. She had nearly killed the *doryantsvo* with a flick of a wrist.

This moment when her magic was depleted made Mikhail want to fight anyone who *looked* at her wrong. He knew that she was capable of everything the Romanovs were afraid of and then some.

Anastasia was made for her magic, and she didn't need him to use it. In these moments, when it was just the two of them, and he was allowed to see the Anastasia that no one else did — he lived for them. It scared him.

"We should move," Mikhail kept looking over at the door behind him. He was waiting for the Tsar to burst back in at any moment with the entire Russian cavalry behind him. "Can you do it?"

Anastasia's eyes had already fluttered closed, and she blinked them back open. "Move?"

"I don't think we're safe here," he said quietly, "In the palace."

"We don't have any choice," Anastasia's voice was fading as heavy exhaustion threatened to drag her under. "If we leave, he'll burn down the city trying to find us... People would die."

"Do you really think he's just going to let us stay here?" Mikhail's voice rose a little, making Anastasia's eyes squeeze closed.

"Please, I have an awful headache," Anastasia sighed, her

head lolling on the pillow, "And yes. He wants his enemies under his nose. He would wait to find the most opportune time to strike against me — find a way to make it propaganda. He'll do nothing today."

"No," Mikhail shook his head. He felt a discomfort, an anxiety that had him suspended in a fight or flight response.

Something was wrong; he could feel it in his bones, though he couldn't place what it was. There was no reason for them to stay in the palace after an argument like that.

The Tsar would want to strike quickly. His reputation had already been damaged. He was a man with every resource at his beck and call, and now, he had a daughter whose powerful magic he had *seen.*

"Trust me," Mikhail pleaded. Anastasia's eyes flew open as she looked at him, going up on one elbow.

They had already made several stands against the monarchy together. Rumors about them were indeed already spreading.

She had saved his life now — twice — and no one had helped her find her magic the way that he had. Yet... he had left her, more than once, at pivotal times whenever they seemed to cross a line they wouldn't be able to return from.

He was only in her chambers right now because she had killed his mother, and *her mother* had hired him. It wasn't exactly a recipe for lasting trust.

Anastasia stopped her thoughts as she felt her heart threatening to cave in on itself. It wasn't the exhaustion caused by her magic either, but the terrible realization that she truly did trust Mikhail.

"I do trust you," the words came falling out of Anastasia's mouth before she could stop them. "I think I trust you more than anyone else in this world, Mikhail."

She continued, her eyes wide at her admission. Mikhail stared at her, and for a moment, she thought that he might leave again.

I swear to God, if he walks out of here one more time when I say something fucking vulnerable, my heart won't be able to take it.

"I promise," Mikhail's voice was slow as if he was being cautious about his word choice, "I'll never give you a reason not to. Never again."

Anastasia nodded, heat flooding her cheeks as she fidgeted with the sheets. The moment felt intrusive. It was as though they were doing things all out of order.

Both of them were afraid to admit their feelings — admitting to trust was terrifying enough.

"Where should we go?"

"Back to the boarding house," Mikhail grinned at the flush that overtook Anastasia's face, distinctly *not* from exhaustion, "We can stay there for a night. Okay? Then we'll figure out where to go."

"We can't let anyone get hurt, Mikhail, please. If someone is caught harboring us..." She gripped his forearm and squeezed it. It was a gentle embrace for someone so tired, and it brought Mikhail's attention back to how exhausted she was.

"We won't," he shook his head, "I don't want that to happen any more than you do. Just one night. You'll be able to sleep in peace."

"Are you sure?" Her voice was tired, and Mikhail could tell that she was fading fast. He couldn't ignore the protective instinct rising in his chest, and he knew she wasn't safe here. She needed some time — at least one night — to get a solid night's rest before their world imploded.

"Yes, Anya," he gave her a soft grin, leaning forward and pressing a soft kiss to her cheek, "One night. Then we'll come back here so they won't send anyone after us. Give me one night, okay?"

"Mikhail," Anastasia sighed and said his name like it was a prayer. The soft tone in her voice made him go nearly blind with the desire to get her out of the palace and keep her safe.

She sat up and leaned against him entirely. "I have an awful feeling that I would give you every night of my life."

❦❦❦

The walk to the boarding house was slow-going. Once they were a few streets away from the Winter Palace, Mikhail caved, leaning down and scooping up Anastasia.

She protested and demanded that she was able to walk, but he could hardly look at the exhausted expression on her face.

It only took a few steps before Anastasia's head was resting on his chest, fast asleep.

Luckily, the innkeeper saw them coming through a window, tossing open the door for the pair as soon as Mikhail climbed their steps.

"Oh, darling, is she alright?" The woman's voice was full of concern as she looked over Anastasia.

"Just tired," Mikhail grinned, his voice barely above a whisper. "Long day. Would you mind terribly putting us up again?"

"The Grand Duchess is the only Romanov allowed here," the innkeeper said proudly. She smiled at the pair and led them up to the same room they had stayed in prior.

"Shall I have some food sent up for you?"

"If it's not too much trouble," Mikhail said with an easy smile, Anastasia still dozing against his chest.

"Absolutely not! I'll send it shortly," the innkeeper glanced once more at Anastasia and, with a warm smile, made a quick exit.

Mikhail walked over to the bed, gently lying Anastasia down. He tried to move as steadily as possible as not to wake her, but she stirred when Mikhail pulled away from her.

"Are we here?" She asked groggily, her voice tired and eyes sleepy. Mikhail had to admit to himself that it was one of the most beautiful things he'd ever seen.

"*Da,*" he sat down on the bed next to her, grabbing her hand and squeezing it. "Go to sleep, Anya. They'll be food shortly. You need your rest."

Anastasia stopped, looking up at him with an expression on her face that he couldn't decipher. She let out a small sigh and pushed herself up to a sitting position.

The atmosphere was drastically different from the last time they were sitting on the bed at the boarding house — Mikhail couldn't keep his eyes off of her.

"I meant what I said," Anastasia's voice was quiet and steady. "I don't know if you feel the same way. Honestly... I would be surprised if you did. I meant it. I trust you, Mikhail, and it's a whole lot more than that. I don't even know what I feel... I haven't felt anything in *years,* then you broke into my life and shattered it all —"

Mikhail flinched, and Anastasia shook her head rapidly before continuing.

"— in the *best* way. I lived an awful life. I don't know how you could ever forgive me... I could never blame you for that... you should know."

"Know what?" Mikhail couldn't help but push her, dying to hear the words come out of her mouth.

"I... I don't even know if I have words for it. It's true. You asked me for just one night, but I'd give you all of them for the rest of my life."

There was a silence that settled over the small room. Anastasia bit down on her lip and felt her stomach begin to turn.

After a mere heartbeat of silence from Mikhail, she was convinced that she was indeed the *stupidest* woman alive.

You dumb child! You're Romanova! You might have a shared goal, one man comes into your chambers, and you go head over heels for him like —

"I'd give you every moment of my life, Anya." Mikhail's voice cut through her thoughts as she turned and stared at him with a wide-eyed expression. "I don't know what it means either... we don't have to know."

"You mean...," Anastasia was afraid to ask the question, but she needed to know before the conversation went another second further.

"I forgive you, Anya."

"I trust you."

Mikhail leaned forward, one hand pulling Anastasia closer by the waist, the other cupping her cheek.

They crashed against one another in a passionate kiss, pouring everything they had been withholding from one another into it.

Anastasia leaned back, dragging Mikhail with her by his hair when they were interrupted by a sudden knock.

Startled, they sprung apart just as the door opened, and the innkeeper stepped in carrying a massive tray of food with a smile on her face that looked like the dawn.

"Dinner!"

17

True to his word, Mikhail brought Anastasia back to the Winter Palace the following morning. He felt wrong. A nagging feeling sat in the pit of his stomach as they made their way back through the gates.

They weren't sneaking around this time but walking through the front door felt like asking for trouble.

They made their way through the palace unaccosted and reentered Anastasia's room, noticing everything was how they had left it.

The floor was covered in blood and shards of glass and ceramic. The candles and lamps were burnt out, and a heavy curtain was hanging off-kilter above the window.

Mikhail studied Anastasia's face as she looked over the damage, concerned that the messy scene would bring back dark memories for her.

The realization that they had really, truly, stood up to the Tsar and Tsarina was sitting on top of both of them like stone. Anastasia simply smoothed down her skirts, looked around, and with a wave of her hand, had the room back in its original state.

Mikhail stared after her with a shocked look on his face,

amazed at how her powers seemed to be developing — and how fast — now that she'd stepped into her identity.

They knew that they had to find more allies or come up with a plan at all if they were going to finish what they started — seeing the damage of the room solidified in both of their memories that they had poured the gas and lit the fire.

The next day they stayed in her rooms, Anastasia stealing nervous glances towards the door every time someone knocked even though only food was delivered to her rooms, per usual.

At first, Mikhail was just happy that the kitchens hadn't received any orders to stop sending meals. By the second day, that changed.

When breakfast arrived, Mikhail grabbed a cloche and knew that it wasn't their normal fare from its chilled surface. He lifted it to reveal Anastasia's old breakfast — cold oatmeal, no fruit, no sugar. Only water, no coffee.

Anastasia let out a long, controlled breath, and he eyed how she clasped her hands together to keep them from shaking.

This was about more than the food. It was a reminder of the years that she had spent entirely under her family's thumb. They would stop at nothing to trigger her and gaslight her into doing whatever they wanted.

"It's alright," Mikhail had moved towards her and grabbed her hands. "They can't control you, okay? Look at me. Talk to me."

His gaze was imploring, hoping that she wasn't slipping away from him at this dreadful reminder of how captive she had once been.

"I'm okay," she smiled softly and looked up at Mikhail, the expression not quite reaching her eyes. "I still expect them to walk in with a firing squad — cold breakfast isn't too bad by comparison."

They ate in silence, both of them occasionally tossing glances at the door. They weren't surprised to see that lunch and dinner were the same familiar cold, bland food that Anastasia had been malnourished with for years.

Mikhail was concerned that it had her in her head more than usual, but she shook her head each time and offered him a weak rebuttal. There was only so much that he could do while she denied it.

By the third day, Mikhail was desperate to find out something. *Anything.*

They assumed that the Tsar still held out hope that he could manipulate Anastasia to his side. It was either that, or he was determined that their downfall would be public and used as propaganda. Both reasons made a good cause for him not to attack them privately in her suites.

Still... there had to be rumors of what he might be planning.

They knew that Nikolai Ruzsky, the man they wanted Anastasia to marry, was speaking out actively against the Tsar. If they could make contact with him, somehow, maybe they could strategize a way to get this brutal regime to end.

At least if it involved force, Anastasia could make an appearance at Ruzsky's side. Mikhail knew that she didn't want to be used as a weapon, but he hoped that her presence and the threat of her gifts would be enough.

"I'm going out for a few hours," Mikhail told Anastasia about his plan to seek out Ruzsky. "Surely, some of the servants know something. I still know my way around the palace. I'll be back before noon."

"Please don't go," Anastasia looked up at him with genuine fear in her eyes. "I'm frightened here, Mikhail. Please. I don't like the idea of us being apart."

"It will be okay," he assured her, leaning down to kiss her forehead. "I'll be back in just a few hours. We must start planning a move, or we're going to be stuck in a stalemate with your father on *his* turf."

Anastasia nodded, "Hurry back to me... please."

"I will, Anya. Always."

He hurried out the doors to Anastasia's suites, both already counting the minutes until they could be back at one another's side.

After an hour, Anastasia was desperate. Anxiety crept up her spine like a cold, shameful feeling that she couldn't seem to distract herself from.

Now that they had put aside their pasts, the idea that they were apart in such hostile territory was enough to make her pick at the scars on her knuckles.

She found herself working towards a fever pitch, her thoughts spiraling out of control when a harsh knock cut through the silence of the rooms.

Anastasia almost vomited on queue at the sound, knowing that Mikhail wouldn't knock to enter. There wasn't even a moment to bid them entry before the door swung open.

The Tsar stepped into Anastasia's room. He shut the door behind him and stared at her, a softer expression on his face than the last time she had seen him.

It had been three days, but his nose was still purple and silently bent, something she knew was probably driving a prideful man like him mad.

"Anastasia," he nodded, his voice solemn. "May I sit?"

She nodded in response, her entire body tense. She eyed him from across the room. Both were eyeing each other like predators sizing up their opponent.

Anastasia wasn't naive enough to believe that he was here to apologize. He had come alone and had likely waited until he knew that she was alone, too.

She took a deep breath attempting to slow her heart rate without Mikhail at her side, feeling intimidated by the man who had abused her for years.

The Tsar said nothing, both of them waiting for the other to speak to break the tension. Neither did. Anastasia kept her mouth in a tight line, hoping to hide her fear.

The Tsar leaned back in the chair, one hand stroking his beard. Anastasia raised an eyebrow in a challenge, and he sighed.

"You'll never know what it's like to be the Tsar," his voice was almost contrite as he leaned forward, putting his elbows on his knees. "It is the greatest pressure that a man can know."

"I would imagine that struggling to feed his own family outweighs it." Her voice was quick, cutting, as she thought of the fathers she had met who couldn't feed their own children. It was a burden that she wouldn't wish upon anyone and one that the Tsar had never come close to knowing.

His eyebrows went up slightly in surprise as if expecting Anastasia to be more agreeable without Mikhail standing behind her.

"Everyone in Russia is the Tsar's children," he tilted his head to the side, their chess match officially engaged.

"Then you must be fraught with worry," Anastasia fought to keep her voice calm, "Knowing that all of your children are starving."

"Sometimes the best thing a parent can do for a child is let them find their way."

"Is that what you did to me? *Let me find my way?*" Anastasia snapped back too quickly, cursing herself as she struggled to remain cool-headed.

The Tsar held up both of his hands in mock surrender and leaned back against the overstuffed chair, picking at the velvet. "You did find your powers, didn't you?"

"*I* did. No one else. Certainly not because of anything *you* did." Her voice rose in pitch as she moved her hands behind her back to hide her golden magic beginning to flare.

"Let's not fight," the Tsar tutted. "I came here to speak to you cordially."

"I believe we are far past cordial, *moi Tsar.*"

"We don't have to be," he shrugged, looking effortlessly put together in the stressful situation, making her blood pressure spike even higher.

Mikhail, dear God, if there was ever a time to read my thoughts, it's now. Please come back!

Sweat was breaking out on Anastasia's palms, and her magic was getting harder to tamper down as she stared down her father. Even just looking at him threatened to pull her back into that traumatic place in her mind, a place where she was caged and prodded, bound by her own gifts.

"I'm listening."

The Tsar looked at his daughter, "You should wed Nikolai," he held up a hand to keep Anastasia from interrupting, "It will not be permanent. We can have the marriage annulled once you... dispose of him."

"Yes, your confidants made it very clear how they thought I should approach that situation."

"And I saw you with my counselors when they suggested it. You can do the same to Ruzsky. Don't you see?" He stood and took a few steps towards her, an enigmatic smile on his face. He was the trickiest of predators, ones who knew how to wield charm like a weapon.

What would I have done as a child to see a smile like that on his face? Anastasia's thoughts were beginning to slip.

"It will be so easy," the Tsar got closer, holding out an arm for her. "You can handle Ruzsky, and then everything will be simpler for us. The threats against our family will be dissipated, and we can focus on making things better."

"Better for who?"

"For everyone. You don't have to be in hiding. You can wed your darling Rasputin if you'd like. We'll make you a commissioner for the people. A liaison. Whatever you'd like!"

Dangerous glimpses of hope danced in Anastasia's vision,

but the words coming out of her father's mouth tasted like poison. She knew she could never trust him. Hearing him say it out loud caused her fragile heart to crack in her chest.

"We could be a family again," he grinned, now only a few steps away from her. "Wouldn't you like that? It's been years since we had all of my children at one table."

She couldn't help it as tears sprung to her eyes. The loss of her siblings, one by one, hurt her the most over the years.

They all trusted their parents and slowly had given up trying to visit or write to her while she was exiled to her apartments under the same roof.

"I had a family," Anastasia hissed as she took a step back. "I had Asya." She felt her hands start to shake as gold sparks flickered off of them towards the floor. The Tsar noticed and tutted his tongue, shaking his head.

"Ah, yes, dear Asya… we don't want any more accidents like that, do we?" Anastasia's blood ran cold as her breath came in shaky gasps. "You can handle Ruzsky and then never use your magic again if it would help."

"No…," Anastasia shook her head. "No, I was a child. That wasn't my fault. It wasn't my fault!" Panic began to descend on Anastasia, and rational conversation began slipping away from her like smoke.

The Tsar grew frustrated, seeing only weakness in his daughter. He had to get her to agree to this, and quickly, before that damned *priest* came back.

"It was your fault!" The Tsar yelled, his booming voice echoing in her empty apartments. His thin grasp on control snapped. He had never had to coerce someone for more than a few moments before they fell to the will of the great Tsar.

"Stop it!" Anastasia shrieked, the tears now fully streaming down her face and her magic flicking across her fingers like a current. "*Stop it!*"

"It was *your* fault we had to kill that damn woman!" As soon as he said it, the Tsar stopped himself. He took a step backward, cursing under his breath and gritting his teeth together. Anastasia stood frozen to the spot, unable to move. All of the blood rushed out of her head, and she was wavering on weak legs.

"What did you say?" She looked at the Tsar, her voice deathly quiet as a decade of guilt came crumbling down around her, threatening to knock her down with the stones of her mental walls.

"He said that they killed Asya." Mikhail's voice cut through the deathly quiet, Anastasia's head snapping to the sound as she realized he was standing in the open doorway.

She didn't know how long he had been standing there but clearly long enough to hear the end of their conversation. His face was etched in fury, an expression that Anastasia had never seen. She thought she was going to be sick.

"For fuck's sake," the Tsar yelled, looking between the both of them. "You couldn't keep a lid on your damn magic, Anastasia. When it exploded, we had no choice."

"Of *course* you had a fucking choice!" she shrieked, launching herself at her father.

Her hands found their way around his throat without a moment's hesitation. She clawed at him with the intent to choke the life out of the Tsar. She was no match for the grown man who gripped her wrists and tossed her to the floor without any effort.

Mikhail was shaken from his stupor. He crossed the room in an instant, and by the time Anastasia looked up from the ground, Mikhail was holding a pistol at point-blank range to the Tsar.

"Give me one good reason why I shouldn't end you right now," his voice had a deadly calm to it that even made Anastasia shiver. "I told you once that if you touched her again, I'd kill you."

"You can't kill me!" The Tsar roared, pressing his forehead

up against the barrel in a challenge. "What do you think will happen? I am the *Tsar of all of Russia!*"

"And I'm in love with a woman! Tell me, *moi Tsar*, which one of these do you think has inspired more passion in a man?"

Anastasia gasped, her hand flying to cover her mouth. Amidst the chaos rapidly unfolding all around them, she couldn't believe what she had just heard. The Tsar scoffed, shaking his head.

"Do you really think that she loves you, too? She doesn't know what she wants. She's a spoiled woman who's hardly ever left the palace. She doesn't *know* what love is." The Tsar spoke as if Anastasia wasn't even in the room.

"I do know," Anastasia's voice was shockingly calm as she rose to her feet. The Tsar and Mikhail both turned to look at her. "I knew love when I was with Asya. I forgot... God, I forgot for a long time. Mikhail has reminded me," she swallowed thickly, unable to shake the fact that this was a very high-stakes situation in which to have this conversation. "And I love him."

Mikhail's smile could've lit every lamp in the Winter Palace.

"Ha!" The Tsar shook his head again, "No better than peasants, the both of you, with your ridiculous obsessions." He took a step back from Mikhail and stared at the end of the pistol, which was still aimed at him.

"Let him go," Anastasia murmured, coming up and putting her hand on Mikhail's arm. "His end will be much more *public* than this."

The Tsar sputtered. His face red at the threat, and his hands clenched into fists.

"Go," Mikhail's voice was rough as he waved the pistol in the direction of the door. "You're dismissed."

Anastasia watched as Mikhail tensed, pulling her to his side with a stoic expression on his face as he dismissed the Tsar of Russia from his presence.

18

The sound of the door shutting behind the Tsar echoed throughout the room. Anastasia stared after her father with shock on her face. She was nestled up against Mikhail's side, her arm around his waist in quiet disbelief.

"You just...," she stared at the door, "You just told the Tsar of Russia to fuck off."

"I did," Mikhail nodded. The adrenaline was still rushing through his veins, his chest heaving and his muscles tense. He looked like a soldier ready to jump back into battle but shook his head quickly as if to clear it, tossing the pistol to a chair.

Mikhail's eyes drifted back to Anastasia, his gaze heavy. He stepped away from her, his mind going a million miles a minute. The explosive atmosphere had given away to a building tension between the two of them, revelations settling over both of them.

"Did you mean it?" Mikhail asked, his voice low. He was quiet for a second, biting his lip. "Did you mean what you said?" His stare was hot and Anastasia felt like she was going to burn under his gaze.

"Yes." Her voice didn't waver as she stared right back at him. "Did you?"

"Every word."

"Say it again."

"I love you, Anastasia," Mikhail repeated without a moment's hesitation.

A lingering silence lasted for one heartbeat, two, and then Anastasia crossed the distance between them.

She flung herself against him, her hands tangling themselves in his hair as she pulled him down to her level. She paused for only a moment to take in his face before leaning in to kiss him.

Mikhail made a satisfied noise against her lips before threading his arms around her waist and picking her up.

Anastasia wrapped her legs around his waist as their embrace became desperate, their passions fed by everything that had gone unspoken between them and adrenaline coursing through their veins. Anastasia couldn't stop running her hands over him, tracing his arms and his shoulders.

She let out a squeak of surprise when her back hit the wall, Mikhail pressing his body up against hers until all she felt was his heat against her.

Taking advantage of her open mouth, his warm tongue slipped against Anastasia's, deepening their embrace.

She tossed her head back, gasping for air, as Mikhail began trailing kisses down her neck. He held her up against the wall with one arm while the other began rifling blindly for the edge of her skirts.

"Christ," he grunted, finally gripping the edge of her hems and ripping. Anastasia laughed — a sound that made Mikhail look up and grin. His hand slid through the fabric until he met her calf, slowly moving upward.

Anastasia leaned forward in his grip and captured his mouth again, her hands tugging on his hair like she was trying to close the nonexistent space between them, relishing in the rasp of his stubble against her skin.

Mikhail's hands moved at a glacial pace, leaving trails of goosebumps all over Anastasia's skin. He made his way up her leg, stroking her calves, up her thighs, until his fingers traced over her hip, narrowly avoiding where she needed him most.

She made a small cry of displeasure, bucking her hips against him. He only chuckled, pulling back and giving her lip a bite.

"Ah, ah, ah," he chided, "Don't be greedy, *Anya*. Take what I give you."

"Give me *more.*" There was no venom in her tone, only desperation that sent a hot line of fire down Mikhail's spine. He grasped her waist tighter as she moved her hips, sliding herself over his cock in painfully slow strokes.

"Oh *b'lyad*," he hissed, dropping his head down so their foreheads were touching, "You keep doing that, and this isn't going to last very long."

Anastasia only let out a little laugh in response, slowing her hips. Mikhail's hand traced back down her thigh until he cupped her sex, teasing a shattered moan from between Anastasia's lips.

"You really do need me to touch you, don't you?" Mikhail chuckled, making Anastasia's eyes nearly roll back into her head. "You're drenched for me, *malyshka…*"

Mikhail gently rolled her clit between his fingers, pulling back to watch Anastasia's face, her breath breaking down into shallow gasps. She was practically dripping down his hand when he pulled her tighter and slipped his fingers inside her slowly.

"Mikhail," Anastasia's voice was a breathy whine, "*Please…*"

He only chuckled in response, leaning in to bite her ear. "Say it again. Let me hear you say it." Anastasia knew precisely what he meant.

"I love you, Mikhail," she moaned, her whole body feeling

like a live wire. Mikhail's impossibly large frame was pressed against her in a million ways except for the one she *needed*.

"God," he grunted, easily slipping another finger into her and beginning to curl them with a simple motion. Anastasia was unleashed, riding his fingers while they remained pinned against the wall. Her hand flew down to Mikhail's wrist, and she stopped him, shaking her head.

"No, no, I want more — I want all of you. *Now*." Mikhail grunted in response, gently pulling his hand from underneath her skirts and wrapping both of his arms around her waist. They stumbled into her bedroom, and Mikhail dropped Anastasia on the bed.

She ogled shamelessly as she maneuvered back against the headboard, her tongue running over her lip while Mikhail undressed at the foot of the bed.

He tugged his shirt over his head, tossing it to the side, and Anastasia moaned quietly at the sight of his body, his muscles still tense and his skin damp with sweat. He chuckled — a dark, purely masculine sound — as he leaned down and stepped out of his pants. Anastasia squirmed on the bed at the sight of his cock, desperate to feel him inside of her.

Mikhail reached over and ripped the rest of her torn dress off, leaving her in a corset. Anastasia leaned forward, her breasts nearly spilling out of the top, as she unlaced the back with feverish fingers. Mikhail climbed up on the bed, grabbing hold of the offending garment and tossing it to the side.

As soon as it was gone, Anastasia froze.

"Anya, what's wrong?" Mikhail leaned away from her, wanting to give her space at that moment if she was unsure.

"I... my... my scars," she said quietly, crossing her arms across her chest. Mikhail looked at her, stripped and vulnerable, and knew how difficult that was for her. He nodded softly, holding out his hand to her. When she slid her palm in his, he grinned, stroking his thumb over the scars on her knuckles.

"They're beautiful, Anya," his voice was slow and soothing, as he nodded as he placed her own scarred hand over the scars lacing his torso. "So are mine. So are yours. I promise."

Anastasia nodded, a soft smile spreading over her face. She leaned back on the bed, stretching out her legs, so Mikhail was kneeling between them.

"Touch me, *please*," Anastasia whined, the desperation returning to her voice as she relaxed entirely around him. Mikhail's hands began to move up and down her sides ever so slowly.

When his hands reached her back, she tensed on instinct until his thumbs gently kneaded little circles into each muscle, feeling the ridge of each scar as she became putty in his hands. Her whole body shuddered underneath him as he trailed kisses up her chest and neck.

Mikhail's hands moved down her legs, bringing them up and hooking them over his broad shoulders in one swift moment.

Anastasia moaned, his cock poised at her entrance. Mikhail could feel her heat radiating, and it took everything in him not to bury himself in her.

"Mikhail," Anastasia said again, staring up at him under heavily lidded, lust-filled eyes. "I love you."

That was all it took to snap the last of his control. He pushed into her, Anastasia's back arching off the bed in pleasure.

The feel of him made her eyes roll back into her head — glorious and hard, enough to make her forget entirely how only his fingers had felt. He was thick and *perfect*. Anastasia felt like she could die at that moment as she adjusted to the breadth of him.

Mikhail began to slowly thrust, letting out an animalistic sound at the fullness and warmth of them together — the feel of them finally joined so closely.

Their eyes met, and the low thrum of Anastasia's magic

began filling the room with every move, drenching them in soft, golden light.

Mikhail picked up speed until Anastasia's hands were fisted in the sheets as she cried out, the sound making him lean down and begin tracing slow circles over her clit.

"Anya," he cursed under his breath, uttering the closest thing that he had ever said to a prayer. "*Fuck*, you feel incredible."

"More, please, please, just more —" Anastasia's voice kept breaking off as she gasped for air. Mikhail gave her a devious smile as he lowered her legs and pulled out of her, causing Anastasia to cry out in frustration at the sudden loss of him. He was back on her in a moment, crawling up her until he was on top of her, covering her with his body from head to toe.

Mikhail cupped her face and kissed her again, a messy embrace that was all tongue and biting. Anastasia threw her leg around his waist and pulled him towards her, indicating exactly where she wanted him. Mikhail chuckled, his hand gently cupping her breast until his fingers were pinching at her nipple.

"Mikhail —" Anastasia was cut off as Mikhail sheathed himself in her in one quick moment, making her moan out at the sudden feeling of him again. He began rocking against her, her hips rising to meet his thrusts as his hand slid down from her breast to her clit, circling it and adding just enough pressure to make Anastasia writhe.

Anastasia's hands tangled themselves in his hair, feeling for the cord that held it in its knot. She tugged at it, eliciting a groan from Mikhail before it snapped.

She sighed her approval, running her hands through the lengths as she used her grip on his hair to direct his mouth back to her breasts. He obliged, sucking her nipple into his mouth before giving it a bite and switching to the other one.

Her orgasm snuck up on her, building from the moment that he touched her, and then suddenly releasing all at once. It was his name on her lips as she came, arching almost entirely off the bed.

Mikhail swore, feeling her clench all around him and hurtling him towards the edge. His cock throbbed, spilling himself inside of her as she finished. Sparks exploded from the lights around them as Anastasia's magic swelled, showering them in golden flecks that disappeared as they hit the floor.

His head fell to the crook of her neck, both gasping and reeling from the aftershocks. Their bodies were soaked in sweat, hot, and pressed up against one another.

Mikhail stayed inside of her, with half a mind to linger there forever. He bit at the skin of her neck gently before running his tongue over it. Anastasia let out a small gasp of air, a pleasant buzz settling into her limbs.

Mikhail chuckled before pulling out of Anastasia as she hissed lightly at the absence. He laid down next to her and tugged her to him, arranging them, so his chest was to her back. His arms cuddled her body tight, neither of them bothered with the sweat and heat evaporating around them.

"Not bad... for a priest," Anastasia grinned, turning over her shoulder to look up at Mikhail. He let out a laugh — a loud, genuine, carefree sound — before leaning down and kissing her once more.

"You can help me repent later... a few times more tonight, actually." Anastasia smiled into the kiss, her hand going up to stroke his jaw.

"I love you," she said softly, her eyes fluttering as she began to slip into a doze.

"I know," Mikhail nodded, pressing kisses over her face, "I love you, too." The two of them drifted off, the embers of Anastasia's magic still glowing around the room.

❧ 19 ❧

Tsar Nicholas II paced in his office, a position he found himself in more often than he would like and one that he was very much hoping to strategize himself out of.

His three *dvorysvasto* were once again sitting around him; they had been at his side for the past twenty-some years, and it was now the only troupe that he trusted.

These three honestly had no opinions of their own but knew that their best interest was to act as an echo chamber for the Tsar.

Over the years, they had approved everything from black magic rituals to political hangings, and whenever something went wrong, the Tsar blamed his council. When something went right, he took the credit for himself. It was too tumultuous of a time to pry themselves from the favor of the Tsar.

"Her weakness is the priest," one of the men spoke up, "If she truly loves him."

"She doesn't," the Tsar snapped in response, "She just thinks she does."

"It works for us either way," the man continued, chewing on

the end of an old cigar. "If that is her weak point, then we must go after the priest."

"No one knows who he is," another one of the men agreed. "It will be easy to fabricate something and get the people talking. You know how everyone feels about religion these days. A false priest? They'll demand his execution."

"He's right," the final *dvorysvasto* spoke up, wanting to make sure that his voice was heard, "And a false priest setting up in the palace? With the family blessed by God to govern Russia? Why, they'll label him as bad as Judas."

"We still need Anastasia to cooperate," the Tsar grumbled, sitting down at his desk. "Even if the public cries for the execution of a false priest, she'll never believe it. She's not pious. If we execute him anyway to satisfy the demands of the crowd, we'll lose every chance of getting her to our cause."

"We'll have to ruin his reputation in more ways than one," the second boyar shrugged. "Go at it from two sides. Drive a wedge between them while we find ways to make the people cry for his execution. When it becomes a fever pitch, strike where the iron is hot."

"She'll cave under pressure," the first man agreed. "She claims to be for the people. If her heart is broken, Anastasia will turn to the only other thing that she says she loves... the people."

"And if they're crying for the execution of the man who broke her heart...," the Tsar murmured in agreement, snapping his fingers. "She'll have to agree."

"Excellent, *moi Tsar*," the third man nodded happily, "You have it all figured out."

"A wonderful plan."

"Truly, none of us could have thought of it."

"I have just the idea," the Tsar grinned lecherously, pulling out sheets of paper from his desk. "She thinks his love is true? I can't imagine that she'll feel very well discovering that he's also in bed with her mother."

The *dvorysvastos* all chuckled delightfully like a perverted chorus. "How shall you do it?"

"It's simple," he shrugged. "Fetch my wife. Tell her I am in need of her penmanship."

It only took twenty minutes for the Tsarina to appear at the door of the Tsar's office. She had very seldom been invited in before and never when he was meeting with his council.

The Tsarina had always turned to her priests and acolytes to deal with the resounding truth that her husband had no need or want for her.

"*Moi Tsar*," she curtsied appropriately, using the formal tone with her husband.

"Alexandra," the Tsar's smile was as charming as ever. "We need you to pen some letters for us." The Tsarina's face contorted in confusion as she looked around the room, seeing the grins of the three old men that sent chills down her spine. She had always hated the councilmen.

"Of course," she nodded, sitting down at another table in the office. A lady-in-waiting behind her produced the stationery. "What do you need it for?"

"I need you...," the Tsar's voice was calculating, "... to fake sexually explicit letters to the priest Rasputin."

The look of horror that spread over the Tsarina's face was almost palpable. The councilmen sniggered like schoolboys. The Tsar shut them up with a singular look before turning back to his wife with a soft smile.

"It's for the good of our family and reign, Alexandra," he tilted his head to the side. "Certainly, you can understand that?"

Alexandra shook her head, pushing the papers away from her, "I will be *ruined!* How do you expect this to be for the good of the family? My reputation will never recover!"

The Tsar's attitude flipped immediately — for a man who

had spent his entire life being told 'yes', the fact that the *women in his family* had started to disagree with him was too much.

"You have not been of value to this court or me since Alexei came of age, and I had no more need for an heir." The Tsar's voice was cutting, and Alexandra stifled a gasp. She was under no illusions that they had a loveless marriage.

The Tsar's quest for power had always accommodated her; she had assumed that they had a sort of companionship, at the very least. At the end of the day, there was nothing that would stand between him and his quest for power.

"You will do it," he said again, taking one step towards her. "You can ruin your reputation with these fake letters, or I will *ruin your reputation with a very real scenario.*"

The Tsarina felt all of the blood rush from her face, the councilmen once again chuckling as the Tsar threatened his wife with assault.

"Alright," she swallowed thickly, picking up the pen in front of her. "What will you have me say, *moi Tsar?*"

The Tsar cleared his throat, standing tall as if he was giving a Shakespearean monologue. "I kiss your hands and lay my head upon your blessed shoulders… all I want to do is to sleep, sleep forever on your shoulder… in your embrace."

The Tsarina felt like she would be sick as her pen moved of its own accord across her stationery.

"Careful now," one of the men warned, "You don't want to go so fast that your penmanship doesn't look like your own."

"Maybe that's best," another one of them laughed. "It looks like she is writing in an impassioned plea for her lover."

The noble's voices prodding her on made the Tsarina feel like the pawn she was, acting in a sideshow of power for these corrupt men.

Suddenly, all of her religious games started to feel dreadfully silly as it dawned on her all at once that the Tsar never cared.

As much as he had encouraged her to do it 'for the good of

the empire,' she could see now that it was only ever to keep her distracted. She swallowed thickly and put the pen down before looking up at the Tsar for further instruction.

The Tsar had poured himself a glass of vodka and was sitting on the edge of his desk. He looked every inch the Tsar who was enjoying himself.

"My darling, my one true star...," the Tsar carried on, the councilmen bursting into laughter as they cheered him on, "How I weep the nights you spend apart from me... each moment your body is away from mine, I tremble for you."

The Tsarina had to bite back a gasp at the words, her hands growing sweaty as she scrawled out the letter exactly how the Tsar had dictated.

This went on for well over an hour while the Tsarina scratched out line after line — growing increasingly explicit — of fake letters to Rasputin.

Eventually, one of the *dvorysvasto* volunteered to write for Rasputin, and the whole cycle of laughs started again. The men got increasingly drunk, forcing the Tsarina to stay in the room as they tossed ideas back and forth to one another.

In the end, there were well over twenty letters of correspondence between the Tsarina and the priest. The Tsar and his *dvorysvasto* were rip-roaring drunk. They began passing the letters around the room, jeering and cheering with one another whenever they reread a sentence they found particularly enjoyable.

It was late in the evening when they finally dismissed the Tsarina who fled the room. She hid in her chambers and refused to come out for three days. Meanwhile, the letters had been strategically dispatched and began to circulate.

♚♚♚

On the other side of The Winter Palace, Mikhail looked down and grinned at the sight of Anastasia sleeping in his arms.

For the first time, he didn't feel as if they were standing on some fragile precipice. It had always been two steps forward and one step back with them, each of them afraid of something that they hadn't been able to admit.

Mikhail had struggled to let go of the idea of whom he *thought* Anastasia was, a spoiled woman whose tantrum had murdered his mother.

Even in the face of the truth, the exact opposite, that she was a prisoner of her own circumstance — like he was — his brain struggled to rewire its conditioning.

He felt as if he was a traitor to his mother's memory every time he looked at her. It was only when he had been able to accept that people were flawed, accidents happen, and to move past his own *hurt...* he had seen who she really was.

And God, she's magnificent.

Anastasia's powers were something that was a new mystery every day. They were inherently hers. There was nothing that Mikhail could truly do to control them or change her. Every spark, every flicker — it was Anya. *His* Anya. That's what he loved about it.

The only thing she ever needed to step into the full extent of her power was an unwavering sense of herself.

Mikhail was the first person to admit that all he ever did to help her find her magic was simply show her to herself.

Sure, sometimes that involved a little bit of antagonizing, but only when she had been able to set free of the jailed bars that she had around her heart and soul was she able to discover who she truly was.

If Mikhail had to spend a little bit of time making her angry enough to pull at the cage — he was more than happy to do it.

Anastasia stirred, blinking her eyes and finding herself bliss-fully entombed in an embrace. She didn't know when she'd been held like this last... if ever. She had half a mind never to leave Mikhail's arms.

Her magic had never flowed as easy as when she was around him — but it was only because of the support that she felt with him behind her. He couldn't do anything directly for her; at the end of the day, she knew she'd always been able to summon her magic. He simply pointed her in the direction of herself.

"Mikhail," Anastasia's voice was sleepy as she reached up and stroked his face, "Do you think we're on borrowed time?" She hated to ask the question.

For once, their relationship felt like the foundation beneath her feet, and it was everything else that was beginning to crumble. It was creeping in on her.

"No," Mikhail shook his head, leaning down and kissing her forehead. "I don't. I think we finally have a chance."

"How can you *say* that?" Anastasia tilted her head to look up at him. "We're sitting in The Winter Palace, for God's sake."

"Anya," Mikhail said softly, "I know that you're frightened. I know it... I am, too. You have got to get away from this fear of your father. This fear of *who you are*. That will trip you up before we ever go head-to-head with the Tsar."

"No," she shook her head, "I'm one person! You can't put this all on me."

"I'm *not* putting it all on you," Mikhail sighed and rubbed a hand over his face. The conversation was not going in the direction that he had planned. "You need to know who you are, or other people are going to tell you instead."

"People like my father," Anastasia muttered, years' worth of pain etched into her features.

"Look at me," Mikhail said softly, hooking his fingers under her chin and pushing up until she made eye contact with him. "Do you know who you are, Anya?"

Anastasia sighed, feeling a tremor of anxiety run through her gut. "Why don't you remind me."

"No," he shook his head softly, "You have to do it. You have to know who you are beyond a shadow of a doubt, do you understand?" Anastasia sighed before squirming uncomfortably and moving a little farther away from Mikhail. There was something written on her face that he couldn't quite decipher.

He cursed under his breath, once again frustrated that something had come along to ruin their moment. He didn't feel like they were on borrowed time until they had started to discuss what they were up against.

Mikhail didn't want to encourage her that they would do it together — even though they would, he'd follow her to hell — but he wanted her to believe in *herself*.

Not that she needed him behind her. She'd always be able to find her magic without him, and he needed to prepare her for that day… should it ever come.

"Anya," he chided, "What's that expression on your face? Tell me."

"No," she shrugged it off, shaking her shoulders as if she could physically rid herself of the emotion. "It's… it's stupid. Let's just forget that I brought anything up."

"Let's not," he said, kissing her again. She tried and failed to stifle a smile when his beard brushed against her. "Tell me."

Anastasia said nothing, and it suddenly dawned on Mikhail. How long had it been since someone had told Anastasia to trust herself… and meant it? Her entire life had been people sent to capture her secrets.

They had just gotten over themselves enough to admit that they loved one another — he knew that she trusted him, but that didn't mean that she was comfortable with it.

Mikhail did the only thing that he could do. He moved down until he was wrapped around her like a blanket, capturing her in his arms and pressing his body up against hers.

"Anya," his voice was low and sultry, "Will you please tell me what's wrong?" His hands began to gently run down her ribcage, attempting to soothe her through his ministrations.

"Are you trying to seduce me into being vulnerable with you right now?"

"Technically, I've already seduced you. Let the record show that."

"Alright, yes," Anastasia couldn't stop from laughing the smallest bit, "You're avoiding the question, which is very damning."

"Fine," Mikhail let out an exaggerated groan, "Yes. I'm trying to seduce you into being vulnerable with me. Is it working?"

Anastasia sighed, leaning back against him and letting her hands tangle in his hair. "Well, I am a sucker for men with hair longer than mine." There was a teasing lilt to her voice that Mikhail wanted to make sure it never left.

"You love it," he smiled down at her, kissing her nose.

"Alright," Anastasia sighed, looking away, "I... Mikhail, I feel like a burden. Every step of the way, I feel like I need you behind me, and I just... I can't stand it."

"You can't stand... what exactly?" Mikhail looked down at her, utterly thrown for a loop by her confession but desperately wanting to make sure that she kept sharing. "All of your magic — all of it — that's all *you*, Anastasia. Can't you see that?"

"I can't do it without you! Don't you feel like you're stuck following around some helpless Romanova who doesn't know how to use her magic?" Her voice escalated, and Mikhail could see fear flooding her eyes.

"Okay, okay, okay," Mikhail shook his head quickly, getting ready to cut off her derailed train of thought. He maneuvered her around so she was looking at him once more.

"You can use your magic without me. You *have*. You've used it to save me when I was entirely indisposed. You've helped those people in the city without even looking at me. You just need a little reminding of who you are."

"That's so... I should know. I shouldn't need you reminding me constantly," tears were beginning to slip down her cheeks.

"Anya," Mikhail's hands went to cup her cheeks, "Look at me. You have needs. You're a person. You've been through trauma, and you need a little reminding of who you are."

"No, stop it —" She squirmed, the conversation veering towards an emotional vulnerability that she was terrified to approach but was in a runaway train towards.

"I won't," Mikhail shook his head. "You're *human*. And what... you feel bad because it's nice to have support? My sweet Anya," he dropped his voice low and made sure that the words were especially for her, "You've lived for so long without anyone supporting you that you don't know how to accept it."

No sooner were the words out of Mikhail's mouth did Anastasia break into a small, choked sob. She buried her head in his chest as he began soothing her, rubbing his hands up and down her back over the scars she was once too scared to let him see.

They stayed like that for a while. Mikhail refused to give her any space, wouldn't let her turn away from him, and was determined to keep her next to him.

Once Anastasia had calmed down, he brought his hand up to her cheek and wiped away the last of her tears.

"Come on now," he said softly, his smile encouraging, "Tell me who you are, Anya."

Anastasia looked up at him, a slow flame licking at her pupils, "I am Anastasia Nikolaevna Romanova," her voice was firm.

"What do you want to do, Your Grace?"

"I am Anastasia Nikolaevna Romanova... I'm going after my father... with my magic."

20

Anastasia and Mikhail made their way toward the side exit of The Winter Palace, ignoring everyone they passed.

The boyars were constantly huddled in either public ballrooms or private hideaways, leaving the halls surprisingly empty.

They were in the unfortunate place of not knowing how secretive they needed to be but erring on the side of caution.

The Tsar wouldn't move against them in the palace. Of this, Anastasia was sure. She knew that with his flare for religious fear and political propaganda, he would never pass up the opportunity to make a spectacle of her and Mikhail in public.

The one thing they needed to do was to try and find Nikolas Ruzsky: the man her father wanted Anastasia to marry.

If he was gathering support against the Tsar and speaking openly against the dynasty, he was their best chance at swaying public opinion enough to get her father to concede.

"Reform or revolution," Anastasia had nodded her head as if she was swearing herself to the idea. "It will be one or the other."

"Are you prepared for either, though?" Mikhail pushed her quietly, wanting to make sure that she understood the outcome of an all-out revolution would not be good for her family.

"My sisters are spread out across the continent with their fat husbands," she waved a hand dismissively. "Alexei... I want to find him. If I could just talk to him... he has spent a long time in my father's shadow, and I'm... I'm prepared to face the reality of what that might mean."

The drive to meet with Ruzskyled them back toward St. Petersburg. Mikhail had gathered intel from the servants he ran into — some of whom remembered Asya fondly — that Ruzsky was relying heavily on public opinion to stir into a mob mentality.

Anyone who worked with him was constantly out on the city's streets, commenting on the conditions and encouraging people to begin hoarding all of the weapons and grain that they could.

Anastasia and Mikhail knew things had been nothing but desperate for years, they both were surprised to hear that the consensus among the people was that the city was headed for a full-on revolution.

"Incredible," Anastasia had whispered with a stunned look on her face. "They eat until they're sick and host balls until their feet bleed... but they have no idea the people are assembling weapons outside their gates."

"We'll let them know," Mikhail had squeezed her hand supportively. "We'll let them know."

They managed to slip out the side door once again, intent on going into the city and spending some time at the boarding house.

They assumed that it — or any boarding house — would end up as a bit of a gathering place in times of need. If they could determine where Ruzsky was hiding, they could hopefully seek out an audience with him.

He had been the Tsar's head general but had quickly gone into hiding after he began speaking out publicly against his mock political executions.

The streets were busy, as always, and the pair blended in seamlessly amongst the crowd.

They had dressed in simple clothing, Mikhail hiding in plain sight wearing priest robes even though he refused to wear the collar. He couldn't help himself as he grabbed hold of Anastasia's hand, pulling her to him and walking arm-in-arm through the city.

They did make a rather strange couple when anyone managed to look them in the eye; an alleged peasant woman making eyes at a priest without his full vestments.

Although the religious fervor was at a peak in the country, strange priestly behavior was par for the course.

The couple approached the steps of the boarding house. The door swung open as if the innkeeper had a sixth sense for their arrival. She greeted them with a smile and ushered them into the sitting room dotted with a few other men and women speaking in hushed tones.

"Do you need a room, dears?" The innkeeper asked them kindly, grabbing hold of Anastasia's hands.

"No, no," she was always enamored by the warm, maternal energy of the woman. "We were hoping to —"

Mikhail quietly stepped in and cut her off, "We were just hoping to spend some time outside of the Palace. You know." His easy grin was so charming that the innkeeper hardly noticed he had cut Anastasia off.

She nodded, "Well, you must eat while you're here. I'll fetch something." She tottered off, humming to herself. Anastasia looked up at Mikhail in confusion, and he looked around to make sure that no one was clued into their conversation.

"It's probably best to not walk into a public space and start asking for Ruzsky," he gave her a grim smile. "We should assume your father has as many spies as Ruzsky does out here."

Anastasia felt herself blush with embarrassment, worried her naïveté was showing through, and making her uncomfortable.

Mikhail, as always, seemed to sense whenever she started to retreat into herself. His hand slid up her back as he gently pushed her towards the center of the room, navigating towards a table where they could both eat and eavesdrop.

As soon as they sat down, Mikhail grinned as he reached across and wrapped Anastasia's hand in his own.

"I think eating dinner at this boarding house is a bit of a tradition for us, Anya."

"Do we have traditions?" Anastasia winked at him. "I would think that we haven't even been together long enough to have traditions."

"We have each other."

"Oof," Anastasia made a mock grimace, "That was a bit cliché."

"You love it."

"Do I?"

"I know something you do love —"

Anastasia cut him off with a small cough as she raised her eyebrows at the innkeeper before Mikhail said something that she didn't want the older woman to overhear.

They dug into their food, both of them starving now that the Tsar had insisted on dictating what food was being sent to Anastasia's chambers once again.

Eating in relative silence, they both tried to catch glimpses of the conversation around them and appear as open as possible should someone want to strike up a conversation.

Once their plates were empty, the innkeeper came over, refilling their glasses and taking their plates.

"How was everything, *solntse*?" She said warmly, looking

down at Anastasia with a hopeful expression that made her heart clench.

"Don't bother with us," she shook her head. "Please. How are you doing? You haven't let us pay the past few —"

"Do not insult me," the woman said. "It is an honor to help you, Anastasia, because you are the kind of person who takes that and goes and helps others." Mikhail turned to Anastasia when the innkeeper said this, a grin spreading over his face that said *told you*.

"Besides," the innkeeper's eyebrows went up, creating as close to a salacious expression as she could probably manage, "I can't imagine what it's like living with the Tsarina."

There was a weight to her words that made them both pause that there was something even more unusual to spark the innkeeper's comment — and there were already unusual stories that circulated about the Tsarina and her religious fervor.

"Yes...," Anastasia nodded in agreement, hoping that the innkeeper would be encouraged to keep going without realizing that they had no idea what she was talking about.

"Can you believe it?" She laughed, squeaking a little and her eyes going wide. "The Tsarina and one of her priests! Right under the Tsar's nose!"

Something in her tone made Anastasia's stomach begin to roll, a sinking feeling that went all the way down to her toes.

"How are they so sure this time?" Her voice was betraying her, but the innkeeper took no notice. "You know," Anastasia forced a grin on her face, "Since she has always had such a penance for her priests." She waved a hand in front of her face, trying to seem nonchalant.

Even Mikhail had stiffened, sensing something was wrong. It was a little too easy. The Tsarina had always had priests, acolytes, and conjurers around her. Why now? The innkeeper was nodding, rifling around in her pockets before she pulled out a scrap of a newspaper.

"It's in all the papers!" She could barely contain her joy, laughing at the downfall of the Tsarina's reputation. "She's been writing love letters to the Priest Rasputin! They have published the letters and — Oh, my goodness. Are you alright, dear? You look quite sick."

Mikhail looked over at Anastasia and saw her transform in front of his eyes. It was as though he was watching her walls fly back up, bricking over the expression on her face. Her hands began to tremble, and her face was pale.

"Anya," he said harshly, harsher than he intended, as he tried to get her attention. He was losing her to her panic and fear. He could see it, and something animalistic in him wanted to claw her away from her anxiety's grip.

"Anya," he said again, "Look at me. Look at me right now. Look me in the eyes..."

"*Shut up!*" Anastasia screamed, her head whipping around towards Mikhail. The entire boarding house went quiet, everyone turning to look at the sound of her outburst. The innkeeper gasped quietly before taking one look at Mikhail's garments and slowly backing away.

"Don't you dare believe that!" He hissed, his brow furrowing as he stood without realizing it. His shoulders began to tighten, and Anastasia could feel the tension between them. "Not even for a second. How could you? *Svo-lach!*"

"Look at it!" Anastasia shrieked, her magic flaring and sending a small shockwave through the room.

Plates rattled and some cups fell as candles flickered out. People around them gasped and quickly dispersed, not wanting to be caught in magical crosshairs.

They cleared out remarkably quickly and left Anastasia and Mikhail squaring off against one another across the dinner table.

"There are *letters*," Anastasia grabbed the newspaper where the innkeeper had dropped it in her quick departure. "Look at this! That's my mother's handwriting... She hired you! She... she was the one who... she brought you back..."

Anastasia's anger was quickly dissipating again as her mind began to fracture, her power flickering off and on through her fingers like a lightbulb on its last legs.

A cold sensation crept up the back of her spine while her face flushed with heat, a pit beginning to spin in her stomach that made her want to be violently ill.

No... no... no... stupid... stupid... stupid... stupid girl... stupid... stupid... so stupid...

"Anastasia," Mikhail's voice was firm as he bent down on one knee in front of her, grabbing her hands. Anastasia didn't even realize that she was speaking out loud. "Stop it. Stop it right now. It's not true."

"So stupid," Anastasia ripped her hands from his grip and buried her face. "I'm so *fucking stupid*! I fell for this shit! How could I believe that anything — anyone — they sent wasn't part of a plot!" Her whole body began to quake with sobs as her mind ran through everything Mikhail had ever said to her.

"No," Mikhail grabbed Anastasia's shoulders and turned her until she was facing him. "It's a lie! I meant every word. This — us, it's real, Anastasia, it's real!"

"Did you get what you wanted?!" Anastasia shrieked in his face, pushing against his chest with all of her might. Her magic was still sparking like a forge, sending flickers of sparks all around them until it started to singe Mikhail's robes.

"Burn me, Anya," he said stoically, barely even flinching as the sparks began to spread across his chest. "Burn me alive if you have to!"

"Stop!" Anastasia screamed as loud as she could, a wretched and terrifying sound, and her voice cut out nearly halfway through. She was openly sobbing, her tears falling onto her hands and hissing when they hit her magic.

"How *dare* you! Did you get what you wanted? Did you get

my fucking magic, you —" Her screams cut her off, the feeling of her chest physically ready to heave in two, taking her ability to speak.

"It's not a lie!" Mikhail's whole body felt like a live wire, and his expression was frantic. His hands found Anastasia's wrists as he tried to keep her from hurting herself. "I mean it... you can end me, set me on *fire* if you must... but don't you ever believe for a second that you can't trust me. I love you!!"

"S-stop," Anastasia pulled her wrists from his hands and buried her face in it one more, the magic ebbing and flowing down her arms. "You're so awful... so *cruel* of you!"

Mikhail felt his anger rising as he stood up and took a step back from her. His shoulders were nearly shaking, and his hands ran through his hair. Every ounce of him was now ready for war, but he didn't know whom to fight.

Sparks of Anastasia's magic were flying in the air all around them, singeing the ends of paintings on the walls and flickering around the remnants of their dinner.

Mikhail barely even noticed the few embers that were still latched onto his clothes. He felt nothing as he stared at the woman he loved destroying herself with fear and the idea that her hard-earned trust had been misplaced. That her feeling of safety with him had been an illusion.

"Anya —"

Anastasia jumped up from her seat, the heat of shame turning to the ice of rejection in her veins. "Don't *fucking* call me that, *Rasputin.*"

Her voice was like stone.

Mikhail stopped.

They both sat there and stared at one another, the past crawling its way through the sparks and the floorboards to drag them both to hell.

"That's not my name," Mikhail's voice was devoid of emotion as he squared off with Anastasia.

"Is it only for my mother to call you, then?"

"You don't call me *that*," he yelled, "I wouldn't respond to it when the priest beat me, and I won't respond to it when you say it. You're hurting, but you don't have to be. You're choosing this!"

"Why would I choose this! I love you!" She hissed, "I don't want to anymore, but congratulations, your con worked perfectly."

"Did you *ever* stop to think," Mikhail growled, his voice taking on a dominant tone that made Anastasia pause and stand up a little straighter, "That it isn't exactly easy for me to trust either?"

The simple question made Anastasia's mind come to a screeching halt. She had been so blind to anything but her fears. She hadn't realized how hard this had been for Mikhail, too.

"Oh God," she gasped quietly, her hand going up and covering her mouth.

"I *love* you," Mikhail choked out, fighting back his own frustrated tears, "And I had to get over the idea of hating myself for falling in love with someone I had spent decades learning to despise. Anastasia, please..."

Mikhail dropped to his knees, and Anastasia let out a choked series of gasps, trying rapidly to blink away tears. "This is a *lie*. It's the Tsar — it has to be."

Anastasia's clarity came crashing through her like a battering ram, and she realized how painfully obvious it was that this was a ploy. She had let herself descend immediately into her fears and pushed Mikhail to the limit in the process.

Anastasia sent herself crashing into Mikhail's arms. He let out a strangled cry of relief as she buried her head into the crook of his neck.

"I'm so sorry," she was sobbing, the strength of her cries shaking her entire body as she brushed the remaining sparks off him. "I love you, I love you..."

Mikhail sank against the wall behind him, scooping Anastasia into his arms and holding her to his chest. They sat there until they both had caught their breaths, drying each other's tears and taking turns petting and fretting over one another. Both of them were almost too embarrassed to speak.

"My Mikhail," Anastasia's voice was soft as she sat up a little straighter, cradling his face in her hands. Her fingers brushed against the stress lines around his eyes and forehead as she kissed him over and over. "You'll never be the person they paint you to be. Ever."

They both knew what she meant. The identity that he had fought his whole life against. Anastasia leaned her cheek against his, her hand pushing some of the hair out of his eyes.

"I'll always choose you," she whispered it like a vow. "May nothing separate us."

Mikhail let a soft smile overtake him, enjoying the soft touches and pieces of affection he knew were hard-won from her.

"I think, Anya... that is the wisest thing you've ever said."

21

Mikhail and Anastasia lost track of time as they sat in the sitting room of the boarding house.

After the noise died down and the magic in Anastasia's fingers had flickered out, the innkeeper slowly made her way back into the room.

She said nothing, ignoring the sight around her as if it was perfectly normal. Anastasia untangled herself from Mikhail as he stood first, helping her to her feet.

"The course of true love...," the innkeeper smiled and gave them both a little wink as if she was keeping a secret to herself. Anastasia blushed as she looked around at the remnants of some of the chaos.

"One moment," she turned to the woman and smiled, "I'll fix this." The woman nodded as if she was never concerned with this in the first place.

Anastasia began quietly moving around the room, a wave of her hand and a flick of a finger helping to repair the burnt edges of paper and scorch marks on the furniture.

Mikhail watched — perpetually in awe — at how easily her magic came to her now, no matter the scenario. He stopped when the innkeeper appeared at his side, gently putting her hand on his sleeve.

"*Da?*" He turned to look at her, wondering how much they were going to owe this woman at the end of this.

"She will always come back to you," the woman's voice was quiet, almost trancelike. Mikhail took a step closer and realized that her eyes were glazed over, "Remember, Mikhail, all you need to do is help nurture her magic. She will do the rest. She will do everything. Just love her."

The words rang into Mikhail like they were aimed straight at his heart as his mother's words from years ago rang back at him.

He leaned down and studied the innkeeper's face, his hand going to her shoulder as he peered into her gaze. He felt his breath catch in his throat.

"...Asya?" He dared to speak his mother's name, but it broke whatever spell had been over the innkeeper. She blinked rapidly and looked up at Mikhail with a slightly confused smile.

"Can I get you something, dear?"

"No, no," Mikhail stood up to his full height and looked around for Anastasia. "That's alright. Thank you, you've done enough." The woman, satisfied with the response, slipped off into the kitchen.

Anastasia was sitting on a couch in the sitting room waving her pointer finger in a circle as her magic restitched the edge of some stitching.

"Good as new," Mikhail murmured, coming up behind her and going to put his hand on her shoulder. He paused for a moment, suddenly cursing as he found himself now hesitating to be as intimate with her as freely as he once was.

"Don't pull back from me now," Anastasia looked up at him with a small smile, the irony not lost on her that she was the one now encouraging *him* to trust her. He couldn't help but let out a deep chuckle, nodding his head as his hand slid effortlessly to her shoulder.

"Are you ready to go?"

Anastasia nodded, following him towards the door — the innkeeper somewhere in the kitchens as they slipped out.

Once they were back out on the street, night had fallen, and people were moving about more freely under cover of dusk. The air was oppressive.

Groups huddled near trash cans with lit fires, under street lamps with broken lights, tattered clothes moving about them like ghosts.

They could see people infiltrating groups, speaking momentarily, and then sliding away. The spies for both sides were painfully obvious to spot.

Amongst the poor man's espionage and the scattered clusters of light, people and dogs were fighting over the same scraps of food.

What had once been a crowded, quaint street had become overrun as society was caving in all around them. Dozens of people seemed to hang out of door frames and windows, every house turning into a shelter. There were young boys no older than fifteen tossing rifles to one another from second-story windows.

Anastasia felt her heart clench as she saw the children hanging off their mothers and pleading with grown men for scraps of food.

Mikhail and Anastasia exchanged looks, both looking somber as they took in the chaos that the city had descended into.

Anastasia thought that she had seen it before when she had snuck out over the years, but it had never been this bad. She was pulled from her thoughts, a sudden commotion breaking up the crowds of people as a massive Delaunay-Belleville touring car pushed through the crowd.

A troupe of imperial soldiers marched in front of the car and behind it shoving people out of the way. It took only a moment for Anastasia to recognize her father's favorite touring car. The soldiers aimed at the civilians, pushing them out of the way and threatening them when they didn't.

She grabbed Mikhail's hand and tugged him further off the sidewalk, desperate to make sure they weren't spotted. Of course — that assumed that the Tsar was looking. So many soldiers surrounded the car it didn't seem as though he could even see the street he was driving down.

Maybe that's the whole bloody point. Anastasia grumbled, another wave of righteous anger rising in her. *Does he think that everything is fine? They're organizing a rebellion in the street around him!*

A shot rang out. The sound was sharp and hollow, followed by chaos as the crows scattered. No one knew who fired first — but someone *had* fired.

Screams came from the soldiers, their bayonets stabbing wildly into the crowd as more shots rained down, this time from above. Men had grabbed rifles and were hanging out of windows, firing aimlessly into the crowd.

Anastasia watched with a panic-stricken look of horror on her face as her father and his men pushed through the masses as if they were cattle.

"Come on," Mikhail urged quietly, his arm moving around Anastasia's waist as he attempted to tug her out of the chaos. "We don't want to get caught in the crossfire. Let's go!"

His voice grew louder as Anastasia fought to hear him amongst the rising madness happening all around them. It was chaos. It was hellfire.

The soldiers had begun firing at will into the crowd, the crowd moving like a hive, sending wave upon wave on top of the soldiers, only to be met with fire and blade. Bodies began to pile up as the street ran red.

Anastasia nearly vomited as the car made a sickening thumping sound, and she realized it was the sound of the Delaunay-Belleville running over bodies.

"No," she turned and looked at Mikhail, her mind made up. "I need to help."

"How?!" Mikhail looked at the crowd. "This is chaos, Anya. No one emerges from fights like these. Please, I've seen them. Live another day with me, please!"

"Like this," Anastasia squared her shoulders and looked at him in defiance. "Are you with me?"

Silence fell between the two of them as the sounds of the skirmish faded away. They looked at one another, and Asya's words rang in Mikhail's head.

Encourage the Romanov magic.

Mikhail looked at Anastasia and wrapped his hand around the back of Anastasia's head, pulling her closer. He kissed her in a way that let the past and the future fade away from them, Mikhail letting out a grunt against her lips as he forced himself away from her just as quickly.

"I'm with you," he nodded, and Anastasia grinned. She turned on her heel — facing the worst of the fray — and threw her hands up in the air.

A sweeping wave of magic began rolling up towards them from behind, feeling like the beginning tremors of an earthquake.

Mikhail ducked and nearly fell as the force erupted from behind them, Anastasia's hands throwing it forward. The air seemed to move around her as her hands exploded in bright, golden light, grabbing the attention of all of those around her.

Some people squealed and others screamed as Anastasia looked like an Orthodox saint reborn for vengeance. She screamed as she controlled the sweeping waves of magic, sending the forcefield into the line of soldiers.

It hit them in a crash, sending them falling and scattering

like bowling pins. The other soldiers around them fell over, almost in shock.

A few attempted to stand again, the men who had been hit with her magic looking dazed and confused. The people around Anastasia began to cheer as they realized that she was fighting for them. Her hair was slipping out of its braid, and she had a manic look on her face.

Mikhail stood behind her — always faithful and watching her back — as his mind drifted to how her body was holding up under the constraints of using such power. Once the group of soldiers had recovered from the shock, it only took a few seconds for them to all train their rifles on Anastasia.

"Anastasia!" Mikhail shouted from behind her, wrapping an arm around her and pulling them both to the ground. Her concentration on her magic broke, sending another shockwave through the ground around them.

Peasants and soldiers alike for blocks fell, window panes shaking against the walls. As soon as they hit the ground, a volley of bullets went buzzing past them in the air.

Anastasia jumped up to her feet; her mind consumed with one thing as her magic danced across her hands. The soldiers were so dumbfounded by what they had seen that they began tripping over one another to get away from her.

There were cries all around them: from the peasants who believed her a saint and the soldiers who were convinced she was a sinner. The mysterious priest without his collar with her only sent the crowd into a Revelations-inspired panic.

The car began to gather more traction as people cleared away, stray bullets still flying all around her. Anastasia didn't know if her father had recognized her — but the soldiers certainly had.

Anastasia's magic was no longer a secret. It was one thing to help people in the shadows, but this open act of warfare against the Imperial troops was a declaration made public.

Both Anastasia and Mikhail needed to be prepared to face the consequences. The word would spread: Anastasia Romanov had magic, a mysterious priest at her back, and used her power *against* her father.

Soldiers moved to follow the car, their command more focused on protecting the Tsar than worrying about returning violence against the revolutionaries in the street.

The bullets had died down, but the people began throwing things at the retreating motorcade. The crowds swarmed the streets as they collected their loved ones and helped those who were injured. The ground was streaked with blood as protestors slowly stood and began dusting themselves off.

Anastasia's eyes stayed with the bodies that didn't get up, the ones being covered by shrouds, sheets, or shirts — whatever was on hand.

"Anya," Mikhail stood, his hand reaching for her shoulder. She was still primed for a fight, looking around as the magic flickered between her fingers.

Down the street, the motorcade had cleared the densest part of the crowd, picking up speed and disappearing on its way back to the palace. He knew what the expression was on her face. It was one that he had experienced a million times over during his time at the monastery.

She was unable to control the adrenaline coursing through her, her chest heaving with the effort to get enough air into her lungs; she couldn't see that the threat was gone, not when there was so much death.

He maneuvered in front of her and put his hands on both of her shoulders, rubbing her arms up and down.

"Release it," Mikhail said softly, ducking down so he was able to look her in the eye. Anastasia's expression was wild, her nose bleeding. "Let go of the anger. It's over. You can't hold on like this when the fight is over or you'll hurt yourself."

He gave her shoulders another squeeze, and Anastasia

started blinking rapidly as if she was coming back into her body.

"They fired into the crowd," she hissed, "At innocent people. They only have weapons to defend themselves! Why is he even out here?"

Mikhail opened his mouth to respond when a middle-aged woman ran up to them, interrupting.

"You!" The woman's face was flushed and her clothing was torn as though she had escaped from the very middle of the fray. "Please, come help, my son —"

Anastasia nodded, beckoning the woman to show them the way. Mikhail and Anastasia followed her through the streets, past the carnage that had plunged the block into further desperation than it had been in not even twenty minutes ago.

There were bullet holes through almost every remaining window, glass was shattered, people were bleeding openly as they pushed for space inside to shelter themselves. Men ripped off their sleeves to bandage their children, and women were tearing out their underskirts to bandage their lovers.

They were in the middle of a war zone on the streets of St. Petersburg, her own family oblivious to what they had just started amongst the people.

They followed the woman for another block, Anastasia fighting to not stop at every person she saw to try and help until she disappeared into a small lean-to.

Anastasia followed inside blindly, not concerned that she might be considered a target if people didn't understand her alliances. Mikhail ducked under the small door frame and followed her in.

It took a moment for Anastasia's eyes to get used to the darkness, but once they did, she saw a young man lying on the ground, only a few years younger than Anastasia.

His face was dirty and his clothes were torn, but the lower half of his pant leg was sticking to his leg. The smell of blood was heavy in the air. He grimaced and stifled back a moan, sweat dripping down his forehead as he was in immense pain. Two other men sat on either side of him, gripping his arms and trying to keep him as still as possible.

"I can't stitch it up," the woman's voice was panicked as she looked from her son to Anastasia. "Th-there's a bullet in his leg." Her eyes were wide as she shook with fright, the events of the afternoon catching up to her as she tried to keep her emotions at bay for her son.

"I... I can try to help," Anastasia nodded, tugging up her sleeves slightly and kneeling next to the man.

"Anya," Mikhail squatted next to her. The two of them found themselves echoing one another in movement and mannerism more and more with each passing moment. "You've never done this before..."

"It will work." Anastasia nodded, needing to hear the words out loud. "I just have to picture it like I do everything else."

Mikhail tensed. He believed that her magic could do it, but he had never seen her heal anyone with an injury like this before. She had saved his life once, yes, but that had happened when she wasn't attempting to control her magic.

She wouldn't hurt the man in any way — but if she couldn't help and failed, he knew that it would take an emotional toll on her that would far outweigh any physical wound.

Mikhail sat silently and watched as Anastasia leaned over the man's leg, her magic already sparking to life between her fingers, with no fear or hesitation in her eyes.

She was enraptured with her own process - he could see the confidence building in her eyes. The magic leaped from her hands to the man's leg, wrapping it around it like a golden coil as it started to glow with a soft light that lit the entire room.

It spun around and around as if the wound were the center of a maypole, and the man's expression relaxed as some of the tension left his body. The others in the room looked on in awe.

It happened so quickly that if Mikhail hadn't been staring, he would've missed it. Suddenly, the fragment of a bullet shot up into the air, spinning around like a top before disseminating into sparks.

Anastasia let out a sudden gasp, jerking back as though she was shocked back into reality. Everyone looked down. The man's leg was healed. Even the blood had been removed from his pant leg. Not only had she removed the bullet, but her magic had also mended the wound as if it had never happened.

The man looked up at her, meeting Anastasia's face with a shocked look. It was almost as if he was looking upon a holy relic.

"Sankta Anastasia."

22

Anastasia shook her head.

"*Nyet*," she grabbed the man's hands and gave him a warm smile. "There are no *sanktas* here. I just want to help."

He grinned up at her before removing himself from her grasp and jumping up to his feet, letting out a whooping sound as his smile spread from ear to ear.

The young man turned and rushed over to his mother, whom he wrapped in a hug and began spinning around the small space. The woman was openly crying, hugging her son, and weeping her gratitude for Anastasia.

Mikhail's hand was suddenly on Anastasia's back, helping her to her feet as he stared at her with what seemed to be never-ending awe of her abilities.

"Shall we?" He grinned, his hand sliding into hers. She squeezed it and leaned into Mikhail's side, enjoying the physical reminder of his support at her back.

"If he doesn't realize that it was me, my father will know soon enough," Anastasia nodded. "We can't stay here. He'll come looking for us... the safest place for everyone is if we're in the Winter Palace."

Mikhail's brow furrowed as he turned around and gave a small wave of goodbye to the room before tugging Anastasia outside to finish their conversation.

"What do you mean, 'the safest place for everyone'?" Mikhail looked down at her, his gaze seeming to peer through to the very heart of her. Anastasia shrugged.

"It's safest for everyone if we don't draw my father out here. He'll come looking for us now. You saw what happened today in the streets. He'll burn half the city to keep me under his thumb."

"You want to go back to the palace?" Mikhail tried to keep his voice from rising.

He assumed the second that Anastasia had openly used her magic against the imperial guard in public, there would be no returning to the palace for them. It wasn't safe anymore. They had declared war and were now acting on it.

"I don't want to, no," Anastasia shook her head, and Mikhail hated how easily he could detect the fear in her eyes. "It's the safest for everyone."

"You mean it's the safest for everyone *but you*," Mikhail corrected her.

They were standing close enough that Mikhail had to look down at Anastasia to meet her eye. She still had a few flecks of blood around her nose, and her braid was only half-assembled. She looked tired but not drained.

"Yes," her voice was slow, "but I couldn't... you know that I'm right."

Mikhail made a frustrated, grunting noise, running his hand over his face.

"This time, yes. I know that it's what we have to do. I need you to get out of this headspace that *what is right for everyone* doesn't include *you*. What's best for you matters, too."

Anastasia nodded, focusing more on the fact that Mikhail had agreed with her than what he was saying. She had spent so long denying herself that she was apt to neglect her own needs — whenever Mikhail presented them to her, it made her uncomfortable.

She trusted herself more every day, but the thought of doing it without him behind her made her anxious. She knew she'd never fully understand herself or her magic until the idea of doing it without anyone's help didn't matter. For now, it did.

Mikhail could tell she was lost in her thoughts and also knew, unfortunately, it wasn't the time to bring it up.

The streets around them had returned to their state before the skirmish, which wasn't to say that they looked much better, but at the very least, there were fewer people.

Windows had already been boarded up, and there were no bodies in the road. Neither of them wanted to think about the losses that had happened that day as they moved through the city.

Anastasia paused for a moment and let Mikhail step in front of her, holding her hand as she let him lead her through the streets.

Once they got a few blocks away and closer to the palace, it grew quieter. There were fewer people as though they all had a subconscious sense to avoid the property and everything that happened within it. As they approached it... the silence started making Anastasia uncomfortable.

"Mikhail...," she started, stepping a little bit closer to his body, "Do you...?"

"Yes," his voice was tight, and he stood up a little straighter. The air around him changed as he looked down the block, analyzing everything like a predator. "Something's wrong."

"The streets have been cleared out," Anastasia whispered back. Her eyes went wide in fear. On instinct, the magic began to spark around her fingers. Her heart rate skyrocketed, and the sparks evolved once more, turning to wisps of flame.

The light caught Mikhail's attention as he leaned down and raised an eyebrow at Anastasia.

"That's new," he nodded with a small smile towards her magic, trying to lighten the mood. "Flames?"

"Apparently," Anastasia looked down at her hands and willed it to calm down, her magic muting itself just as easily as it sparked.

"You're getting good at —"

Mikhail's voice was cut off as a sudden gunshot sent a bullet flying past them and ricocheted off the ground.

"*Move!*" Mikhail yelled, grabbing Anastasia's hand and pulling her through the streets.

They ran blindly towards the Winter Palace, not sure who was shooting at them. Anastasia covered her head with her hand on instinct, even though it did nothing for her.

They were nearly tripping over their feet on the rough road, the bullets pinging around them.

"Where is it coming from?!" Anastasia yelled, trying to look up at Mikhail as they fled.

"I don't know, just — *blyat,*" he hissed as a bullet hit dangerously close to his foot, "We have to split up —"

"NO!" Anastasia shook her head as Mikhail wrenched himself free of her hand. "What are you *doing?*"

"I think they're only shooting at me," his voice was hoarse as they looked up, only a few blocks now from the palace. "You can't get caught in the crossfire!"

"If you think for one second —"

There was a momentary pause as all the unseen riflemen seemed to need to reload simultaneously, causing Anastasia and Mikhail to duck into a nearby alley for a moment's security.

"Listen to me," he grabbed Anastasia by the shoulders. "I can't have them shooting you, do you understand me? The people will need you. On my count, I want you to run like hell towards the palace."

"Are you crazy?!" Anastasia slapped him on the chest. "I won't leave you! I won't —"

"You have to! I will catch up with you, I *promise.*" They both stood still for a moment as they stared at one another, their chests heaving with exertion and fear.

"How can you promise that? What if they shoot you?"

"Then I'll find you in the next life, my Anya." Mikhail pulled Anastasia closer to him before she could respond, crushing her into a kiss that was all heat and consuming passion.

Anastasia wished with all of her body that she couldn't taste the fear in him as well. Mikhail released her with a look on his face that Anastasia couldn't decipher. She tried to read the look in his eyes as he suddenly pushed her out into the open street.

Anastasia had no time to react. *That fucking bastard!*

As soon as she was out in the open, her survival instincts kicked in, and she sprinted. Mikhail knew this and forced her hand, driving them in separate directions.

For a few mere seconds, there were no sounds — no gunshots, just the sound of Anastasia's feet slapping against the pavement as she ran. She could see the gates of the palace now, just out of reach.

They didn't even know if the shooting would stop once they got there, but it was the closest thing they had to cover.

A single gunshot rang out.

Anastasia froze, her feet coming to a complete stop as her momentum nearly drove her onto the ground. She turned around and saw that Mikhail had emerged from the alleyway.

They were shooting at him again as he started running through the street, purposefully moving in and out of doorways. He took a less direct route to the palace, moving at almost a jog and not a run.

He's distracting them. Anastasia felt her chest clench. *He's offering himself up as bloody fucking bait until I get to the palace.*

Whoever had sent the shooters, it was true: Mikhail was their target, not Anastasia.

I'll be damned if he's the only one who gets to play this game. Anastasia's mind turned to violence. She had had enough arms raised at her over the years.

If Mikhail wanted her to use her magic, then she was going to use it. Her hands flew up on their own accord, the magic already sparking between them.

"Let's see what else you can do," she whispered to the sparks as they rose into flames on her command. She flicked her wrists forward, and the telltale shockwave of magic spread out from all around her.

It shattered a window nearby, and she could've sworn she heard a hidden gunman falling over in a second-floor apartment. She warped her magic, twisting it until the air spun in a golden circle in front of her.

It took everything in her to push the magic forward, to send it *away* from her as she manipulated it.

Time seemed to slow down. Her magic went hurtling down the street until it wrapped itself around Mikhail — as if it was all too willing to rush to Mikhail's place in her stead. He stopped moving, looking up with wild eyes as he saw Anastasia three blocks away holding her hands up.

Mikhail didn't even have a moment to panic as the magic wrapped all around his body, enveloping him; his vision was like looking through gold-colored glasses.

The magic held for a few precious seconds and then — another shot. Mikhail flinched at the sound and held his breath, closing his eyes… sure that he was hit while standing still. One second. Two.

He slowly flickered his eyes open and realized that nothing had hit him.

A second gunshot.

A third.

My god, Anastasia... What is this? Mikhail was too stunned to move as she wrapped around him as a bulletproof shield. The bullets were deflecting off of her magic, one by one, as they increased in speed.

Mikhail found himself standing in a firestorm of bullets, completely untouched.

"Mikhail!" Anastasia's voice sounded like it was coming from underwater. *"Run,* you idiot!" Her voice hissed at him through her sparks, "I can't hold this for long!"

Mikhail snapped out of his wonderment and bolted toward Anastasia as fast as he could.

They were both vulnerable out here like this, and using her magic always made her somewhat of a static target. He could see her tight expression, her nose beginning to bleed again, as he got closer.

Two blocks left.

One.

Then, almost just as suddenly as it had started, the golden light around Mikhail flickered out. He didn't stop running.

As his vision cleared from the magic, he cursed. He was hurtling towards Anastasia — now only a block away at the gates of the Winter Palace — and she had a knife to her neck. An imperial guardsman had come up behind her, holding her hands back while the blade glinted in the late evening light.

"No, Mikhail!" Anastasia screamed, wincing as her shout caused the blade to dig into her skin. She wanted him to take cover, to hide, to run in a confusing pattern. He needed to do anything other than run at her in a straight line.

There was another gunshot. It seemed to sound final. Mikhail stumbled, falling. Anastasia let out a heart-wrenching cry, beginning to shake and fight against her captor, knife be damned. As soon as he had emerged from the darkness, the man holding her was gone. She was free.

Their objective had been accomplished — Mikhail had been shot. The offenders slunk back into the darkness, rifles stowed, knives sheathed.

Anastasia raced towards Mikhail's motionless body, face-down on the road. This was now the third time she had stared down the idea of a future without him, and the thought terrified her.

"No, no, no," she tossed herself down on her knees, her hands shaking his shoulders as she grunted.

She struggled to turn his massive body over, screaming as she did it, her eyes scanning over him as her magic lit up her hands once more. She was desperate to try and find the offending bullet, to rip it from his body with her magic and pull him from the claws of death once more.

"Fuck, fuck, fuck!" She cursed as her hands ran over him. She couldn't see where he had been shot, and she began to panic. Her hands were shaking, and she had to keep wiping at her eyes so she could see.

"*Mikhail,*" she sobbed, grabbing his face and leaning over him, "Where is it? Where did they shoot you? Where, where, where? I'll fix it, I'll fix it —" She stopped, nearly screaming when Mikhail's eyes blinked open, and he grabbed hold of her wrists.

"Ssh, Anya," his voice was muted and quick. "Come on. Let's get out of the street. Hurry now." He hauled himself up to his feet almost immediately, leaving Anastasia blinking through the remnants of her tears and kneeling on the ground.

"Were you... were you fucking playing dead?"

Mikhail leaned down and grabbed her hands, helping Anastasia to her feet. She was too stunned to negate him, letting him guide her body and telling her what to do. He wrapped an arm around her protectively and walked them the remaining few feet to the palace gate.

They slipped inside, Anastasia walking forward like she was comatose. The shock written on her face was palpable.

She felt numb as she watched on, Mikhail then maneuvering in front of her and leading her towards the door. She followed him inside, not bothering to even notice that they had been left alone.

A few tense moments later, they made it back into Anastasia's rooms; Mikhail immediately moved over to the fireplace and stoked it. He turned around to see Anastasia still frozen by the door.

"Anya," he said quietly, moving towards her as if she was a spooked animal. "It's okay. I'm right here. I had to give them what they wanted to make him let go of you."

Anastasia nodded dumbly, her face incredibly pale. When she said nothing, Mikhail moved forward a few more steps, dropping his voice low to a tone that she never heard him take outside her rooms.

"I was faking it," he said softly, closing the gap between them. "I'm alive. I'm right here."

Mikhail grabbed Anastasia's hands and gently led her towards the center of the room. He sat down in an oversized chair in front of the fireplace, tugging Anastasia into his lap.

She fell into him without hesitation, curling her body around his, and tucking her head into the crook of his neck. His arms wrapped around her, rubbing up and down her back and periodically squeezing her tightly. He waited until every last bit of tension seemed to seep from her, turning his head to kiss her forehead.

As soon as he did, she let out a soft cry. The tears came quick and sudden as her breath struggled to keep up. Mikhail sat with her for as long as she needed, letting her acclimate. He held her as she finished the grieving that she no longer needed to do but had to see through.

"Here," he said softly, whispering in her ear. He grabbed her hand and brought it to his chest, sliding the collar of his shirt to the side as he placed her hand on his heart.

"It's beating, Anya," he kissed her softly, coaxingly. "It's beating for you."

23

The fact that they were back in The Winter Palace felt wrong. Anastasia had openly attacked the Tsar earlier that day. They both understood that the Tsar tried to have Mikhail shot coming back to the palace, likely to get at Anastasia once again.

As they sat in front of the fireplace, Anastasia had fallen asleep in Mikhail's lap. He went over their options in his head, but there weren't many.

They needed to seek out the leader of the resistance, Ruzsky, and hopefully join forces. If Anastasia didn't want to leave the palace because she was afraid they'd draw fire onto the people... Mikhail didn't like either option. Regardless, they were sitting ducks, even more so in the palace itself.

"Anya," Mikhail murmured, shaking her awake. "We need to talk, *malyshka*." He waited until her eyes blinked open and she sat up, a confused look on her face.

"What you did today...," he sighed, knowing that the conversation was not going to end well. "You can't do it again."

Anastasia tensed, sitting straight as her back went as firm as a rod. "Excuse me?"

"You can't do it. You can't stop, ever. You can't turn back for me, Anya." His chest hurt as he got the words out.

"Why the fuck wouldn't I? What are you trying to say?"

"It isn't best for either of us. This isn't going to be the last attack on us, and if we end up in trouble again, you need to just keep moving —"

"Do you not *want* me to turn back for you?" Anastasia felt her blood run cold. The thought of rejection, of broken trust, crept back into her mind and settled in. Mikhail wanted to scream. Every time he thought that they had made headway, the smallest of things would cause Anastasia to fall back into mistrust. She could never believe — never trust — that he wanted her the way that he did.

"No, no, no," he sighed and shook his head, adjusting her in his lap. "Don't go there, Anya. Don't do this every time. Trust me when I say that I love you."

Anastasia nodded, attempting to pull her thoughts back. Mikhail continued.

"It's because of how much I care about you. I need you to look after yourself. I couldn't watch you die," he said quietly, dropping his lips to her ear as if he could speak the words into her bones. "And I *love* you. I need you to believe two things. Can you do that? Just two."

Anastasia nodded, staring straight ahead as his voice did wicked things to her.

"I need you to believe that you can do it. Whatever it is, whatever happens. Whomever you're with. Can you do that for me?"

Anastasia nodded her head, and Mikhail shook his. "Not good enough. Say it out loud."

"I believe that I can do it."

"Whatever it is?"

"Whatever it is."

"Good girl," Mikhail squeezed her body once more, pressing

a kiss to her neck. "Now, the second part. I need you to believe that I *love* you, Anya. More than anything in the world. Can you please believe that? Can you trust me?"

Anastasia nodded, more resolute this time. She pulled away from him slightly, looking up into his eyes. He saw the fire there once more as she nodded again.

"I trust you. I believe you." For the very first time, there was no hesitation in her voice as she stared at him. "I love you."

Mikhail grinned, leaning down and capturing her mouth in a kiss. One of his hands began to drift down her leg, searching for the end of her skirts... when suddenly, the doors to Anastasia's rooms burst open. The two ripped apart from one another but not away. They looked up as both of their arms tightened around the other. Anastasia stifled a gasp.

The Tsar was standing in the middle of the doorway, looking as calm as she had ever seen him, and it was terrifying. The next moment, a stream of soldiers began pouring into the room.

Anastasia and Mikhail struggled to separate their limbs from one another as they jumped to their feet.

Soldier after soldier filed in and began lining up around the walls until they were surrounded. They both looked around and quickly realized there was no escape or weak spots.

Anastasia slowly turned her head towards her father, raising her chin and meeting his stoic stare.

"*Moi Tsar.*" There was no emotion in Anastasia's voice. The Tsar chuckled. It was a sick sound, the kind of sound that a predator made before devouring its prey.

"I see you're still here," The Tsar nodded towards Mikhail. "That's rather contrary to the reports that I had received."

"No thanks to you."

"I retaliated in kind." He waved his hand in the air as though he was brushing off the thought. He turned his attention to Anastasia. "You fired first."

"I did not," she hissed, taking a few steps *toward* the Tsar.

"Your men were brutalizing civilians so you could go for a bloody drive."

"There were people on the road. What kind of city planning is that?"

"City planning?" Anastasia looked at him as though he were delusional. Frankly, he was. "Truly. You see people starving in the streets of St. Petersburg, and that is what you have to say?"

"I don't want to get into politics..."

"That's *rich* coming from a *Tsar.*" Anastasia cut her father off. For a moment, his facade cracked, and his face seemed to twitch. He quickly recovered and kept talking.

"Like I was saying. I don't want to get into politics. I want to discuss, let's say, the state of our familial affairs. You've openly campaigned against me now. This changes your options quite a bit."

"Bold of you to say that I've had options."

"You have," the Tsar shrugged, taking a few more steps into the room. The soldiers shut the doors behind him, the sound of them clicking shut final. "If you didn't like those options, well, that's a different story. Now there are very few options for me, as a father, which is very upsetting."

"Yes, I'd imagine you're very torn up."

"Anastasia," he snapped, his facade cracking once again for the briefest of moments. "You will either publicly recant, take communion, and kiss my ring —"

"I would rather die!" Anastasia cut him off, her voice sharp.

The Tsar let out a chuckle as he took a seat, far too relaxed for this conversation. "Dying is your second option," the grin that spread over his face was conniving. "I will see you take communion and swear your fealty to God and my kingdom. Or you will be publicly executed. I do so hope you choose the former. Your gifts might still prove very useful."

Mikhail moved closer to Anastasia at the Tsar's mention of

her execution. She felt the warm, steady presence of him at her back and was emboldened further.

"I would *never* use my magic to help you." Anastasia's voice cut through the air like a blade.

The room was crowded with soldiers, all of them still as though they were part of the decor, blending in with their sabers and ornamentation next to the chandeliers and vases. Except Anastasia knew that they were not to be trifled with.

The men would all move on the Tsar's command, and although they were inlaid with gold, those sabers and guns would be used against them.

The Tsar sucked on his teeth, shaking his head as though he was deeply disappointed.

"I really would beg you to reconsider."

"Don't waste your breath," Mikhail cut in, feeling his blood pressure rising as he stared back at the Tsar in front of him. He hadn't forgotten how the man had nearly managed to rip their relationship apart in an afternoon.

"What is your plan, exactly?" The Tsar tilted his head to the side and looked at Mikhail in a challenge. "Anastasia is barely known outside of a few streets of St. Petersburg. *You* have developed quite a fascinating reputation, Rasputin...," a slow smile spread across the man's face. "I suppose I had *something* to do with that."

"It doesn't matter what the people think of me," Mikhail shook his head. "All that matters is that your grip on their livelihoods loosens. We don't care what that looks like."

"That's your problem, young man," the Tsar leaned back and crossed an ankle over his knee. He looked like the picture of relaxation and refinement — his presence deeply unsettling as both Mikhail and Anastasia stared at him with narrowed eyes.

"You have no vision," the Tsar continued, "and you're much too flexible. A man's got to have a plan!" The Tsar made a mock toast towards Mikhail. His stomach rolled.

The Tsar was the picture of everything that he had grown to hate. The opulence, the ultimate quest for power, his unquenched thirst for blood, guts, and glory. He had threatened and gaslit Anastasia *as a child* until she spent most of her adult life impoverished in the same set of rooms.

For that alone, he felt the hair on the back of his neck rise and his hands clenched into fists. If he thought he had an opening to be on the Tsar in a second, without getting shot by the guardsmen first, he was going to take it. If he had to choke the life out of the imperial Tsar with his bare hands — he would.

The Tsar looked over Mikhail's face and let out a low chuckle. She didn't like the way that her father eyed him.

Mikhail had spent enough of his life being boxed around by crueler men and had to fight his way out of every situation they had put him in.

Anastasia looked around the room with a subtle eye, trying to determine if she had an opening to take out her father before the guards could shoot. If she had to choke the life out of the Tsar with her magic — she would.

The Tsar's laugh grew louder until it was manic. He slapped his hands together in a booming clap bringing both Anastasia's and Mikhail's attention back to him.

"How adorable," he crooned. "The both of you are trying to calculate making a move, *da?*" He pointed to each of them. "Trying to size me up for the crimes I've committed against your truest love?"

Anastasia paled. Her father was even more of a formidable opponent than she realized.

"No matter," the Tsar cleared his throat and snapped his fingers.

Everything happened in the blink of an eye. The soldiers lurched from their stock-still positions at the walls, leaning forward and grabbing hold of Mikhail and Anastasia.

Anastasia shrieked as she felt the hands of strange men gripping her arm, ripping her from Mikhail's side. Mikhail turned and wrapped an arm around her, pulling her to his chest. She hid in the crook of his neck while more and more hands emerged from all sides.

Mikhail shook his shoulders and tried fighting back with his free arm against those who were piling up on his back, but it was no use - there were too many.

Anastasia tried not to descend into tears, letting out a strangled cry as she felt more hands gripping her, digging in her tight enough to bruise.

She was brought back to that place that she had existed in for fifteen years with strange men bringing their hands against her time after time. As soon as she was sucked into that headspace, much like how she had been as a child, she couldn't even think about using her magic.

In the end, it was only a few minutes. To the pair, it felt like an eternity. It took seven men to pull the lovers apart. The Tsar watched on with a small grin on his face as if the entire scene brought him sadistic pleasure.

As soon as they were separated, the sound that Mikhail made was inhuman. It was a feral sound, the yell of a desperate man who would burn the world to get her back. He knew that she was too deep in her head to access her magic, that the anxiety of being back at her father's hand might cause her to panic.

The soldiers were sons of nobles and the elite, and Mikhail had spent fifteen years doing hard labor in the freezing cold. If it weren't five to one, it would have been no contest as he tried to fight them off.

He turned, light on his feet for a man his size, sending one soldier flying into the wall with a massive swing. Another jumped on his back, and he tossed his shoulder to the right, sending the man crashing into another one of his comrades.

"Enough!" The Tsar roared above the din. Mikhail kept fight-

ing, both of his knuckles now bloody and his hair loose, looking every part of the possessed priest that he allegedly was. "STOP, or she dies!"

Mikhail let go of a soldier and turned around. Anastasia was being held tightly by two men, one of them holding a knife to her throat. It was a sight that Mikhail had seen too often in recent memory.

He could have gone his whole life without knowing the intrinsic fear that he felt when he saw a blade threatening his lover's neck. It made him descend into the depths of his rage, every ounce of hatred pooling in his body as he prepared to take the way out with violence.

It was the coolness in the Tsar's voice that made him pause. The Tsar would kill his own daughter. He would. So Mikhail froze.

As soon as he stopped, the soldiers were able to gain a proper grip on their weapons. There were four muskets pointed at Mikhail's chest and back a second later. He raised his hands slowly with a sigh of submission. It made his blood curdle.

Mikhail looked at Anastasia, trying to make eye contact. He cursed internally, seeing the look on her face vacant. She was slipping; he could see the anxiety settling over her bones. It was too familiar of a pattern for her. She was staring at the ground beneath her father's feet, not looking at either of them.

"Now," the Tsar drawled his words out as if it was a dessert that he wanted to savor. "No magic or Rasputin here gets a bullet in his heart. As you know, Anastasia's... skillset...," he struggled with the words, "come from my side of the family. I was wed to her mother specifically to lower the chance of this... appearing," he waved his hands in the air, "in any of my children."

"I bet you regret that decision now," Mikhail's voice dripped with animosity. He was like a predator caged only by the business end of four pistols. It still sent a chill down the Tsar's spine, even if he didn't show it. The Tsar kept talking as though he was unaffected.

"I had some of my advisors do a deep dive in our family history, Anastasia," the Tsar pinned his gaze on her. She didn't look up but shuddered. Mikhail wanted to vomit. "Did you know that there was one very particular way that our family kept the magic controlled?"

Anastasia's eyes snapped up. Her expression made Mikhail's chest constrict as he saw the fear in her eyes — pure terror.

"Answer me," the Tsar snapped, standing up to his full height and walking closer to Anastasia. Mikhail stepped forward, momentarily forgetting about the guns trained on him until they pressed into his body. He let out a low grunt, eyeing the men on the other end of the weapons with contempt.

"I didn't know," Anastasia said quietly, her eyes falling to the ground once more.

The Tsar smiled as he felt the noose of control tightening around her neck again. He was concerned that he wouldn't be able to get her under his thumb once more — that her love for this priest would cause complications — but it seemed that he was just another pressure point for her. She still crumbled. Mikhail could nearly read those thoughts going through the Tsar's mind, and he wanted to scream.

She could burn this whole fucking palace down with you in it. She'll find herself, and the second she does, none of these damn mind games and posturing attempts will save you.

His faith in her was still resolute but hinged on her stepping out of her father's conditioning.

"I didn't know myself," the Tsar nodded, stepping forward until he was right in front of Anastasia. "It's fascinating." He turned to look at one of the soldiers standing behind Anastasia and gave him a curt nod.

In a flash, the soldiers holding Anastasia's arms wrenched them forward, pushing her wrists together in front of her.

Another man moved from behind them, quickly stepping in between Anastasia and the Tsar. He snapped ancient, heavy-looking iron manacles around Anastasia's wrists.

As soon as he released them, the weight of them nearly sent her to her knees. She stumbled, and her father caught one of her wrists, yanking her up in front of his face.

There were tears on Anastasia's cheeks now, her face contorted in pain. Mikhail screamed, pushing once more against the mouth of the pistols pressed against his chest. One of the men shoved back and brought the gun to Mikhail's forehead, cocking it.

"Mikhail, stop," Anastasia's voice was quiet, but she shook her head rapidly. Mikhail was breathing heavily, his body vibrating with the desire to crack the skulls of everyone in the room. They both turned to look at her father. The Tsar was smiling from ear to ear, grinning with a prideful look like the cat who got the cream.

"Iron," he smiled as though it was obvious. "Iron manacles bind your magic, Anastasia." His smile was positively sadistic as he leaned in until Anastasia could feel his breath on her face.

"Please," she squeaked, all traces of her confidence gone. "I can't feel it…" The irons bound her hands and drained her magic, making her focus on an empty, pin-prick feeling that started at the base of her spine and threatened to consume her.

"I think you'll find this evens the playing field a little bit," the Tsar snapped his finger, and the soldiers began to file out. "You have a day to consider my offer. I suggest making a decision quickly, or my mood may foul."

He leaned in and kissed Anastasia on the forehead, causing her to grimace and struggle in the arms of the soldiers visibly.

Mikhail broke into a chain of curses, threatening the Tsar's life as the man walked out of the rooms without a second glance. Once all of the additional soldiers had filed out, those holding Anastasia left.

As soon as they had let her go, she sank to her knees — the heavy, thick iron chain hitting her legs as it kept her wrists close together.

The last men to leave were the ones holding Mikhail at gunpoint. They left one by one, refusing to turn their backs to him. The guns stayed trained on him until the last man was out, the door slamming shut behind them.

As soon as they were alone, Mikhail threw himself to the floor next to Anastasia. He pulled her into his lap, running his hands over every inch of her that he could find.

She dissolved into sobs as she tried to put her hands around his body and couldn't. She screamed in a panicked frustration, an awful, heartbroken sound.

"Ssh, it's okay." It took everything in Mikhail to keep his voice steady and low. He leaned down, gently grabbing hold of her arm and bringing them up towards his head. With her wrists bound, he was still able to slip his head underneath her arms. He gently maneuvered her until her hands were around his neck, albeit at a somewhat awkward angle, and she readjusted her head on his shoulder.

Her sobs were coming even harder now. Mikhail stood, words failing him. He brought them to the couch and readjusted both of them, trying to make her as comfortable as possible. He said nothing, feeling like there was no way to take away her pain.

"Mikhail," she cried into his chest, her voice wavering, "I can't feel my m-magic. It's so wrong; it's so wrong —"

"I know, *malyshka*," he leaned down, pressing kisses to her cheeks to try and wipe away her tears. "Don't worry. It's still in you, Anya; it'll never leave. You know it's there… even if you can't feel it."

❦ 24 ❧

At some point, Mikhail brought them both to Anastasia's bedroom. The rest of the night passed torturously.

Anastasia had never felt her magic bound, and it was slowly pushing her towards insanity. It felt like she couldn't breathe or what she imagined it might be like to walk without a limb.

She was a ball of pent-up energy, sweat sticking to her forehead as she fought the warring sensations within her. It had started as a growing pain, settling in her wrists, but was beginning to spread down her arms as the pain evolved into a torturous heat.

By dawn, it felt like her arms were on fire, and her face was flushed red as if from a fever. She stripped down to a nightgown, everything feeling too hot and cumbersome.

Mikhail was out of his mind with worry. He sat next to her all through the night, trying to calm her down and keep her attention on anything but the ancient-looking iron wrapping around her delicate wrists. It appeared grotesque.

He made the mistake of stepping out to get water once, only to return and find Anastasia's fingers nearly bloody as she tried to claw the chains off. He had dropped the glass, sending shards everywhere, and leaped over it to get to her.

He hated how he had to grab her on top of the metal, forcing her hands down. She had collapsed into his chest with a scream.

As sunlight began to seep into the bedroom, Mikhail didn't know how they would make it to this evening. He didn't know how they were going to answer the Tsar's ultimatum. He was preoccupied with making Anastasia comfortable — wracking his mind to try and come up with something to change her focus, even if just momentarily. She was sitting in his lap, her eyes vacant and her cheeks flushed.

Mikhail leaned down, pressing an absent-minded kiss to her forehead... and paused. His lips hovered above her, paying close attention as he leaned down and kissed her again.

More slowly this time, letting his touch graze over her skin, watching her focus shift for just a moment.

Oh.

Mikhail's thoughts began moving and he sat up a little straighter, wondering if he was insane. They were out of options — and he'd give anything a try.

He gently maneuvered Anastasia, lying her down on the bed. Her eyes flickered open as she looked at him, confused, while he swung a leg over her and straddled her hips.

Her eyes grew wider as the implications settled over her. Impossibly, she flushed a little deeper.

"*Malyshka...*," Mikhail leaned down, bracing himself on the wall with one arm as he came close to her face. "Do you trust me?"

Anastasia said nothing. For once, she nodded quickly, without any hesitation. That was enough of an encouragement for Mikhail to keep going.

He nodded, sitting back up. He kept all of his weight on his knees, preventing Anastasia from getting any friction as she writhed underneath him.

"Okay," he nodded, "The moment you say so, this stops. Tell me you understand."

His voice took on a deep, vibrating tone that made Anastasia quiver. Her thoughts were quickly spiraling and turning *far away* from the ache of her missing magic. Anastasia was biting on her lip, nodding her head.

"Say it out loud."

"I understand."

Mikhail grinned, leaning into the opportunity in front of them. He sat up a little bit taller, grabbing his shirt and tugging it off.

Anastasia's breath quickened; the sight of him on top of her — but *so far* from where she needed him now — kept her heart rate elevated for entirely different reasons.

The empty feeling that had consumed her for hours was now wholly focused on her core, making her thighs rub against one another.

Mikhail dropped one hand down and gripped her hip, pinning her waist to the bed while he shook his head.

"No," he chided, a smirk sliding onto his face, "I tell you when to move. You're going to take whatever I give you, isn't that right?"

Anastasia let out a wicked moan, all of her frustration officially focused elsewhere.

"*Yes,*" it was a breathy, relieved sound that went straight to Mikhail's cock. He stopped, staring down at her and slowly trailing her entire body with his eyes — a gaze so hot that Anastasia swore that she could *feel* it. He reached up and tightened the bun in his hair, giving her a wink.

With a shocking tenderness for a man so large, and as turned on as he was, he reached down and picked up Anastasia's bound wrists. He brought her hands to his face, making her sit up a little and rub against him. Anastasia released another uncontrollable whimper when she felt how hard he was.

"Please," her voice was desperate, "I need you. I need..." She was cut off as Mikhail licked one of her fingers before sucking it into his mouth — that wicked tongue tracing it until Anastasia was rocking her hips against him, already close to coming.

"I'll give you exactly what you need," Mikhail grinned, pulling her finger out of his mouth and then tracing around the manacles on her wrist with his tongue.

Anastasia shuddered, and Mikhail grinned, pulling back. He wrapped an arm around her back and lowered her onto the bed. He was still straddling her hips, sitting up and grabbing the irons.

"Look at me, Anya," he growled. Anastasia's gaze snapped to him, and she nearly cried out. He was undeniably male, so fucking *big*. He was so much larger than her, especially when she was underneath him like this, his chest alone almost double her size.

"Good girl," he grinned again, his smile feral, "We're just going to distract you a little bit, *da?*"

Anastasia nodded eagerly, her breath escalating and all of her thoughts focused on the pulsing heat between her legs.

Mikhail grabbed the chain holding her wrists together, leaning forward, and looping it over a rod in the headboard. It stretched Anastasia's arms above her head, making her back arch into Mikhail's chest. He let out a dark chuckle, the sound making chills break out all over Anastasia's body.

"Mikhail," she begged, her voice sounding utterly wrecked, "Please..."

Mikhail sat back up, looking at her with a wicked light in his eyes. "What do you want me to do? I feel like taking my time... you aren't going anywhere, are you?"

He cocked his head to the side and winked at her, biting his lip at the sight of her nipples hardening under the smolder of his gaze. He stood up and got off the bed — making Anastasia cry out in frustration.

Without her legs pinned together by his knees, she took the opportunity to rub her thighs together, trying for any source of friction that she could get.

Her hands tugged at the shackles around her wrist, and before long, she found herself moaning every time she pulled on them.

Mikhail nearly came at the sight of her — flushed and bound and begging for him to touch her. He moved around to the foot of the bed, stepping out of his pants. He was hard as he'd ever been, fighting the temptation to jump on top of Anastasia and pull her onto him.

"Look at me," he commanded again, his voice hard and demanding.

Anastasia blinked her eyes open and let out another *devastating* sound. Her mouth dropped open, and she was panting at the sight of him — naked and hard at the side of the bed, his hand dropped down to fist his cock.

"*Blyat,*" Anastasia cursed, trying and failing to keep her hips from bucking wildly at the sight of him.

"Do you see something you like, Anya? Do you want to touch me?" He grinned again, slowly beginning to work himself over, pumping his hard-on and letting his head drop back at the sensation.

Anastasia was nearly undone at the sight alone, fighting against the shackles as she watched Mikhail touch himself.

"Yes," she begged, completely giving herself over to desire, "Yes, yes, please — *please* touch me!"

The 'please' that did Mikhail in, picking his head up and letting go of himself. He was on top of Anastasia in second, and she let out a strangled cry at how *good* he felt.

Her mind was far away from her magic at that moment. She couldn't focus on anything else other than the now delicious burn of the restraints and Mikhail's weight on top of her, the feeling of his skin hot and nearly burning through the shift she was wearing.

Mikhail sat up for a brief moment — making Anastasia cry out in frustration — grabbing her nightgown and ripping it in half with one movement.

He laid back on top of her, Anastasia driving her hips up and relishing in the delicious grind of him, the friction of feeling his hardness against her aching center. *Fuck,* it wasn't enough.

Mikhail leaned down and sucked one of her nipples into his mouth, making Anastasia's eyes roll back into her head. She was so strung out that a few more touches were going to finish her off.

He bit her breast hard, making her stretch and pull at the shackles once more — his tongue soothing the sting a minute later. He moved to her other breast, but Anastasia was shaking her head.

"No, no, no," she hissed, "*Touch me,* you bastard, or I swear to — *oh!*"

She was cut off with a gasp as Mikhail found her center, cursing at how she was already dripping all over his hand. He slid two fingers into her without pause, sinking into the knuckle while Anastasia made a wholly possessed sound that made Mikhail growl in satisfaction.

He curled his fingers up as his thumb found her clit, making devastatingly slow circles as Anastasia began to ride his hand. He slipped in a third finger inside, leaving soft kisses all over her waist and pubic bone as he studied her face.

He kept a close watch on her expression, making sure that as she got further lost with every second, she stayed present and distracted. The slightest note of her discomfort and he was ready to stop.

Mikhail kept going, moving his fingers in wicked ways — until Anastasia's whole body nearly came off the bed with the force of her orgasm. She let out a strangled cry, her release soaking his fingers and tightening around them. He fingered her through it, murmuring sweet things against her hip bone.

"That's a good girl, sweet Anya," he murmured, leaning down to clean her up with his tongue. "You're so pretty when you come for me, *malyshka*." He looked up at her, finding her head lolled to the side as she fought to catch her breath. She was still flushed, her eyes still wild.

"You're gonna give me one more," Mikhail commanded her, his kisses at her hip turning into bites. Anastasia merely nodded, her head falling back on the pillows.

Mikhail was about to break out of his skin with the desire to be inside of her. He slowly moved up her body, his hot mouth pressing kisses and licking up her stomach... her breasts... her neck... biting at her jaw, and finally capturing her mouth in a devastating embrace.

One arm wrapped around her back, the other slapping against the wall as he braced himself.

"Lift your hips for me," he smirked, and Anastasia obliged. She wrapped a leg around his waist and pulled him down to her, dictating exactly what she needed.

Mikhail was poised at her core, feeling the heat emanating off of her — he pressed the head up to her entrance, making Anastasia groan with frustration.

"Mikhail, if you don't *fucking* —"

Mikhail laughed a dark and twisted sound near Anya's ear and thrust inside of her in one movement. He was completely enveloped in her heat to the hilt as he let out a massive groan at the feeling of her around him.

They were both insanely worked up, Anastasia already on the cusp of her second orgasm and Mikhail ready to burst. He began thrusting wildly, watching Anastasia's eyes the whole time. As they fluttered closed in bliss, he picked up his pace, knowing that she was on edge.

He leaned in, pressing their sweaty bodies together, staring to whisper in her ear.

"You take me *so well, malyshka,*" he growled, biting the shell of her ear, "Every last bit of my cock."

Anastasia moaned, turning her head away from him for a moment as if she couldn't handle how hot his words made her.

She pulled once more against the restraints, her whole body flushing at the delicious friction it gave her and how completely at his *mercy* she was. She was so turned on she couldn't speak — the first orgasm doing nothing to take the edge off. Anastasia was pinned underneath his massive body and completely at his mercy, not even able to touch him in return.

Mikhail's hand dropped down and began tracing circles against her clit. As soon as he touched her, she exploded, dropping her head back as she pulled against the manacles and wrapped her leg even tighter around Mikhail.

He let out a groan, dipping his head to the crook of her shoulder as he felt her tighten around him. He kept fucking her through the last throes of her orgasm before he finished with a shout, slamming his fist against the wall above them.

They both lay in total silence, recovering. After a few minutes, Mikhail picked his head up and looked at Anastasia — only to find that her breath had evened out and she was already fast asleep.

Mikhail's eyes widened in a little bit of surprise at how his plan had, well, worked. He slowly pulled out from her, eliciting only the smallest of noises from Anastasia, and detangled himself from her.

Mikhail stood up and went to the bathroom, grabbing a towel and coming back to the bed. Anastasia stayed fast asleep, her face now a pleasant blush instead of the near traces of fever that she had earlier.

He cleaned them both up, before reaching for the shackles. He detangled them from the headboard and brought them down to her chest, making sure that she was comfortable and none of her was cramped in an awkward position.

He slowly slid into bed next to her, daybreak now fully streaming through the window. They still had the Tsar's ultimatum to deal with. This was far from over. Her magic was still bound. Anastasia was sleeping, finally, with a well-fucked expression that made a primal part of Mikhail's chest swell up.

He leaned down and pressed a kiss to her forehead, unable to help himself. He smiled when she barely stirred. He stretched out his legs, flipping over on his back and gently bringing Anastasia's head to rest on his chest.

Selfishly, he just wanted to feel her body next to his as they came down.

There would be enough to deal with when they woke up — but the important part was that they would wake up. She could sleep. There was no fear in her eyes anymore, and she had been well and thoroughly... distracted.

🕸 2 5 🕷

By the time that Anastasia and Mikhail finally woke up, the sun was beginning to set.

Anastasia fidgeted on the bed, her hands absent-mindedly going to fidget with the irons. Mikhail stopped her, running his thumb over the back of her hand to keep her focus elsewhere.

"What are we going to do?" she asked quietly, looking up at Mikhail. There was concern etched in her features, her gaze distant.

"What do *you* want to do?" Mikhail's question hung between the two of them. Anastasia looked up at him, confused.

There had only been a handful of times in her life that someone had handed the power back to Anastasia — it wasn't lost on her. She had felt herself backsliding when her father delivered his ultimatum to them. All it had taken was a few choice words and it sent her hurtling back to that place.

Without the feeling of her magic, the pieces of herself that she had been starting to put together felt fractured. Anastasia sighed, putting her head back down on Mikhail's chest.

"I don't know."

"You do know," he squeezed her arms affectionately, "You do. Don't let him get in your head."

"I don't have my magic… I can't feel it, Mikhail."

"So?" He gently put a finger under her chin and tilted it up until she met his gaze. "You're still you."

"Who I am —"

"Don't let them convince you that your only worth is your magic. You aren't their weapon or a tool; you're a person. We have a situation with your father. What do you want to do about it?"

"You make it sound so easy…"

"It isn't," Mikhail shook his head, "It's not easy, but it is simple. What do *you* want to do?"

The silence fell thick between them. Anastasia waited for a heartbeat, then two. She took a deep breath — and regardless of her bound magic — began telling Mikhail exactly what they were going to do.

♜♜♜

When the doors to Anastasia's room were flung open, the pair was ready. Anastasia and Mikhail both sat on one of the couches together, waiting, staring.

The doors were pushed open by two soldiers, the Tsar strolling in casually behind them, his posture relaxed. His hands were held behind his back, walking in as though he was visiting for afternoon tea.

Only Anastasia could see the telltale signs of his frustration. Whatever had happened in the past twenty-four hours for the Tsar, it had not been good.

His mustache was slightly askew, not the usual picture of precision that it normally was. There was a wrinkle in-between his eyes, and his glance jumped around the room.

The Tsar always had a glaring stare. He would focus it on

people and could make grown men weak in the knees, but his gaze was now unfocused.

The way his eyes pivoted around the room let Anastasia know that his mind was distracted, too. She felt herself biting back a smile, feeling a little bit more confident in herself with every passing moment.

No one wanted to speak first. The Tsar came in and opened up his jacket, sitting down in a chair opposite Anastasia and Mikhail.

The couple had decided that no matter what it took — they would force the Tsar to speak first. They sat there, calm and collected, but careful to keep their faces devoid of any emotion. At one point, Anastasia slid her hand into Mikhail's.

Everything was intentional; each moment had been planned. Mikhail had encouraged her in the few hours they'd had before the Tsar's arrival to do whatever it was that she felt would be the right choice. He would support her, not decide for her.

They knew that if they were already sitting hand-in-hand when the Tsar entered, it wouldn't have as great of an impact as watching Anastasia willingly reach for him. She was right, and it broke the Tsar's silence.

"I'm waiting for your answer, Anastasia," his voice was quieter than she expected, tired. She was no less afraid of him — a cornered predator is the worst kind of predator.

"I will marry Ruzsky," Anastasia cast her eyes to the ground as if she was embarrassed.

A smile spread over the Tsar's face as if it was the first good news he'd heard all day. Mikhail stiffened next to her as if he was not prepared for her answer or just still didn't like it.

"A very wise decision, daughter," the Tsar couldn't keep the glee from his voice. He stood quickly — maybe a little too quickly — the atmosphere in the room didn't change.

There were only a handful of guards with him this time.

There was still a panic in the Tsar's eyes that Anastasia couldn't identify.

Something about it was setting both her and Mikhail even more on edge than they already were. The Tsar turned on his heel and was already moving to leave, re-buttoning his jacket.

"Father," Anastasia purposefully called him by the moniker, marking the first time she did so in years. He stopped, turned, looking increasingly agitated as he was trying to leave. She stood up slowly. "The... the irons, please."

Anastasia kept her voice pitiful and extended her arms out towards him. The Tsar made a calculating look, his expression turning stony. He shook his head.

"I think it's best that we wait," he said gruffly — clearly not trying to push Anastasia into choosing rebellion, frightened of her without the irons on.

"Please," she said again, letting a crack slide into her voice, "I can't feel it anymore. I don't know if it will work, and I... I need to make sure it does."

She looked up at her father and pleaded with him, giving her voice an angle of desperation like a child crying for their parent's approval. The Tsar's lip twitched and he adjusted his hands in front of him.

Finally, he turned to one of the soldiers and nodded in Anastasia's direction. The soldier moved quickly, pulling a pair of keys out of his jacket and going over to Anastasia. She could almost feel the relief cascading over her at the idea of the dreadful pieces of metal coming off.

As soon as he went to turn the key in the lock, the Tsar's voice rang out. It was sharper this time.

"Wait," he snapped, some of his fury returning to him. He stopped and turned around, lifting his hand and beckoning a few extra soldiers into the room.

Anastasia couldn't help but notice that they were much younger. In fact, all the guards in the room seemed to be fresh graduates. As compared to their last meeting, the Tsar had not brought the upper echelon of his men. Something was afoot.

"The man comes with us," the Tsar commanded, pointing at Mikhail. Mikhail stood up immediately, bracing himself for a fight — his hands fisting at his side. He fought the urge to move closer to Anastasia, he knew that she needed to stand on her own.

Anastasia fought back a gasp before looking at her father with confusion. A few of the guardsmen went to stand near Mikhail, but they looked like they could hardly grow a mustache, let alone restrain someone of Mikhail's size.

"What is this?" Anastasia looked at her father, her hands still in the grip of the guard. "You said that —"

"I don't trust him," the Tsar shook his head once. He looked towards the door, itching to get to something beyond it.

Anastasia bit back a response, trying to play the role of ashamed daughter dutifully. She sent a glance over to Mikhail — who was obediently following the soldiers towards the door.

Anastasia felt a pang of panic at the sight of him retreating from her, but wasn't overcome with fear like she once was at the thought of doing something without him next to her.

As Mikhail stepped away from her, the soldier finally turned the key, and the heavy iron manacles fell to the ground with a thud.

Anastasia jumped back from the cursed metal as if they were a dead animal. She felt her magic rushing through her like blood returning to her fingertips. The Tsar turned his back on her to leave. The screaming began.

Anastasia immediately let her magic loose. It exploded all around them as if a bomb had gone off. It spilled not only from her hands but erupted out of the fireplace and poured from the walls. Her rooms looked as though they were flooding from the outside in with spirals of her golden magic.

The few soldiers in the room immediately collapsed to their

knees, hands flying to their throats as they clawed for air. Mikhail was spared, the glittering tendrils snaking up his legs and around his torso like her magic recognized its lover.

The Tsar spun around, his feigned control gone in an instant. Anastasia was screaming as the magic began to spin around her like a current.

Everything happened too fast. The Tsar responded in kind, turning around like he expected this. Anastasia's magic was a second too slow.

The Tsar pulled a pistol from his jacket, placing it to the back of Mikhail's head and pushing him down to his knees.

"*Call it off*, or I will shoot him in front of you." The Tsar's voice was now disturbingly steady. He had been waiting for this moment and found his calm in the chaos, a trait that made him as dangerous as it did murderous.

As quickly as it erupted, all of Anastasia's magic disappeared, swirling up and through the ceiling like evaporating water.

She stood there in the center of the room, breathing heavily as her nose began to bleed. She stared at Mikhail, her eyes wide with worry. She didn't move fast enough.

The Tsar let out a dark chuckle, looking around the room and seeing all of the unconscious soldiers around them.

"I was curious about what you could really do," he grinned, looking over his shoulder and whistling. Soldiers filed into the room, surrounding them.

Oh dear God. Anastasia fought to keep the shock and fear off her face. *It was a test.*

The soldiers kept coming, coming, coming, until they were surrounded. The last man shut the door behind them, creating an awful, final sound.

Anastasia winced. Mikhail said nothing, looking up at Anastasia and trying to keep his expression neutral. He was on his knees, hands in the air. The Tsar was still standing behind him, a pistol nestled in Mikhail's hair.

Only once all of the guards had filed in and had their weapons trained on both Anastasia and Mikhail did the Tsar slowly step away from him and pocket the pistol.

"It seems you do have a stress point, daughter. Good to know just how quickly you'll react when Rasputin is threatened." The grin that spread over the Tsar's face was nothing short of apocalyptic. It made Anastasia's blood run cold.

The Tsar turned away from them and began shrugging out of his jacket. He draped the heavy piece of fabric, all of the metals and ornaments making an inappropriately joyful sound, over the back of a chair.

He began making his way over to one of the soldiers, rolling up his sleeves as he went and adjusting the cuffs, so his forearms were bare.

A sick feeling came over Anastasia as she watched him. The Tsar walked over to a guard, who handed him a wicked-looking knife. It wasn't a dagger or even a combat knife but was a cruel, curved thing — that glinted in the light and looked suspiciously like a butcher's carving knife.

Anastasia felt her heart beating faster as a cold feeling began running down her spine.

"Bind her," the Tsar snapped, flipping the knife in his hands as he walked over to where Mikhail still kneeled on the ground.

Anastasia let out a cry as a guard appeared behind her, snapping new irons on her wrists. The ones at her feet were kicked away, and she forced down another gasp at the feeling of her magic wrestling with itself again.

Whatever new bonds her father had made, they felt wicked — instead of a dull, aching feeling, they felt like hot pokers where they touched her skin. It was only a few seconds before Anastasia couldn't bear it, her back arching as she fell back into the soldier with a scream.

The noise that came out of Mikhail was inhuman. He went

to rise to his feet only to be pushed back down by the pistol at the back of his head.

His whole body was straining, tortured by the sight of her struggle. It took a few moments before the pain in Anastasia's arms settled down to a low burn, and she was able to regain a fraction of her composure. She looked at Mikhail, giving him the slightest shake of her head.

Not now.

The Tsar cleared his throat. "Those are new," he nodded to the manacles. "I had one of your mother's acolytes whip those up. It looks like we'll have to try something *else* to get your attention."

His voice had a joyful tinge to it, as though this was the happiest that he had been in days. He flipped the knife once more before looking straight at Anastasia and bringing it down on Mikhail.

"No!" Anastasia's knees went out. Mikhail had a second to brace himself, locking his eyes on Anastasia's, determined she would be the last thing he saw.

There was a sharp ripping sound and it took them both a second to realize that the Tsar had cut away Mikhail's shirt. It hung off of him in tatters, the cuffs holding on at the wrists.

Mikhail's stomach sank as memories of the monastery came flooding back to him — he had been in this position before.

"Anastasia," the Tsar was still smiling, his eyes wide with mania. He traced one of the scars on Mikhail's back with the blade. "This is for all the trouble you've caused me."

With that, he pressed deeper, cutting open Mikhail's scar and branding him with a fresh wound. Mikhail let out an involuntary shout before cutting himself off.

He shook his head, lifting it to find Anastasia's gaze. She looked murderous, tears running down her cheeks as she squirmed in the guard's hold. He shook his head once.

Not now.

"Anastasia," the Tsar snapped, "Bow to me." He traced the knife down Mikhail's back before he stopped at the next scar.

Anastasia looked at Mikhail as he nodded. She let out a shuddering breath.

"No."

The Tsar grunted and pressed in, ripping open another one of Mikhail's scars. Mikhail stayed silent this time, only allowing his face to contort for a brief moment. Anastasia felt like she was going to vomit.

"Bow to me!"

"No."

The process continued, Anastasia began to feel as though she existed outside of time and space. She couldn't move her eyes from Mikhail, who kept shaking his head, refusing to let her cave against her father. The process happened again. And again.

The Tsar moved in front of Mikhail and found a scar going across his shoulder. With a quick movement, he traced it fresh.

There was sweat beading on Mikhail's forehead now, his back bloodied and soaking the waistline of his trousers. His eyes were starting to glaze over as the deep cuts ran in a wicked crosshatch across his back, each one reopening their own painful memory.

It was as if the Tsar was trying to coax the old hate from underneath Mikhail's skin. He'd never find it.

The Tsar turned around and stared at Anastasia, pointing the knife's edge at her. He was grinning like a wild man, his expression entirely unhinged.

She could no longer feel the pain in the irons, her attention solely gripped by the horrendous tableau unfolding in front of her. It was like she was watching as a passerby, unable to fully comprehend the sight of watching her greatest love cut open, piece by piece.

She felt as though she was walking past the stained glass

window of a bloody crucifixion — violent and full of guilt, but felt nothing to carry on.

"I take no pleasure in being your ruin, daughter," the Tsar tutted, "The *people* you love so greatly have been setting the streets aflame since dawn." Anastasia's eyes widened.

That's where all the guards are... and that's why he's so angry.

"Well," the Tsar scoffed, turning and spitting at Mikhail's feet, "Maybe I take a little bit of pleasure in this." He got down on his knees in front of Mikhail, looking him in the eye as he wagged the knife back and forth in front of his face.

"Let's see if we can't find the heart that my daughter has so aptly stolen, hm?"

Anastasia heard him and screamed — throwing her body to the floor in an attempt to rid herself of the soldier's grasp, but was unable to shake him free.

"*No!*"

The Tsar turned his head and looked at Anastasia, only giving her a wicked grin. He turned back to Mikhail and found the scar over his heart, placing the blade there; he pressed it against Mikhail's chest until he let out a low grunt.

The blood ran down his chest until, with a sudden cry of frustration, the Tsar dug deeper and ripped the knife across his heart.

Mikhail lurched backward and let out a shout that threatened to shake the chandeliers, a horrendous sound full of pain and anger.

His head fell back as he sank to the ground, unmoving. Anastasia stared in horror as his limbs went lax and his eyes shut.

"*Mikhail!*" Anastasia wailed, the tears now coming so hot and fast that she could barely see through them.

She was fighting against the guards like mad, clawing at the heavy chain around her wrists, and didn't even hear the sounds that she was making. She hadn't realized that it another two guards now were forced to hold her back.

No, no, no.

The Tsar stood, standing over Mikhail's body like a man on a hunt. He wiped the bloodied knife on his trousers before tossing it to the ground. He nodded to two of the soldiers, who grabbed Mikhail's arms and began pulling him out of the room.

"Where are you taking him?!" Anastasia screamed, her face twisted into a holy rage that momentarily sent a pang of fear down the Tsar's spine.

She was scorn, she was fury, she was wrath. She watched in prolonged agony as the men took minutes to pull Mikhail's heavy body from the room, his back leaving bloodied streaks along the floor.

She paled when the last of him disappeared from view. He hadn't moved.

The Tsar stared at his daughter, slowly returning to his unaffected state. "Go look outside, *doch*," he jeered. "The people are furious as to why God has abandoned them. They wonder how this Rasputin has managed to escape death and bewitch the Tsarina."

"That has nothing to do with why they're starving!"

"Bah," the Tsar waved a hand in front of his face, "They don't know that. They are starving... they'll eat up anything I give them."

Anastasia's blood ran cold. "You won't."

"I will feed them the man who has distracted the Romanovs from their greatness," his smile was exuberant, "And I will let the people decide what to do with what is left of your dear Rasputin."

"He's just a man! They'll never hurt him!"

"They will act as jury and executioner," the Tsar hissed, "and you will have a lovely view from your window."

The smile left his face as he descended into his madness. He looked at the guards holding her.

"Make sure that she watches. Don't let her turn away — she will watch as she learns what happens when you cross a Tsar. You think you know power, Anastasia? You're about to learn what it truly looks like."

Anastasia bit back another scream as her father exited the room, and she was alone with a handful of guards. She turned to look at them, the fire inside of her feeling like it had been dosed in gasoline, refusing to consider the possibility that Mikhail was dead.

One of the guards gripped her elbow and tried to force her over to the window, Anastasia digging her heels into the ground. She spun towards him, and spit in his face.

"I will go," she hissed, "You would do well to remember that I am still Romanova."

There was something that had changed in her voice. The way that she was standing. She didn't have Mikhail with her, and she didn't *need* him — she *wanted* him.

She was going to get out of these manacles and burn everything to the ground on her way to get him back, to finally get her revenge against her father. They had been dancing around one another for too long. It was time.

The guard's eyes widened as he released her and took a step back, wiping his face with his sleeve. Whether her magic was bound or not, she realized that they were still afraid of her.

Good. She thought to herself, looking around the room. *I will make sure that they all fear me. Fear what they have taken from me.*

"Go on then," one of the other guards lazily waved a pistol in her direction as someone else pulled the heavy curtains open. Anastasia took a few steps towards the window and gasped.

From her vantage point, she could see the front doors and the lawn of The Winter Palace. The city looked like it was burning. In the past day that she and Mikhail had been held up in their quarters, the Tsar had not been exaggerating. St. Petersburg's revolution had begun.

As far as the eye could see, smoke and flame rose from different parts of the skyline. It was the crowd. *The crowd.*

Thousands of people were pressed up against the iron gates of the Winter Palace. Some had torches, others waved knives, rifles, even sticks or pieces of metal.

It was as though the entire city had grabbed whatever they could find and was posed ready to rip down the luxury that stood in front of them.

The contrast that it provided was stark; the Winter Palace, with its gilded inlays and hundreds of rooms versus the thousands of people in front of it wearing shoes with holes and torn coats. Anastasia couldn't help but find herself hoping the crowd would break through.

There was a sudden, rising cry from the crowd. It sounded like a natural disaster, the sound of a thousand desperate, angry people.

Anastasia felt her blood run cold as she scanned the crowd and prayed that she didn't recognize any of the faces within it. It was too dangerous.

It all deserves to burn, but so many of you might go with it!

The crowd grew even louder, shaking their weapons in the air, and a few of them fired off into the night sky.

Anastasia turned towards the front door, seeing what had

sparked the cry. Her father had emerged on the steps of The Winter Palace.

Oh my God... he'll be shot. The thought didn't bother Anastasia, but she wanted to make sure that he was held accountable for his chaos, for his ruin.

Everything that had been done to her, she wanted to look her father in the eyes and make him know that he was responsible for each child that went to bed hungry. A stray bullet taken on the steps of his monument to opulence was an ending fit for cowards.

Her heart stopped when she realized that he was pulling Mikhail forward, his bloody body stumbling, barely conscious from the looks of it. He was alive.

The Tsar had him gripped under the arm as they descended the steps, tossing Mikhail on the ground in front of him. The crowd let out a voracious roar as if they were watching gladiators.

They do want to kill him... they think he truly is the legendary Rasputin.

The realization spread cold over Anastasia. Every time he had escaped death, every time she had saved him, the forged letters... a master of his craft in public opinion.

Her father had painted a picture of a man possessed, a man with *her* magic... and he was going to let the people tear him apart in a religious frenzy.

♛♛♛

Mikhail attempted to stand up on shaky legs before he collapsed back down onto the cold ground. It had started to snow, but his body was on fire. He was weak. The Tsar had cut him to the quick, both physically and mentally, as he ripped open his old scars. Mikhail looked up at him, his face full of contempt, unaware that Anastasia watched on.

"Are you the one they call Rasputin?" The Tsar proclaimed, more of a declaration than a question. He raised his hands out as if he was Pontius Pilate himself.

"It seems that you have already said I am," Mikhail hissed. His eyesight blurred. He was beyond pain.

"Do you not know the charges brought against you?"

Mikhail did not answer, not responding to a single comment. The Tsar stared at him in a befuddled and angry confusion. He turned to the people, ever the showman, deciding that he would make the people choose him — whether they realized it or not.

The crowd was screaming for Mikhail's blood, only half of them believing him to truly be a man possessed who had led the Romanovs astray. The others were ready to rip the gates down and burn the inequity at the root. The Tsar turned towards the crowd.

"Who do you want me to send to you?" His voice dripped with pompous sanctity. "This Rasputin? The man who calls himself a priest?"

The Tsar was no fool; he knew only the most religious zealots in the crowd were the ones calling for Mikhail's head. He wouldn't give them a second option to lock onto.

There was a sudden noise as the front door to the Winter Palace swung open, the crowd going into an absolute frenzy, as the Tsarina stepped out to join her husband. He turned and looked at her, rage coating his face while his back was turned to the crowd.

"What do you *want?*" he hissed, stepping towards her and grabbing the Tsarina's arm, "*Go inside.*"

"I don't want anything to do with this man," the Tsarina's voice had a deathly tone to it. "I've had a vision —"

"Oh, for fuck's sake," the Tsar hissed, gripping her tighter instead of shaking her visibly in front of the crowd, "Not another one of your blasted visions."

"I'm serious," she looked up at him with wide eyes. "He's innocent. This man has done nothing wrong, and it will bring about our ruin if we let this happen. Think of Anastasia..."

"I'm the only one who has ever considered Anastasia," the Tsar countered. "Everyone else simply lacks *vision!*"

The Tsarina paled as she looked at the crowd that had gathered behind the Tsar once more, seeing Mikhail struggling to breathe on the ground as he bled out into the snow on the steps. She was overcome. The Tsar turned back to the crowd of people as though he was a ringmaster.

"Who do you want?" He raised the question again, this time turning around and grabbing the Tsarina's wrist and raising it in the air. "This demon they call Rasputin or your Tsarina, who he has tricked?" His voice was loud enough to ring out in the smoky night sky.

The Tsarina paled further as she looked over to her husband, the fullness of his depravity washing over her. If he tossed her into this mob, they would rip her limb from limb. The crowd roared at the offering of the Tsarina. And yet, their choice was clear.

"Rasputin!" The din from the people seemed to shake the ground. The Tsar seemed a little disappointed but shrugged.

"What shall I do with the one that they call Rasputin?"

"Execute him!" The cries were impossible to ignore. It was a crowd that was starving, for both food and violence, who had lived off of political executions more often than bread.

"Do you know what he has done?" The Tsar yelled out to them. He leaned down and ran his hand down Mikhail's exposed back before flinging his blood out towards the iron gates like a perverse priest and holy water.

"He has avoided death. He had corrupted my darling Anastasia. He has seduced the Tsarina with his wickedness!"

"Execute him!" The crowd was officially lost to their madness as they gave in to the mob mentality. The hunger ate them alive, and they were thirsty, but in a crowd of thousands in a burning city, they could no longer tell that they wanted food and drink.

The Tsar turned and looked at Alexandra, "I am innocent of this man's blood. They chose him over you. If anything, you shall bear the responsibility."

His grin was infectious as he turned back to the crowd. He raised his hands in the air, and a cheer went out. He was a master manipulator, able to take advantage of each wayward emotion.

Mikhail heard the roars and his only thoughts were on Anastasia. He could barely remember where he was, hissing in pain when he felt the Tsar's hand on his back. He didn't know how much blood he had lost but it wasn't going to improve.

For the first time in Mikhail's life... he prayed. He prayed for Anastasia. He prayed for the time that they did not have and what little they did. He prayed for her magic, and he prayed for her heart. That the two would never be separated again.

He prayed for her future and her past, that the latter would never intrude once more on the former. He prayed that he would be nothing but an encouraging footnote on her destiny, on the full life that she would live.

In his heart of hearts, as he heard the crowd of people on the streets twisted and manipulated into calling for his blood — the blood of a name that he had never taken — Mikhail prayed.

The Tsar turned on his heel and walked back towards Alexandra, nodding towards the front door.

"Get the fuck inside and be grateful I've saved your reputation."

There was a moment where it looked like she was going to push back against him, but Alexandra took one fleeting look at Mikhail, her eyes filled with pity, picked up her skirts, and fled inside.

The crowd cheered and hissed as the Tsar grinned, turning

back around to the masses, and waving to the soldiers who lined the gates. Two of them stepped forward, and once again, Mikhail found weaker men dragging him by the arms away from where he needed to be.

The crowd was growing toward a fever pitch, rattling up against the iron as parts of it creaked. Guns shot into the air. A flaming torch was thrown over the top. They got louder and wilder, their voices and stomachs clamoring for blood.

The Tsar didn't show a moment's panic as they pounded at the gates, some of their hands reaching through the bars to grab for Mikhail's body as it came closer.

The soldiers could barely pry the metal apart, multiple soldiers holding it in place, so it opened just enough for them to toss Mikhail into the crowd.

His body disappeared from view like dark magic, hands grabbing at him from everywhere, in every which direction, raining down on him as the last of the light absconded from his eyes.

He was in the middle of a crowd, torn down and pressed up against bodies all around him. He didn't hear the clanging, empty sound of the gates as they locked behind him, only managing one last glimpse of the sky as he angled his head to see if he could spy Anastasia's apartments — the crowd descended, and breath left him as the earth shook.

♛♛♛

Anastasia watched from her bedroom window. She refused to believe that the people were going to call for the murder of Mikhail - she couldn't. They had been so focused on her father that they hadn't considered the seeds he was planting behind their backs.

Neither of them could play the court game of intrigue like he could, warping all gossip that arose around Anastasia and

Mikhail's magic usage. All that was left was a twisted, dark, cruel reputation for the man Rasputin. A man who didn't even exist.

When her mother appeared on the palace's steps, she felt a dangerous hope for a moment. As she watched her father ask the crowd who they would rather take, her heart sank.

Anastasia had been unable to keep her eyes off of Mikhail, muttering prayers under her breath. Genuine prayers for the first time in her life. Her chains rattled against the glass panes of the window as she slammed her fists against it, watching her father torment and touch Mikhail's broken body.

I will murder him — I will murder him and I will end everything that he has ever brought about.

Anastasia felt her heart slowly disintegrating and rip apart in her chest, a panicked feeling threatening to consume her.

She was tired of her own idle threats. She was tired of affirming that she would do something against her father. She was tired of saying one thing and doing nothing. She was tired of letting herself slide backward in his presence, of letting his fear overtake her.

It didn't matter that Mikhail wasn't with her now. She knew who she was, and it was time for *vengeance.*

She watched in horror as time slowed down. Her father's soldiers grabbed Mikhail and pulled him towards the iron gates.

Her heart began beating wildly in her chest, her hands slamming against the windows again and again — she didn't notice that her fingers were bleeding.

The soldiers in the room had started backing away slowly as she threw her body against it when her hands failed her. She screamed, haunted, breaking sounds.

"Mikhail!" The glass cracked. She threw her body against it, a glass fragment cutting her forehead.

"Mikhail!" Another thud, another crack. One of the soldiers dropped his weapon and left. She was possessed. The shackles around her wrists started to bleed. She was the ghost of her demons.

"Mikhail!" Another thud and the glass shattered. Her body was bleeding in places where the glass had ripped at her, but she didn't feel it. The iron gates were open.

People were grabbing for him, desperate to pull him apart. From the open window, she could now hear the chaos and the din of the crowd unbuffered. They were mad. Her father was controlling them all like the ringmaster he was.

Mikhail's body disappeared amongst the people. Anastasia was in a frenzy, half hanging out of the broken window as she released a blood-curdling scream.

It was an earth-shattering, world-ending kind of sound that haunted the soldiers who heard it for the rest of their lives. It was a broken woman at the edge, being reborn. Anastasia's vision reduced to a single point, the last place she had seen Mikhail's body disappear into the people.

Her scream continued, rippling over the night sky — when suddenly, the earth shook and the windows of the Winter Palace facing the street shattered.

The sound came in a bang, lights flickering out while some exploded in bright bulbs of light and smoke. Fires started in some of the dark rooms with broken windows, sending the entire scene further into chaos.

The Tsar looked up; his eyes fixed on Anastasia's window. He saw her, half hanging out of the windowpane, bloodied and screaming for her lover.

The irons that he had specially made were glowing hot around her wrists but did not seem to be burning her, and if they were, she did nothing to betray it.

Her eyes were centered on the crowd, her magic sending a shockwave over the palace that shattered the windows. He stumbled back, falling down the steps as he looked up at the half-ruined palace.

The crowd had gone silent for only half a second before the screaming began again.

"It's an act of God!" Someone cried, their voice laced with panic.

"We've chosen wrongly!"

"This man is innocent!"

"We should have taken the Tsarina!"

Echoes started to ripple through the crowd, no one noticing Anastasia as the soldiers finally got their wits about them and yanked her back inside.

All they saw was the blood on their hands as the glass rained down on them like a new wave of a plague.

Anastasia was ripped from the window, crying and bellowing out for another sight of Mikhail. She refused to believe that he was dead even as her nose bled and her head ached from the sudden outburst of her magic.

My magic! Her eyes went wide as she pushed against the soldiers who were still acting like they were afraid to touch her for too long. *The chains my father had made...*

They don't work. The voice inside of Anastasia's head was not her own. She started looking around the room like a woman possessed, searching for the woman's voice.

"Asya?" She cried out, looking crazed. "Asya!"

One of the soldiers dropped her arm. "I've had enough of this," he backed away, making the sign of the cross. "She's possessed!" His comrades agreed with him, and they fled.

I'm here, child. Asya's voice returned. *Those shackles will never work. Your father tried to invoke magic he knows nothing about.*

Anastasia fell to her knees, weeping softly into her hands. "What do I do? Mikhail —"

Take the shackles off, Anastasia. Asya's voice rang clear as anything she had ever heard. *Free yourself.*

The voice went away, fading out softly, just as abruptly as it had come into Anastasia's awareness. She looked around the empty room and down at the chains around her wrists.

She held all of her focus on them, imagining herself free of the restraints. She felt herself rising above everything that had ever happened to her.

"I am Anastasia Nikolaevna Romanova," her voice was steady, "and my father cannot keep me in chains."

She felt the bonds begin to vibrate, heating up continually, although they didn't burn her.

Anastasia sat up taller, feeling a great swelling in her chest as she heard Asya's words echoing in her head and remembered the calm touch of Mikhail at her back.

"I am Anastasia Nikoalevna Romanova... and my father cannot keep me in chains!" The bindings turned an even brighter orange, the joints where the metal was forged beginning to melt. Drops of molten iron hit the marble floors underneath Anastasia and hissed.

"I AM ANASTASIA NIKOALEVNA ROMANOVA. MY FATHER CANNOT KEEP ME IN CHAINS!!" She screamed it, yanking her wrists apart and letting out another cry when they snapped in half.

There was an explosion of golden light as her magic came flooding back to her, erupting from her fingertips and bathing the room with its electric current.

Anastasia sagged, covered in a gold cloud as the chains dissolved in front of her. She tried to stand on weak legs, her adrenaline fading as her injuries caught up with her.

"I am Anastasia...," her voice cracked, her throat sore. Anastasia collapsed to the floor of her suites, drenched in her magic, and lost consciousness.

❧ 27 ❧

Mikhail felt the earth-shattering around him as he surrendered himself to the masses. There was nothing left for him beyond seeing Anastasia's face once more — and with her away in the palace, there was nothing left.

There were hands on him, grabbing and tugging, but he was beyond pain. He was still shirtless, the cuts on his body bleeding on the hands of those who touched him.

The voices were muffled. He waited for death to take him, his senses dulled. He was uncomfortably jostled and pulled through the crowd once more... suddenly finding that his senses were growing clearer. And clearer. The edges of his vision began to return.

She's waiting for you. His mother's voice slid in from the din all around him. *She lives, she's free. She's waiting for you. You'll have to get to her yourself.*

He no longer hesitated when he heard his mother's voice from the ether these days; as soon as he heard it, he kicked his legs out and tried to get his bearings. The crowd shuffled around him like a living thing that he was fighting against.

"Stop!" A voice rang out near him, the first clear voice that he could hear. "I know this man!"

Mikhail felt the hands disappearing from his arms, blinking feverishly against his blurred vision.

He was on his hands and knees in the street, a small circle had formed around him. He was still shirtless after being ripped straight from Anastasia's rooms and tossed into the streets.

"How could you?" A voice hissed nearby, sounding angry and ready to fight. "Do you know who this is?!"

"It's the Priest Rasputin!" Another voice from somewhere around him. The more that he was coming to consciousness, the more he was aware of his wounds.

He took a deep breath and sat back on his knees, looking up and getting a glimpse at the crowd for the first time.

The faces that looked down at him ranged from inquisitive to enraged. As soon as he blinked his vision clear, the cacophony started again.

"What do you have to say for yourself?!"

"Kill him!"

Mikhail let out a low growl when someone emerged from the crowd, pointing a rifle at his chest. When Mikhail finally spoke, his voice was hoarse.

"I'm getting really tired of people pointing guns at me today," he deadpanned, looking up to see the nameless man who was insistent on sending him to hell for his sins.

"I'm not who the Tsar says I am," Mikhail said slowly, speaking to the whole crowd but looking directly at the man with the rifle. "Would you truly trust that man? The one who has left you all to starve in the streets?"

"We have no business trusting the Tsar —"

"You saw what happened to the palace! God is watching."

"God hasn't watched over St. Petersburg in a long time."

A barrage of opinions rose from the crowd, each of them

valid in their own ways. Mikhail could tell that everyone was confused, frustrated, *angry.*

They needed something to believe in, whether it was that the Tsar had been bewitched or that it was finally time to overthrow the empire. Mikhail had to admit that he was partial to the latter.

"I'm not that man," he said again. "There are dark things in the palace. Of this, I will not lie to you. You must believe me. I am not this Rasputin that they say I am."

"Well, then, who is?" Another voice in the crowd jeered, tossing a handful of rocks in the circle.

"There is no Rasputin," Mikhail let out a heavy sigh, feeling his body grow tired. His hands sagged down by his sides, "My name is Mikhail. Mikhail Ivanov."

"How are we supposed to believe that?" Another voice. Mikhail was growing frustrated. He didn't know how to explain this to an angry mob. He was lucky enough that they hadn't killed him yet.

He didn't know what they were talking about when they mentioned what had happened to the Winter Palace, his view blocked from the ground by the crowds.

"I don't know what to tell you, other than you have been lied to..."

"You are the one lying to us!"

"My name is Mikhail —" He was cut off as another round of disparaging cries came up from the crowd.

His mind began to turn, his body exhausted. He was almost put back in that place, that monastery; the struggle to maintain the one part of his identity that had always been his, the rejection of this moniker.

He thought back to the one time that Anastasia had ever called him by that name, how it had broken him. He heard the cocking of a rifle and sighed. He had made it this far only to die now.

The crowd jostled around him, guns shooting into the air once more and another rock flying at Mikhail. The crowd was ready now. They were bloodthirsty. They were hungry for *atonement*. It didn't matter who was doing it or what it was for.

"My name..."

"Stop!" A man's voice broke through the chaos of the revolutionaries. His command carried enough intensity to make them all quiet down.

Mikhail looked up, blinking once more through blurred vision. The speaker broke through the barrier, walking over to stand in the center of the circle near Mikhail. Mikhail didn't recognize him.

"I know this man." The man's voice was clear, calm. He had a presence that was able to settle the people around him, "He is not this Rasputin that the Tsar would have you believe."

"Who is he?"

"Yeah, why was he at the palace?"

"He must know something!"

The jeering from the crowd resumed almost immediately, their skeptical minds and hungry stomachs driving their need for any semblance of justice.

The man seemed unbothered as he looked around at his countrymen. He looked each one of them in the eye, almost as though he was disappointed. They slowly calmed some of their ire.

"I know this man," he repeated, "He speaks the truth. His name is Mikhail."

"Well, then, why —" Someone interrupted him only for the man to hold up his hand.

"I will finish if you would let me." Silence fell over the crowd. "His name is Mikhail. He is a companion of the Grand Duchess Anastasia. I have seen them together. Surely, some of you have heard of or know someone whom she has helped."

There were murmurs of assent. While they had not been

able to accomplish much, Anastasia had spent years sneaking into the city and helping wherever she had been able. If they were in another city, at the Summer Palace...

Mikhail cringed to think of how this scene could have gone differently. This was St. Petersburg. Her home. *Their* home. They knew these people. Surely, someone was now going to be able to speak for him — and someone was.

"She was just trifling with us," one voice dissented, his tone angry. "So one of the daughters of the Tsar performs parlor tricks in the city. That doesn't mean anything!"

"Do not call them parlor tricks," the man's voice was edging towards anger for the first time. "Anastasia saved my son's life. She pulled a bullet from his leg after fighting her own father's soldiers in the streets. Whatever you heard to the contrary was contempt strewn by the Tsar. He grows afraid of his own house."

"Who is Rasputin?" Someone cried. "We all saw the letters!" Mikhail couldn't help but cringe at the reminder of those damn letters. The thought of Anastasia's pain made him snap to attention.

"Those were a *lie,*" his voice was deadly. "The Tsar fabricated them. They were written by the Tsar himself."

"The Tsarina..."

"She was in on it!" Another voice cried out. "Who are we to trust the palace's lies?" Mikhail let out a brief sigh of relief as the tide of the crowd began to turn.

"Trust me," Mikhail found some of his voice, the last of his strength flooding his body as he stood on shaky legs. The man next to him offered Mikhail his arm, helping him rise.

Mikhail looked around the crowd seeing faces and experiences that mimicked his own. Too well did he know the hurt and frustration they were feeling, the helplessness. He found his body shaking, staring at a sea of people who were now listening to him speak.

"Trust me," he started again, "There is no love lost between Anastasia and the Tsar. You have seen what she can do." Faces and heads began to nod in recognition. "Her father has kept her a prisoner in that palace for fifteen years. She had never known kindness. No one understands the cruelty of the Tsar greater than his own daughter."

Mikhail paused, seeing the people's expressions around him contorting. They moved from anger, slowly slipping into confusion, then disbelief.

He coughed a few times, desperate for the last of his strength to carry him through. Something in him was flickering, his wounds unattended to, and there was a sinking feeling in his gut that this was the last that he had to offer. If he could ignite the energy around him with the sparks in the air, they could end things.

If there is even an 'us' left. Mikhail's thoughts were intrusive, and a chill went down his spine. *I don't know where Anastasia is or in what state the Tsar left her.*

"She has been plotting against him for weeks," he found his voice again, extending his hands out in a plea. "If you have heard the whispers or seen the wonder of Anastasia — please, believe me. They are true. Every wonderful... every wonderful thing is true. We are all flawed. Anything you have heard to the contrary about her has been a lie. Her father holds her captive now, held in her rooms, her hands in chains. Because she dared to seek out and find your revolution."

"The Tsar has captured his own daughter!"

"He holds his own family captive!"

The crowd was cresting, the wave of their sentiment about to crash to the cold stones all around them.

People had begun pushing against the gates. The metal was groaning, soldiers attempting to shove back with rifles from the safety of the courtyard. Shots rang out — but there were only a

handful of ceremonial guards at the front gates of the palace
and it seemed that all of St. Petersburg had arrived.

"Help me!" Mikhail implored the crowd, his voice growing
stronger. "The Tsar laid waste to your homes, to your fields, and
he has forgotten what the heart of this country is about."

A cheer erupted from the crowd. They raised their rifles in
the air, everyone's attention turning from the gates momentarily, and fixated on Mikhail. His eyes were wild, his hair tangled
and matted, standing shirtless in the snow before the crowd of
thousands, blood still drying on his back.

He was every bit the soldier and commander; for the very
first time, he was the picture of a man sent by God to fight a
holy war.

"Bring this devastation to his door," Mikhail yelled, pointing
towards the gates. "Help me. Feed your families with the gold
from his table. Save those who he has held captive. Free all of us
from his rule. Help me. Help yourselves. Help all of Russia rid
themselves of this disease in her heart!"

A cry sprang up from the crowd as they began to cheer,
turning towards the gates once more. Mikhail was nearly
knocked off by the rush of people running towards the gate. He
was almost worried about being trampled as the horde began to
throw themselves at the barrier.

The gates creaked and groaned, already waving and bending
dangerously under the weight of hundreds of people.

There was a warm hand on Mikhail's shoulder and he
turned, the people jostling around him. It was the older man
from earlier who had vouched for his identity. Mikhail leaned
forward, and the pair embraced, the man careful of his shredded
back.

"We should move you to the front," the man nodded, having
to lean in to shout near Mikhail's ear so he could be heard. "The
people will follow you."

"Follow me?" Mikhail's eyes went wide. "No, that's the last thing I want — I need to get inside. I need to find Anastasia."

"We all need Anastasia," the man nodded. "You best be the one to make sure that she isn't caught in the crosshairs. She is still Romanova," the man's expression was grim. "This crowd cannot be controlled."

Mikhail nodded as a new sense of purpose flooded him. He turned, and the man began shouting on his behalf.

The people moved easily, parting for him as if they were being divinely guided. Far too quickly, Mikhail found himself standing near the front of the crowd as people threw themselves against the gates. They turned to him and cheered, making even more room for him.

Someone tossed him a gun, and Mikhail caught it mid-air. He made a rather imposing figure; standing at the front of the palace gates, a rifle in one hand, fresh wounds crossing his body.

Mikhail turned and looked to the few guards who were still standing there, fear etched into their faces, most already having abandoned their post.

The Tsar had inspired very little loyalty, and when they saw how large the crowd was growing, they left. They wanted nothing to do with this revolution.

The city of St. Petersburg was burning behind them, and the palace was next. Mikhail looked up and saw the building was already under attack; half of the windows were blown out, and flames were licking up the walls. The ground was sparkling like a shattered diamond, snow and glass shards mixed around it.

Anastasia! His heart stopped, adrenaline pumping through his veins. Mikhail looked up and sought out her window, praying that he would find it intact. Praying that he'd see her, unharmed and waiting.

As his eyes passed over the pieces of glass and broken window frames, he finally located Anastasia's window, and his heart stopped. It was shattered — but it looked different than all of the other windows.

While most looked like the glass had been blown out, pieces of the wooden frame were hanging off hers. It was as though someone had battered their way out of it.

Or like someone had been thrown out of it. A dark thought crossed his mind, possessing him until Mikhail forced himself to turn back to the guards that were staring at him.

There were even fewer of them now, feebly holding up their rifles. The crowd was roaring behind him like a sea of animals. He watched as the flames began to consume more and more of the palace.

His thoughts turned from revolution to revelations as the only thing that occupied his mind was finding Anastasia.

"I would suggest," Mikhail's voice echoed over the empty palace courtyard as he stared at one of the guards, "That you put down that gun."

He nodded in the soldier's direction, his eyes wild. With the people behind him, his figure backlit by the night sky and the flames, he looked every inch of the cursed priest — like the dreaded man they called Rasputin.

"You do not want to see what becomes of you.o you know the sound a man makes when a demon enters him?"

The threat was idle but landed with its intended effect. The soldiers within earshot immediately dropped their weapons and ran. Those who hadn't heard Mikhail over the din saw their fellow comrades leaving and departed swiftly.

Mikhail laughed, turned to the crowd, and raised the rifle above his head. "Tear it down!" He pointed to the gates behind him.

Now that no rifles were pointing at them from the other side of the gates, the people rushed at it without hesitation. The crowd surged upon it like a tidal wave, moving as one as hands gripped the metal and began to pull.

One woman held the lock steady while another man smashed against it with the butt of his rifle. It took one... two... three cracks before it broke apart. The gates swung open and part of the fencing fell, eliciting a cheer from the crowd.

The ice was melting all around them as the palace began to burn, a third of the windows now lit with flames. The city was on fire. The air was hot. Sparks, embers, and ash rained down on them like snow.

Mikhail stood on the center of it all, bursting forward as the gates fell. He wasted no time and ran through the front doors of the burning palace, a thousand people at his back.

People immediately began looting the palace, ripping frames off of the walls and pulling gold from the baseboards.

The front hall was empty only mere moments later. Mikhail didn't care in the slightest... He was off, running down the hallways, bending under smoke and collapsed statues. He was looking for Anastasia.

Mikhail ran through the palace, grateful for once that he knew each wicked turn by heart.

The people flooded in behind him, and with each step, he heard the building being dismantled piece by piece.

It brought him a sick sense of satisfaction as he thought of the Tsar and Tsarina's precious finery being torn down, ripped away, and the rest of it burned. His thoughts were occupied by Anastasia, growing anxiety sinking into his gut as he raced towards her suite.

As he passed through the halls, Mikhail grew more anxious, the flames spreading around him. Some of it was contained to rooms, smoke billowing out from underneath the doors, and in other corridors, it raged openly.

Boyars and royals were fleeing from their bedrooms and hideouts, people in various stages of opulent undress flooding the halls. He heard their shouts of surprise and cries when they ran into the mob that had amassed behind him.

Mikhail paid none of them any attention as he picked up his speed, clearing over rubble and fallen drapes. He finally turned the corner and found Anastasia's wing, the doors shut. He said a quick prayer when he realized that these rooms didn't seem to have been touched by the fire.

A man possessed, he stormed over and kicked the door open. Weakened by the heat and the flood of Anastasia's magic, it collapsed and fell forward with a loud thud. Mikhail pushed inside, his eyes immediately scanning the room. It was empty.

God damn it! He cursed, tearing through the rest of the apartments. He checked each door, ripping the bedrooms apart and tossing the furniture to the side.

"Fuck, Anya," he muttered under his breath, realizing she was nowhere to be found, "Where are you?"

Mikhail left the suite, jogging back into the hall and following the sounds of mayhem. The entire palace now looked like it might come down around them at any minute.

There were people everywhere — it was as full as he had ever seen it — and even though he had only been in Anastasia's rooms for a few minutes, the world around him seemed to have transformed.

It was chaos, like a living thing around him, as the smoke gathered at the tops of the halls and the noise threatened to drown out his thoughts.

No one paid him any attention, the full strength of the impoverished crowd descending upon the seat of a dynasty.

All of its trappings, hangings, ornamentations, anything that could be carried out, was gone. Some men were standing in the middle of the madness, the butts of their rifles dragging on the ground, as they wept at the finery.

They had starved for so long, the idea that this had been just beyond their reach for decades pushed them to tears.

People were calling out to one another, emerging and disappearing into rooms, each of them crying out for the Tsar. Apparently, he had yet to be found.

There was a massive shattering sound — the sound of a

thousand stained glass windows breaking at once — coming from the ballroom.

The ground shook as a sweeping shockwave went through the palace. Anything that was remaining on the walls came tumbling down, Mikhail dodging to avoid a crashing curtain rod.

Anya! Mikhail's heart jumped. He knew the feeling of her magic as it ripped through the palace. He went running through the halls, tracing their steps towards the ballroom.

As he rounded the corner, he saw that the doors to the ballroom were standing wide open. There was smoke pouring out, a few boyars in various stages of undress running out of the room. Mikhail ran against the tide of the crowd, sweeping into the ballroom.

His heart leaped at the sight of her. She was standing in the very center of the room, magic flooding out from her fingers while a barrage of guardsmen aimed their rifles at her from the perimeter of the room, none of them firing. They seemed to be repeatedly trying to get them to load.

The glass windows all around the ceiling shattered, leaving the room a minefield of glass shards.

Mikhail barely noticed them as relief flooded his body. Anastasia was alive. Not only was she alive, she was *fighting.*

She had freed herself. The chains that he had watched the Tsar put on her were gone. She didn't even seem winded now, the sparks and golden elixir of power circulating her like a personal ecosystem. And she was *laughing.*

Her hair was wild, tossed out behind her, barefoot on the shards of glass below her.

She's magnificent when she's burning. One of the first things that Mikhail had ever thought came rushing back to him. As he gripped the banister of the balcony overlooking the scene, a quick movement caught his eye.

He turned and saw one of her father's most trusted

dvoryanstvos sneak up quietly behind Anastasia — a blade glinting in his hands. He was only a few feet from her as she was dangerously distracted, keeping all of the guardsmen's rifles from being able to fire.

"*Anya!*" Mikhail's voice rang out through the ballroom, echoing off the walls, sounding as clear as a bell. Anastasia whipped around to find his face, the spinning motion causing her magic to flick around her.

The offending rifles were all ripped from the soldier's grips and tossed haphazardly onto the floor. Her eyes caught Mikhail's and she gasped, her face lighting up brighter than the golden magic exuding from all around her.

She was only distracted for a moment as she caught sight of the *dvoryanstvo* in front of her, the blade raised and ready to drive into her heart.

Anastasia laughed — she *laughed* — and Mikhail rejoiced at the sound. It took a single flick of her fingers and the knife went hurtling towards the edge of the room.

With a second twist of her wrist, its wielder followed. Anastasia turned and picked up her skirts, running haphazardly across the ballroom towards Mikhail.

He turned and started running down the steps as she leaped up stairs, taking them two at a time. They crashed into each other like two great forces, colliding in the center of the grand staircase.

They sank to the floor, unable to keep their grasps off of one another. Anastasia ran her hands over Mikhail's bare chest, as gently as she could, tears springing to her eyes.

"You're barefoot! The glass!" Mikhail scolded, his eyes pouring over her to check for any injury. She didn't let him.

"You're shirtless... why are you shirtless?" Anastasia's brow furrowed in confusion; she struggled with the emotions that were pouring out of her.

Mikhail couldn't help but laugh, the strength of his mirth

making his head drop back. "That's the question you have right now?"

"I'm not complaining. It's just curious."

Mikhail leaned forward, wrapping his arms tighter around Anastasia and kissing her as though they had all the time in the world.

Anastasia made a soft noise that nearly set him ablaze as she sank into him. After a moment, pausing to catch their breath, he smiled.

"I didn't have time to stop and change." The situation settled over Anastasia and her eyes fluttered, tears suddenly threatening to spill down her cheeks.

"Oh god, oh God, Mikhail, I *saw you*," the smile evaporated from her face as she began to cry. "You were dead!"

Mikhail let her hands roam their fill as he reached up to cup her face gently. He only winced slightly as she traced the fresh wounds, the scars that had been reopened. She needed to feel, to *touch*, to know that he was real. His thumbs moved gently across her cheeks as he wiped the tears away.

"Me?" He scoffed, "You know that it would take much more than that to kill me, Anya."

He gave her a wicked smirk as she let out a small laugh through the tears streaking her face. She leaned forward, tenderness forgotten, and wrapped her arms around him tightly.

Mikhail's arms went around her body and pulled her to him, adjusting her gently so she was straddling his lap in the middle of the ballroom.

They sat there for a few precious moments, the smoke and sounds of the revolution just outside the doors, touching and petting and reminding one another that they were alive.

"What happened?" Mikhail finally leaned back from her and gently tilted Anastasia's chin up to meet his gaze. "You unleashed your magic."

His grin was infectious. The pride swelling in his chest threatened to break out of him and flood the room with as much light as her power. She hadn't needed saving — not for a moment.

Even when he had been mutilated and ripped away from her side as she was left bound in chains, he had come back to find her fighting.

"I did," she grinned, looking up at him with a fire in her eyes that finally seemed to be at its fullest blaze, "I... I got a little reminder from someone. I decided my father's chains wouldn't hold me anymore." Somehow, they both knew what she was talking about.

"How curious," Mikhail nodded, leaning in and pressing a kiss to her forehead, "I had a bit of a reminder from someone, too."

Anastasia pulled her body closer to his, leaning her head down on his shoulder and catching a few precious moments to breathe. She wanted nothing more than to disappear with him, forever. As if he was reading her thoughts, he responded.

"We just have one more person to find."

"I know. Did the gates fall?"

"They did. Did you shatter half the windows of the Winter Palace?" Mikhail asked with a small grin as if it could've been anyone else. Anastasia sat up straighter, putting her hand ever so gently across the fresh cut over his heart.

"I did, as soon as I saw my father give you over to the crowd... I set his world on fire." She looked up at him, and it was Mikhail's turn to be breathless. He knew it had been Anastasia but he hadn't known what had caused her ire. She had done that for *him.*

"I have a feeling I'll never deserve you, Anya," he said softly, his hand going up to stroke her hair.

"Let's find my father," she kissed him quickly, "Then I'm happy to spend the rest of my life letting you try and prove it."

She winked at him, and they both stood. They slowly disentangled themselves from one another as if they were rising from bed, not the floors of a palace on fire.

No sooner had they stood than a swarm of people began flooding into the ballroom. It was a group of men, all of them in tattered clothing while wearing jewels that they had pillaged from the palace making for a curious sight. Less curious were their rifles, now pointed at both Mikhail and Anastasia.

"I'm getting *really* tired of having guns pointed at us," Mikhail grunted, his hand instinctively wrapping around Anastasia. It was Anastasia who took a protective step in front of him, her magic flaring at her fingertips.

Mikhail stood once more at her back, speaking first to let them know where their allegiances lay.

"We're looking for the Tsar," Mikhail looked at the men, "Has he been found?"

One of the rifles cocked and re-aimed directly at Anastasia. Mikhail made another sound from somewhere deep in his chest, feral.

"She is Romanova," one of the men shouted. He was a boy, barely of age, with yellowed teeth and dull eyes. Anastasia felt even now, as he threatened her life, a sympathy for the fact that he was likely starving.

"I have no allegiance to my father," she said calmly, holding up her hands and willing her magic to go out. She had no desire to fight with these people. They were victims of her father's cruelty just as she was. "We are looking for him so that we might see him deposed."

"Or to escape!" Another one of the boys yelled, who looked even younger than the first.

"Trust us," Mikhail said, stepping forward with his hand out. "We are on your side."

"You're the one that the Tsar was with!" The first boy said, now aiming at Mikhail. "You're Rasputin!"

Mikhail cursed under his breath. He knew that he hadn't been able to win over the entire crowd, but he had hoped that they had seen through that charade.

"I'm not," he forced his tone to stay neutral, "There is no one by that name. It was a lie. She is not like her family," he continued, trying to get the boys to understand, "You must believe us. She is here to help."

"He's the one with the dark magic!" The boy pointed a finger at Mikhail, and it took everything in him not to roll his eyes in response.

"Actually," Anastasia cut in, "That would be me."

She let her magic flare to life, taking the form of open flames that danced above her palms.

She watched as it reflected in the eyes of the teenage revolutionaries in front of her, having no patience left for seeing her lover threatened. The boys shouted in surprise, taking a few steps back, but kept their rifles up.

Anastasia didn't want to use her magic, she didn't even want to make them feel powerless or to take their weapons, but they were losing precious time. If the Tsar hadn't already left, he had a million ways to sneak out of the palace.

Don't forget about Alexei. Anastasia's thoughts took a sharp turn, and her stomach lurched. She had barely seen her brother in years. She didn't know what side he would take, for or against them. If he was in the palace, she needed to try to find him.

"They're working with the Tsar!" One of them cried, "They have to be!"

"Have you found him?" Mikhail asked again, trying to distract their line of questioning.

"Yes," one of the boys looked down at Mikhail, "Not that it is any of your business. She will be joining him soon." The boy cocked his rifle and nodded towards Anastasia, "You are coming with us, Romanova. You will see your father." He said her name like it was a curse.

Anastasia paused, letting her magic go out. She stood frozen for a second before picking up her skirts and taking a few delicate steps towards the boys. Mikhail let out a grunt of surprise, his arm moving to grab Anastasia.

"What are you doing?" He hissed. "They want to execute you with your father!"

"I will not harm innocents," Anastasia whispered back, looking up at Mikhail. "I won't become him. I won't let them shoot me. They'll take me to him."

"This is a bad idea," Mikhail shook his head, his grip tightening ever so slightly on her arm. "Please. They're desperate, trigger-happy men. They aren't thinking clearly and you're a royal." Anastasia put her hand over Mikhail's, her fingers gently stroking him as if to soothe.

"I am a royal," she nodded, "I am no fool. Do you trust me?" Anastasia met Mikhail's gaze.

He bit back a sharp retort, letting out a long breath. He didn't like it. He didn't like this plan for a moment. He had only just found her, and now, Anastasia was ready to play prisoner to some revolutionaries with rifles they had stolen off bodies of her own family's dead guards. The answer to her question was simple.

"I do."

Anastasia gave him a wink before turning and moving slowly toward the steps. She raised her arms and kept her magic sequestered.

When she reached the top of the staircase, one of the boys reached forward and grabbed her arm. Mikhail felt his chest tighten as he fought to keep his breathing in check and obey Anastasia's wishes. He trusted her.

She wasn't the woman that he had met just a few short weeks ago. She was entirely self-possessed. If she had a plan, he believed it. That didn't mean he had to *like it,* especially when it involved anyone else laying a hand on her.

One of the boys kept a gun trained on Mikhail as the others pulled Anastasia out of the ballroom, letting the broken door swing shut behind them.

Mikhail chose that moment to let out a strain of curses, once more separated from Anastasia. He counted to twenty before he went running after them.

❧ 29 ❧

Anastasia followed the group of boys through the palace, looking around at the remnants of what was once.

She couldn't help but smile. Maybe it was perverse to grin at such devastation, but when it had represented everything that fought to keep Anastasia in a cage her whole life, she was thrilled to see it burning.

Partygoers and priests were still being smoked out of their hiding places as they passed, more than one of them accosted and stripped of his bejeweled garments by revolutionaries. She laughed, causing other boys to turn and look at her with a confused look on his face.

Finally, she saw that they were winding their way through the palace to the Tsar's chambers. She bit back her shock. Even *she* had never been inside the Tsar's private rooms. If they had made it that far, then her father's grip on his dynasty must have collapsed entirely.

Once again, Anastasia only smiled. She was in a slight predicament at the moment, but the idea of her father running for his life at the sight of the people who he had willfully starved only elicited joy.

"In there," the boy commanded, pushing the door open with one hand and keeping his rifle raised with the other.

Anastasia took a few steps inside, observing the room at a glance. It was the waiting room of her father's apartments, all lined with mahogany paneling, looking more like a hunting lodge than a statesman's suite.

Her father was sitting on one of the large chairs, facing a lit fireplace. He seemed to be unaffected by the fact that half of the palace was on fire.

He was staring deep into its flames as if they could predict the ashes of his empire falling around him. There was hardly a hair out of place on his head, and he was still wearing his damn jacket.

Although, Anastasia noted with an internal smile, all of his medals and sashes had been ripped off of him. Even the Tsar himself had been looted. He was so deep in his concentration, he didn't hear her step into the room.

Anastasia turned her head and found her mother, on the other side of the room, staring back at her.

The Tsarina looked small and frail. She was down to just a dressing gown and underskirts, her jewelry having been tugged off of her neck and out of her ears.

It pleased Anastasia, potentially a bit too much, to see her disposed of the finery that she depended on.

"Anastasia," her mother gasped, with a shock that couldn't quite be deciphered. "You're alive."

"What did you think happened?" Anastasia scoffed, taking a few more steps into the room as the revolutionaries followed in behind her. "I'm certainly not alive because of anything you did."

The Tsar then turned, his eyes raking over Anastasia as he let out a deep, disturbing laugh. "I see you couldn't save yourself after all. The people have risen against you," he sat back down, and Anastasia could see him fighting to keep his composure. "You never should have stood against the family."

"You say that as though there was a family to stand with," she hissed, her voice full of venom. She walked right up to her father, standing in front of him while he sunk further into the chair, looking deflated.

"I was never yours," she spat. "I hope this means they have taken everything from you." She let a small flickering of her magic out, the flame dancing across her fingertips and making the Tsar's eyes flash in something resembling fear.

"That's enough," one of the boys snapped, waving his rifle around. "Separate chairs, all of you."

"Let us go," the Tsarina wailed like a child, "By God's graces, just let us go — you can take everything..."

"Silence, Alexandra," the Tsar's voice was cold. Anastasia was sad to see that it still greatly affected her mother, who obeyed and averted her eyes. "There is nothing that they can take from us. Russia belongs to us from God — and the rest of the country will see us restored!" Anastasia turned to look at her father in bewilderment.

He was gone, entirely lost to his delusions of grandeur, his eyes red and wild. He now paced in front of the small fireplace in a ripped jacket, dressed in the remnants of his empire.

Anastasia's desire for revenge was slowly seeping out of her. She had it; watching her father locked in his rooms as she had been for years... Anastasia had a heavy realization that these men would likely never let the Tsar see the sunrise.

She turned and looked at her mother. "Alexei?" She tried to keep her voice down. The Tsarina shook her head and Anastasia's eyes widened. The Tsarina realized what she had implicated and shook her head harder.

"No, no, he's alright," she kept her voice low. Anastasia

moved closer so her father and the other men wouldn't hear. "I sent him away before the gates broke. I couldn't bear it."

"He's safe?"

"He is safe. He took some money and I told him to disappear." The statement hit Anastasia... hard. Her mother was not expecting to survive this and her father was waiting on the rest of Russia to show up and declare him their one true Tsar.

"Your magic," her mother shrugged, looking up at Anastasia with a shocked expression. "You could get us out of here..." The Tsarina reached for Anastasia's hand, but she pulled it away in disgust.

"Of course," Anastasia let out a dark chuckle, "Now is the time that you want me to use it. No. I won't have any of these people harmed."

She was pulled from her thoughts as the doors to the apartments swung open again. A handful of men stormed in, much older than the teenagers who had been keeping an eye on them. They pushed in the room, barking commands. Whoever they were, they were the ones in charge, and they had no fear.

Anastasia counted five of them, swallowed thickly as they dispatched the teenagers. She didn't want to use her magic, but if she was forced to... she would not die next to her father.

Anastasia quickly scanned over their faces, stopping at the last man who entered the room. She fought to keep a grin off her face.

Mikhail stepped inside — dressed now, much to Anastasia's disappointment — standing a head above the rest of them. He was holding a rifle in his hands, looking every bit the furious revolutionary as the other men.

His gaze flickered to Anastasia for just a moment, sending her a wink, before one of the men broke the tense silence in the room.

"Nicholas and Alexandra," his voice was gruff and heady with exhaustion. "Consider this your trial by fire. Your reign is over. Accept it, and you will be taken as prisoners of the new state. Deny me, and you will die."

The Tsarina shrieked, her hands covering her face. Nicholas was frozen. It was the first time in her life that Anastasia had ever seen her father taken by surprise.

He stood slowly, his eyes burning with hatred as he looked over the men. There was contempt in his eyes and Anastasia knew he was evaluating them as "lesser" men, even when they had toppled his dynasty.

"Never."

The man grunted, turning with military precision on his heel and cocking his rifle at the Tsar. "I will give you one more chance, which is more than any grace you have given Russia or her people. Hear me now, comrade, I will shoot."

The Tsar's eyes started to move over the men once more, his gaze finally settling on Mikhail. He began to sputter, his face turning red.

"This demon!" The Tsar bellowed, pointing at Mikhail. "You let him into your ranks! You saw! I fed him to you people for penance! You are being led by a demon! You know not what —
"

"Silence," Mikhail's voice boomed with an authority that even the Tsar had not possessed. "These men know me. I am one of them. Not even your bread and circuses could distract them from the truth."

Anastasia tensed. A showdown between her father and Mikhail was going to end in bloodshed.

"He is cursed! Cursed! The curse of the Romanovs! Rasputin has ended us all!" The Tsar began shrieking, his voice descending into inconsolable babble. The Tsarina was still frozen in the corner, watching her husband's final dive into the throes of madness.

The next few seconds happened as though Anastasia was watching from outside of her body. The Tsar was ranting wildly, spit flying from his mouth at his claims, all while the guardsmen watched him with wide eyes.

He moved too quickly for any of them to comprehend. The Tsar reached down, pulled a broken shard of glass from his boot, and launched himself at Mikhail's throat.

Anastasia screamed — a sound of fury, not of fear — and leaped in front of her father. She threw her hands up, using her magic to help her block his weight.

She gripped her father's wrists; the power flooding from her fingertips helped her to hold him off. They grappled with one another amongst the shouts of the revolutionaries, now afraid of firing at the moving targets.

The Tsar dropped the shard of glass and Anastasia released her magic, the momentum sending the Tsar to the floor.

Without another moment's hesitation, Anastasia grabbed it. She bent over her father, throwing out her other hand aflame with power to keep him subdued.

"Never," Anastasia's voice was strong, "Will you go after anyone I love ever again — including myself."

Before the Tsar could comprehend the weight of her words, she brought the glass down into his heart. Anastasia felt nothing, not even the blood that covered her hands or the weight of the arms that tugged her off her father's body.

She heard nothing, not the shouts of the guards or the shocked wailings of the Tsarina. Her vision had narrowed to a single point. All she could see was her father on the ground in front of her, bleeding out.

A set of strong arms enveloped her.

"Anya, Anya," Mikhail's voice was in her ear, the familiar feeling of his beard brushing up against her face.

His presence was warm as Anastasia slumped into it; she didn't look at him as she watched one of the guards walk over toward her father. He was still clawing for air, one hand over his chest.

The guardsman kicked his side once, twice. Then positioned his rifle and fired. The noise echoed in the room, making Anastasia flinch.

"The Tsar is dead," the man proclaimed before he turned around and nodded respectfully at Mikhail and Anastasia. "Let it be known that he has been executed for his crimes against Russia." He looked towards his comrades, and they all quietly followed. It was done.

It was not lost on Anastasia and Mikhail what he had done for them — letting the record reflect that her father had been executed by firing squad would give them some semblance of peace, a way to retreat.

Anastasia was in shock. Mikhail gently helped coax her to her feet as she sunk into his side. She was staring at the dead body of her father, something she had imagined in her head for years.

"Don't look anymore," he said gently, encouraging her towards the door, "It's done."

Anastasia nodded blindly, a strange numbness settling over her before it crested away. She sat there for a few more seconds until only a sense of freedom remained. They were free. It was done.

"It's over," she looked back up at Mikhail with a small smile of relief, but one that was devoid of any joy. There would be time for joy later. There was time for everything now. She let Mikhail escort her to the door gently, leaning most of her weight on him.

"Stop," the Tsarina — who had been mostly forgotten in the last few moments — spoke up. Mikhail and Anastasia both turned and took in the sight of the broken woman. Anastasia raised an eyebrow.

"What... What about me?" She squeaked, sounding like a child. Mikhail let out a sound that was akin to a low grunt, and Anastasia raised an eyebrow.

"I'm sure you'll come up with something, mother," her voice was cold, "You always did."

With that, Anastasia and Mikhail walked out of the room. They let the door slam shut behind them and left the Tsarina with the Tsar, where she belonged.

The rest of the night passed in a blur for Anastasia. It was nearly dawn now and the exhaustion was settling into her bones. She couldn't imagine that Mikhail felt much better, but she was more than content to let him lead her through the palace.

In a grand twist of irony, the quickest way that they could escape the remnants of the burning building was through the old side door.

"Do you want to get anything?" Mikhail had asked her gently, looking back towards the hallway where her rooms were, "We will probably never return to the palace again." Anastasia shook her head, looking up at him.

"Let it all burn, Mikhail... let it all burn."

He nodded and escorted her through the door for the last time as they slipped across the courtyard still covered in glass.

Once they made it past the fragments of the shattered gate, the exhaustion and emotional turmoil caught up with Anastasia. She let out a tired sob, overcome with the events of the evening, and started to sink to the ground.

Mikhail caught her in one smooth movement, scooping her

up to his chest. He held her tightly, letting her adjust so her head was in the crook of his shoulder.

"Rest, sweet Anya," he said gently, pressing soft kisses to her face, "You're safe now."

"*We're* safe," she corrected him with a sleepy grin, "Don't think I haven't been keeping track of how often I've had to save your ass."

"It's because you're very fond of my ass."

"Guilty," Anastasia giggled slightly, making Mikhail's chest tighten as the events of the past day started washing over him.

They had made it. The Tsar was dead.

They didn't know what would happen to Russia, and they didn't care. That was for politicians and the people to figure out.

If he had his way, they would leave Russia entirely, but he would do whatever Anastasia wanted. He looked down at her, asleep in his arms, and felt his chest tighten.

He had nurtured the Romanov magic, but she had found herself. The woman he was carrying away from the ashes of the palace wasn't someone who needed him — lest he ever forget he was only carrying her because she'd allow it — and she was magnificent when she burned.

Mikhail walked them through the streets, now quiet, the people dispersed throughout the city, spreading the word of the Tsar's death. Mikhail let his feet take him exactly where they needed to go.

As always, the innkeeper was waiting for them. She tossed the door open once more as Mikhail climbed up the steps, her eyes wet with tears and her smile bright.

"How did you know we were coming?" Mikhail smiled warmly at the woman, who had now shown them kindness thrice over.

"Your mother told me you were coming," she said with a wink, making Mikhail's heart seize.

Tears sprung to his eyes as he thought of Asya fondly — his

mother, not her death — for the first time in years. The woman looked at him as if she knew and took a step back, waving him towards the stairs. "Your room is ready for you."

Too stunned to say much, Mikhail only nodded and made his way up towards their space. Anastasia didn't stir. The door shut behind him and he moved over to the bed, lying both of them down together.

They were exhausted and overcome, but as Mikhail leaned back on the pillows and pulled Anastasia to his chest, there was only peace in his heart.

Anastasia's eyes blinked open as she stirred, wriggling herself closer to Mikhail's body. "Where are we?" She said through a sleepy daze.

"It doesn't matter," he kissed her once, softly, the both of them hurtling towards sleep. "…It's you and me now, Anastasia."

EPILOGUE

The cottage overlooking the sea was small. After escaping The Winter Palace, Anastasia didn't want anything bigger. It was warm, perfectly fit for the two of them, and always had a pleasant breeze no matter the time of day.

Mikhail and Anastasia had wasted no time leaving the city after the descent of madness around them. They would return to Russia eventually, but both of them felt they needed time and space to heal away from St. Petersburg.

The morning after their departure, Anastasia had revealed a few small gems that she had hidden in her clothes — they sold them and used the fare to book modest travel to Paris.

From Paris, they made their way to the coast. As fate would have it, once they arrived in Èze, someone had posted for a groundskeeper. The couple laughed at the surprising versatility of Mikhail's work history at the monastery and applied immediately.

Most days, Mikhail stayed busy on the property while Anastasia helped wherever she could. When there was nothing that Mikhail needed her assistance with, she'd go into town, developing a new reputation for helping people with small tasks and chores. It was a humble existence, one that was lazy for the soul but not on the body.

Some days, Anastasia sat back with a smile on her face as the realization of their freedom settled into her bones. For the first time in a long time, no one was chasing them; no one wanted to hurt them or see them destroyed.

Before the fall of her family's empire, she had spent every day looking over her shoulder — the absence of that feeling was exhilarating.

This particular day — they all blissfully ran together in a kind of monotony that soothed them both — Anastasia found herself looking out the kitchen window, eyeing the path that Mikhail would take from the main house to the cottage. As if she had willed it into being, some movement drew her eye, and he appeared from the treeline.

Anastasia ogled shamelessly, her stare already hot with anticipation. He caught her gaze from the window and started to laugh.

The sound drifted through the glass and brought a smile to her face. These days, they were unabashed, an effect of the sea air and the euphoric feeling of having every possibility open to them now.

Mikhail slowed his gait purposefully, grabbing the hem of his shirt and pulling it over his head before throwing it over his shoulder.

"Oh, *Christ,*" Anastasia cursed under her breath in the kitchen.

This was a game that they had played many times over, but one that she would never grow tired of. He laced his fingers together, stretching his hands above his head, pulling the muscles in his arm and chest taunt.

Anastasia moved away from the window, walking towards their bedroom to wait for him. She pulled off the shift that she was wearing and as she passed the front door, flicked her finger once and threw the door open with her magic.

She didn't bother to make eye contact with Mikhail, feigning impassivity as she tossed the shift to the floor and disappeared into the bedroom.

Anastasia laid down on the bed and felt the growing heat between her legs, sliding her fingers to her core and circling her clit lazily. She let her eyes flutter closed as her thoughts drifted to Mikhail.

He was only a minute behind her, slamming the front door closed and kicking off his pants as he went. He turned the corner to the bedroom, licking his lips when he saw her, waiting for him.

"*Malyshka*," his voice was low, husky. "You couldn't even wait for me, hm?" Anastasia bit her lip to keep the smirk off of her face.

"You were taking too long," her voice took on a playful tone. She bit back a small gasp as she slid a finger into herself, moving slowly against her own palm.

"Hands on the mattress." He went to the side of the bed as he crossed his arms over his broad chest and stared at her.

He was already hard, Anastasia struggling to hold a disinterested look on her face and keep her eyes off of him. She pretended she didn't hear him, adding a second finger and canting her hips faster against her grip.

"Anya," the command was thick in his voice, "Stop it. Now."

Anastasia froze, her hands going to her sides as she cursed herself mentally for her response. It was the demand that did it, snapping Anastasia out of her reverie and pulling all of her attention straight to Mikhail.

"Then touch me," she whined, shifting her hips on the bed.

"I plan on it," he growled. Before she knew it, he was on top of her, wrapping an arm around her waist and flipping her over on her stomach. Mikhail pulled Anastasia up until she was on all fours as he kneeled behind her.

"Are you always this naughty when I'm gone?" His voice was like gravel as his hand moved down her spine, leaving a fire in its wake. She felt each callous on his palm as he skirted around her waist, teasing and refusing to touch her where she needed it.

"Maybe," Anastasia hissed, refusing to give up the game that easily, "Maybe I *need it.*" Mikhail chuckled, hearing the taunt in her voice. He kept moving his hands over her body, letting her talk. "If I wasn't tired after — *oh!*"

Her voice was cut off in a sharp gasp as Mikhail's hand made contact with her ass, spanking her once. He licked his lips, feeling himself get even harder as he watched her pale skin flush red.

"Were you saying something, *malyshka?*" His voice was sweet and cloying as if he had no idea what had cut her off. He brought his hand to her and slowly rubbed over her cheek.

"Please," Anastasia felt like her body was on fire, now fighting against her basest urges as she rocked back against Mikhail.

"What was that?"

"*Please!*" Her voice was pleading and Mikhail tutted his voice in disapproval.

"How many times did you touch yourself without me?"

"What?" Anastasia's voice was breathy and distracted. She could feel the heat radiating off of him, his body almost pressed against hers from behind.

"I think you heard me." She let out a sharp cry when Mikhail's hand came down again on the same spot, the pain blossoming over to something else entirely. "How many times?"

"Three," she gasped out, her head dropping to the mattress, "three times." Mikhail's laugh was dark in response.

"You're almost there already, *malyshka*, isn't that right?" He let his hand slide between her legs, cupping her sex and sliding a finger slowly around her entrance before removing it.

"*Blyat,*" he cursed, losing the grip on his control as he realized how this was affecting her, "You're dripping."

Anastasia whined in response, rocking her hips back once more to make her point. His cock slid in between her legs and his hands went to her waist possessively once more.

"Do something," Anastasia cried out, "For God's sake."

Mikhail leaned over, pressing his body against hers, covering her skin with his, as he bit at her ear, enveloping her completely with his massive frame. Anastasia felt like she was going to crawl out of her body, every sense overloaded with *Mikhail, Mikhail, Mikhail...*

"Honey," his low voice in her ear sent shivers down Anastasia's spine, "I think we both know God couldn't fuck you like this." Before she could even react, Mikhail spanked her ass hard and sheathed himself to the hilt inside of her.

"Fuck!" Anastasia screamed, bucking her back but unable to move, blissfully trapped under his bodyweight.

"Christ," Mikhail grunted, one arm around her waist and the other supporting his weight as he held himself over her. "You feel so fucking good, *malyshka,*" he groaned as he began moving in and out of her, relishing the vice grip she had on his cock. His hand slipped down and began rubbing against her clit, making Anastasia's eyes roll back into her head.

"Mikhail," she whimpered softly, already stretched to her limit as she felt her body adjusting to him and his relentless pace.

"Go on, Anya," he encouraged, already dangerously close to the edge and desperate for the feeling of her coming around his cock. "Come for me," the commanding tone returned to his voice and pushed his hips against hers.

Mikhail pulled out almost entirely before slamming into her

once more, the sensation of him buried inside her, sending both of them hurtling over the edge.

Anastasia came with a sharp cry, collapsing against the mattress as he chased her in his release. Mikhail pulled out of her slowly, dropping to the bed beside her and tugging her closer. He pressed a kiss to her sweaty forehead, making Anastasia break out in a grin.

"We didn't last very long," she critiqued them both playfully.

Mikhail would never get tired of seeing the freedom in her expressions and the deliciously carefree way she lived now.

"We've got all the time in the world, Anya."

ABOUT THE AUTHOR

Molly Tullis would have picked the Phantom of the Opera over Raoul and named her French bulldog Jean Valjean. She only believes in black clothing, red lipstick, and never turns down an iced coffee or tequila. She enjoys writing fantasy, romance, or any genre with an opportunity to insert a dark-haired, morally grey man.

Her debut novel, The Romanov Oracle, was inspired by a love of history and a simultaneous desire to rewrite it with more magic.

When not identifying as an author, she identifies as a woman with bangs, finger tattoos, and a nose ring, who can tell you what planets are making you sad.

Her DMs are always open on Instagram and Patreon (@the-bibliophileblonde), and you can get information on all upcoming projects at www.thebibliophileblonde.com.

Printed in Poland
by Amazon Fulfillment
Poland Sp. z o.o., Wrocław
15 December 2021

e3b77247-73a0-440f-9d6a-9234371c1475R01